Under a Waning Moon

Other Books by Steven

Before the Coming Dawn, book 2 of As the Starlings Fly

Also read about Steven's role in uncovering the story behind the top-secret crash of the plane en route to Area 51 in *Silent Heroes of the Cold War Declassified.*

Under a Waning Moon

AS THE STARLINGS FLY BOOK 1

Steven L Ririe

Copyright © 2025 Steven L Ririe

All rights reserved, including the right to reproduce this book, or portions thereof, in any form. No part of this book may be used or reproduced in any manner whatsoever without written permission from the publisher, except in the case of brief quotations embodied in critical articles and reviews. The views expressed herein are the responsibility of the author and do not necessarily represent the position of the publisher. For information or permission, visit StevenLRirie.com.

Cover design by Miblart
Author photo by Rick Fowler Photography
Interior print design and layout by Marny K. Parkin
Ebook design and layout by Marny K. Parkin

Published by Groundswell Books

ISBN Paperback 979-8-9925832-0-5
ISBN Hardback 979-8-9925832-1-2
ISBN eBook 979-8-9925832-2-9

To the women in my life, who exemplify the qualities of faith, courage, and character innate in my protagonist, Emily. My wife, Marianna; my mother, Barbara; my sisters, Stephanie and Laura; and my daughters, Jessica, Sarah, Victoria, and Briana are my jewels. My wife, in particular, is my partner, friend, encouragment, and greatest source of happiness. To these incredible women, I say thank you.

Acknowledgments

My profound thanks to Eschler Editing, Michele Preisendorf, and others who lent their talents in polishing my words and preserving the message I wish to convey.

A Note from the Author

If you find yourself in New Harmony, Indiana, and look north, you won't see a large mountain. The only Mount Erebus in Indiana is the one found in this story. In Greek mythology, Erebus is a place of darkness in the underworld on the way to Hades. Similarly, if you could go back to just before the American Civil War, a time many people believe mirrors the divided world we live in today, and scan the sky for starlings, you wouldn't see any. It wasn't until 1890 that sixty European starlings were intentionally brought to America and released in Central Park, in New York City.

Both the mountain and the starlings are fictional. Together, they make up an allegory, and Mount Erebus and the starlings, as found in these pages, are but metaphors. There are many additional metaphors, and I hope you enjoy sorting out their meanings.

I happened upon a monster today.
So worried was I to get out of its way.

Yet something whispered that we were the same
In body, in mind, and also in name.

Though different we were, this was true.
I feared the creature the same as you.

Since we moved as if tethered, which came as a shock,
I darted to escape, my way being blocked.

Recoiling, I scowled. "I'm in no mood."
Mockingly it mouthed as I muttered, "How rude!"

Then came a thought. I suddenly realized,
What troubled me most were my own two eyes.

Part 1

The End of Harmony

Prologue

High above the slopes of Mount Erebus was a perfect perch, a place from which to watch over the valley below. At that ideal spot, dark forces gathered in mythical proportions. Thunderclouds boomed, lightning flashed, and from within in the rubble of a long-abandoned fort, eerie voices issued forth.

"It's nearly time, sisters," said the more ancient of the cloaked figures as she stirred the contents of an iron pot with a spoon made of bone.

The three siblings watched the swirl of bubbling entrails and blubber.

"We must be ready when darkness falls," said the second hag in a high-pitched voice as she added several pig ears to their meal. "They're certain to hear us now."

The third, plump and just as devilish as her sisters, added several forked serpent tongues to the pot. "To give it flavor," she said delightedly. "A little favor for us when the dark comes."

"Precisely," said the more ancient one. "From here, we can see our monster and those would-be monsters."

"Yesss! Jonathan and others," chanted the sisters. "Enough to keep us busy."

"Yes, indeed," said the plump one with perverse glee. "Though we must be careful with Jonathan. We may lose him, sisters."

"Rubbish," declared the more ancient one. "You always worry, but when have we ever lost one? We simply cannot send him down into the pit until he abandons hope. It's a matter of time—just a matter of time, no different than all the others."

"Yes," agreed the plump one, "but perhaps he is not all rot. His transgression was for another, not himself. And this one, unlike the others, clings to his memory of the things we've taken from him. How can he remember? How can he know he is not all beast?"

"Right," said the one with the high-pitched voice. "Our hold appears tenuous at best."

"And yet Jonathan will surrender. But first he must believe he is a beast," said the elder. "Then, like the others, down he'll go."

"And if he doesn't?" asked the plump one.

"Though there is an escape clause for him, the beast within will certainly win. And he is still useful, our monster. Worry not."

"But what if . . ."

"Sisters, I hear another. There is another, but this one screams for himself and no other. An alliance is imminent, and our monster has a role to play."

"Who, sister, besides Jonathan? Who is it?" The other two begged her to tell them.

Extending a bony hand covered in tight, leathery skin, the elder dropped a rotted goat's heart into the bubbling pot. "With a heart turned spoiled and corrupt, we'll be acquainted soon enough, but I'll give you his name."

"Do tell! Why keep us waiting?" the younger sisters pleaded.

"All right. His name . . ."

"What is it?"

"His name is Robert."

"Robert?"

"Yes, sisters, Robert."

"And when will we meet this Robert?"

"Soon enough, soon enough. Patience, darlings."

"Splendid," cheered the sisters, the sound of their laughter mingling with the thunder. And those who lived in the valley below were none the wiser when it came to the evil brewing atop the mountain.

Chapter 1

New Harmony, Indiana, 1850

The door slammed behind Ruth as she burst from the house. In a panic and beneath the light of a waning moon, she crossed the front yard and continued to the country road that led north to Mount Erebus and the coal mine. In the dark, she could see the lone figure of a small child dragging her feet in the distance. Ruth hurried toward the child. "Emmy!" she called out. The wind kicked up dust that scratched at her eyes, but she didn't bother to wipe her face or cover her mouth. Instead, she kept running toward the child. Tippy, a border collie with blotches of white and black, came from around the back of the house and ran past her.

It seemed as if time slowed and the air thickened the closer Ruth got to the young girl. Seeing her alone could only mean one thing, a thing Ruth long feared. Something horrible had happened.

Ruth fell to her knees in front of Emily. Then, in desperation, she grabbed hold of the girl's shoulders and shook her to get her attention. "Where have you been?" she asked, her heart pounding. "And your papa—where is he?"

In the faint light, Emily's dusty face showed streaks where her tears, now dried, had run down her cheeks. Unable to utter a word, the girl stared blankly at her mother.

Ruth tried again to stir her daughter out of whatever trance had come over her. "Honey," she urged, "you in there?" But she peered into vacant eyes. "Sweetheart, answer!"

Only then did Emily focus on her mother's panic-stricken face. "Where's your papa?"

Emily answered timidly, as if her words floated upon the wind. "Mama, he didn't come back."

Ruth wiped the moist dirt from under Emily's nose with her apron. With growing impatience, she tried again. "Where did Papa go? Tell me!"

Emily shrugged. "He put me in the tool cabinet, hid me there, said not to come out."

"But why?"

Another shrug. "Papa said to wait, to stay hidden until he came and got me."

"Makes no sense. Tell me! Where is he now?"

"I looked for him, Mama. It got dark, and I was scared. I had to come out, but he was nowhere." Her hazel eyes swelled with tears, fatigue overcame her, and she collapsed onto the road.

Picking her up, Ruth carried her into the house and set her down. "Sweetheart," said Ruth while gently shaking the young girl, trying to revive her. "This is important, dear. Think! Were you alone with Papa? Were there others?"

"No."

"So there was no one there, only you and your papa?"

"No, Mama."

"Who, then?" Ruth's forehead wrinkled, and her eyes narrowed, desperate to make sense of it. "Who did you see? Who else?"

"No one." Emily began to cry again. "Sorry, Mama, but I—"

Impatient, Ruth interrupted. "Then how do you know? How do you know there was someone else?"

"I heard 'em," said Emily through her tears. "That's when Papa put me in the tool cabinet—said to hide and not come out."

"Stay here, in the house, and don't leave no matter what." Ruth grabbed a lantern and disappeared as Tippy jumped on the bed and licked the salty tears from Emily's cheeks.

Ruth rode as fast as she dared, lantern held high. She was grateful at that late hour to see candlelight in the neighbor's window. She knocked louder than intended, then waited until Old Man Taylor opened the door in his long nightshirt. His wife, Amelia, shouted from inside the house. "Who is it?"

"Ruth, darling."

Ruth heard a shuffling inside the house, and Amelia appeared at the door. "Well, don't make her wait on the porch. Invite her in."

Old Man Taylor stepped aside and dipped his head. "Come in if you like, Mrs. Hampshire." Only then did his brows rise in surprise. "What's wrong?"

Not moving, Ruth struggled to speak. With shallow breaths and a racing heart, she answered, "It's my husband."

"Jedediah?"

"Yes! My husband."

"Of course, I'm sorry. What about 'im?"

"He hasn't come home . . . from the mine. Emmy went there earlier in the day. She likes riding home with him. But she arrived home after dusk without him."

Moving around her husband, Amelia took Ruth's hand in hers and drew her into the house. "Oh, my dear, dear," she exclaimed. "Where's your daughter now?"

"At home. She knows not to leave."

"That's good," said Amelia, turning to her husband. "Best go see 'bout Jed. See to it that Lawrence and Otto go with ya. Wake 'em if ya have to."

Old Man Taylor nodded. "All right. I'll dress and be off. Meanwhile, you'll see Mrs. Hampshire home?" When Amelia nodded, Old Man Taylor's kindly eyes focused on Ruth. "We'll find your man, Mrs. Hampshire. Don't ya worry."

Without another word, he disappeared into the house. Ruth heard the sound of rummaging as he looked for where he'd kicked off his boots before retiring for the evening. He reemerged a moment later with his pants and boots on, holding a lantern, rifle, and hat.

"Excuse me," he said as he moved past the two women who watched the light of his lantern fade into the night.

☾

Upon arriving at the coal mine, Old Man Taylor, Lawrence, and Otto ran into the tall, slinky sheriff, Graham Weasley, and the mayor, Robert Owen. The short, pudgy mayor wore a white shirt, and leather suspenders held up his fine-wool, cuffed pants. As the trio rode through the gate, the sheriff moved to cut them off. He waved his wide-brimmed hat, shooing them away like bothersome flies.

"What are ya here for?" hollered the sheriff, placing his hat back on his head and resting a hand on his pistol, finger tapping the hammer. "Ya got no business here. Why ain't ya home in bed?" Sheriff Weasley stared coldly, his gaunt, pockmarked face barely visible under his wide-brimmed hat. He held a lantern high above the brim, the glow casting a shadow over his menacing face. As always, he sounded cross.

"Now, Sheriff," said Taylor, hands up as if to calm the wiry lawman. "We're here 'cause . . . Ruth Hampshire . . . why . . . she came to the house, and, uh, she said Jedediah ain't come home. So we heard, and we come to help is all."

"Don't need none of yer help," the sheriff said dismissively. "Y'all get on home. Mayor and I got this." He turned and started to walk away, a bucket and paintbrush in hand, presumably to mark the tunnels in a search.

"Bucket and brush. Bad omen," whispered Lawrence. "Cave-in, my guess."

"Yeah," agreed Otto. He moved his horse closer to avoid being overheard and muttered, "Or it was the sheriff's doin', he and the mayor. Don't appear a proper search, just them two. Look what the mayor's wearing. He ain't plannin' on gettin' dirty. Why, I bet he's wearin' silk stockin's underneath them pants of his."

"Ya ever seen silk stockin's, Otto?" asked Taylor.

"No. But I heard 'bout 'em. That's what them Chinese wear. I also heard rumor Jed was plannin' on runnin' for mayor."

"Hmm," said Taylor. "I heard that as well. But I would advise against it."

Lawrence and Otto nodded, then turned their horses to leave, anxious to oblige the sheriff. They had no intention of entering a mine prone to collapse, if that's what had happened.

Old Man Taylor, on the other hand, felt otherwise. He was a thin man, unremarkable in stature but scrappy and not inclined to being dismissed. He dismounted and called after the sheriff. "I prefer to help regardless. An extra man can't do no harm."

The sheriff hesitated before turning around. Eyes narrowed on Old Man Taylor, he said, "I recall tellin' you we'll handle this. Didn't ya hear me?"

Reluctantly, Old Man Taylor nodded and mounted his horse. Truth be told, the sheriff held a social status granted by the mayor that allowed blatant disregard for common courtesy. Everyone in New Harmony understood the regretful reality. Taylor pulled the reins to the side and headed back to town, hurrying to catch the others.

Once they'd gone, the light from the sheriff's lantern slowly disappeared, leaving the entrance of the mine dark and foreboding.

Two hours past midnight, Sheriff Weasley rode up to the Hampshire's house with Snip-Joe, Jedediah's horse, in tow. He put the horse in the Hampshire's small barn around back, then walked up to the front porch. Removing his hat, he brushed the coal dust and dirt off his shirt and pants, then tapped his hat with his fingers to do the same before putting it back on. Emily stood behind her mother in the darkness as Ruth peered discreetly from the kitchen window. Looking back at Emily, she placed a finger on her lips. "Shhh." Amelia Taylor nodded and knelt at Emily's side.

At the look of fear in her mother's eyes, young Emily felt a renewed sense of panic. Curious, she crept forward and joined her mother at the window. Emily's eyes locked on the thin man with the stringy hair, unpleasant face, and tin badge. She knew this was not a man her mother wanted to see on their doorstep. Mother had warned her about the sheriff, telling her to stay as far away as possible. Emily froze at the thought of what might come next. To her relief, Old Man Taylor appeared out of the dark and approached the porch, where the sheriff waited. When the dreaded knock came a moment later, Ruth left the window and cracked open the door. The sheriff stood there, eyes pinned to the ground. Then, hearing someone approach from behind, he peered over his shoulder. Noticing Old Man Taylor, he shook his head. "Thought I told ya to get on home! What are y—"

Ruth stepped onto the porch, interrupting the sheriff. She shut the door behind her as Emily discreetly parted the curtains to continue watching.

"So I, uh, come to tell ya that, uh . . ."

"What?" Ruth demanded. "Where is my husband? Where do you have him?"

"There's been an accident," said the sheriff, his gaze darting upward before dropping back to the floor. Emily gasped when her mother's knees buckled, dropping her to the porch. Abandoning her post at the window, she rushed toward the door, but Amelia held her back.

"You mustn't go out there, Emmy," Amelia whispered. "Your mother is not alone. My Henry is there with her. He'll take care of your mother, but you must stay quiet. Your mother needs you to stay quiet. Can you do that?"

Without answering, Emily returned to the window and resumed monitoring the situation.

The sheriff and Old Man Taylor appeared to patiently wait as Ruth struggled to her feet and composed herself, wiping her tears with her sleeves. "Where's my husband?" she demanded. "Where is he?"

"Don't rightly know," admitted the sheriff, shrugging.

Ruth's voice rose, her tone stern. "Then you go and you find him. Bring him here."

"Can't do that," said the sheriff, eyes still glued to the ground. "The mayor's havin' the mine sealed off. Too dangerous. Too unstable to search anymore. Won't be no rescue neither, or . . ."

"Or what?"

"Or recovery, ma'am. Ain't nobody allowed in the mine. It's closed. Don't want nobody else goin' missin'!"

Ruth clenched her fists. "Yeah, can't find him? Why? Unless . . ."

Careful, Mama, thought Emily. *That man frightens me.*

Ruth stepped back and leaned against the door. "Are you certain your threats toward my husband aren't at play here?"

Her words had an edge the sheriff clearly didn't appreciate. A scowl crossed his lips, and his countenance turned stony. He offered no defense.

"You're grievin', ma'am. Not thinkin' right." The sheriff paused, then glanced back over his shoulder at the imposing figure of Old Man Taylor. "For that alone," said the sheriff, "I'm willin' to pretend ya made no such inference. Be advised, however. Pretendin' ain't part of my nature, and there are limits to my—"

He clamped his mouth shut as her mother stared straight into his face, watching as his eyes darted about nervously, still avoiding her gaze.

With the innocence of youth melting away and her world collapsing around her, Emily stared coldly at the man talking to her mother. She had no idea it was all so very fragile.

Where are you, Papa? Mama and I need you to come home.

"How is it," asked Ruth, "that I warned Jedediah this very mornin'? I warned him about you, Sheriff. I told him to leave well enough alone, to not challenge the mayor. Yes, the mayor, and, therefore, you will never allow people to choose who they want as mayor. But Jedediah's conscience would not allow him to stand idly by. Life always had to be fair, or he couldn't live peacefully. But is it fair that he is now missing? Is it fair that I am now alone? So I ask: What have you done with my husband? You tell me—"

The sheriff interrupted her. "Huh," he snorted. "Well, we can't find 'em, so . . ." His words trailed off, and he turned to leave.

Old Man Taylor moved past the sheriff as Amelia opened the door and ushered Ruth inside.

Old Man Taylor went to shut the door behind them, but before it closed, the sheriff mounted his horse and callously shouted, "Things are the way they are, Mrs. Hampshire. Blame who ya will, but it ain't no different for any of us, and you ain't special. We all gotta live with things the way they are."

Emily, still peering out the window, waited a moment before closing the curtains. "He's gone, Mama," she announced.

Through the darkness of the parlor, Emily stared at her mother, not fully comprehending what she'd heard, knowing only that things would never be the same. What worried her most was the tremor in her mother's voice. It scared her. She watched nervously as her mother and Mr. Taylor walked past her, her mother disappearing into her bedroom and closing the door.

Amelia called to her. "Emily, dear, come here, would you?"

Amelia came over before Emily could move, took her hand, and led her into the kitchen. A moment later, Mr. Taylor joined them. A paraffin lamp illuminated their faces as they sat around the table.

"Best we leave your mama alone for a while," said Amelia. "I'll inform the parson and your aunt Margie at first light. Then we'll call on you to make sure everything's all right. Will you expect us?" she asked. Emily nodded. "You watch your mama, dear. If'n ya need anything, no matter the hour, come get us. Knock loud, and we'll wake."

The Taylors put Emily to bed, blew out the candle on the kitchen table, and quietly saw themselves out.

Emily lay in the darkness of her room, wiping the tears from her cheeks. Though exhausted from crying, she couldn't sleep. *Only this morning,* she thought, *I turned eight. How did it all go so wrong?* The smell of cider cake, her favorite dessert, still lingered. *I never want to smell cider cake as long as I live!*

An hour passed and then another, and Emily lay there, staring at the shadows on the ceiling, until she thought she heard a faint whisper from behind her mother's door.

"Emmy?"

Emily sat up and listened. Was it her mother or her imagination? The house was filled with the stillness that only came with death.

"Come in here."

This time, Emily felt certain. She crawled out of bed, swept into her mother's room, and lay down beside her. Ruth pulled Emily close, and Emily snuggled into her. She could tell her mother hadn't slept and that she'd been crying too. A candle on the dresser cast a soft glow into the gray gloom that blanketed the room.

"What happened, sweetheart? Tell me," Ruth said calmly while brushing the hair from Emily's face.

Emily thought back. "Horses, Mama."

"Horses?"

"Yes, Mama. I heard horses, and that's all I heard until Papa hid me in the tool cabinet in the shed. That's when I heard loud voices. But Papa told me not to be afraid. Even so . . ."

Confused, Ruth shook her head. "Men on horses? Did you see them—see where they took Papa?"

"No, Mama. But I heard the one."

"What do you mean? Heard who?"

"The man outside. The one from earlier."

"Mr. Taylor? Is that who?"

She shook her head. "No, not him. That other one. I'm sorry, Mama." Emily started to cry again.

"Calm yourself. My dear, you did nothing wrong. Now, tell me about the other one, the one you heard with your papa. Was it the sheriff, the man you heard speaking with me on the porch? You did hear our conversation. You did, didn't you?"

Emily nodded. "Uh-huh."

"So was that him?"

"I think so, Mama."

"Yes, dear," said Ruth. "I'm sure that's who it was. His voice is like a bleating goat, but he's a wolf. Now listen here." Ruth placed a hand on her cheek, demanding her full attention. "This is important," she said. "Tell no one. Do you understand?"

Emily nodded.

"No one, dear. If you must speak of it, do so with me only. No one else. That man, the one I've warned you about, the sheriff—he's not a good man. Tell me you understand."

"Yes, Mama. I do."

"Not a word. Ever!"

Chapter 2

New Harmony, Indiana, 1860

Ten years had passed since Jedediah's disappearance. No one asked about the circumstances anymore, the memory either stored away or forgotten. The town had long since moved on when the bell above the door at Hyrum's General Store rang and a trio of women entered. One spoke loudly as the others listened.

"What a shame. Whether it be an offense to God or not is not for us to decide," said Abigail Williams, her words full of feigned concern, as was her manner.

In his white cotton apron, Hyrum didn't bother to look up as he straightened several items behind the counter, though he couldn't help but listen. The volume of Abigail's voice made it difficult to do otherwise.

"Perhaps, ladies," she continued, "it may be all too predictable. Ruth Hampshire is, after all, the self-destructive type. Nonetheless, she is to be pitied rather than judged. Is she not?"

Abigail reviewed her list of commodities for purchase—coffee beans, oatmeal, flour, sugar, and molasses. Shadowing Abigail, Elizabeth Howe and Susannah Boyer listened carefully.

"When my Norbert died, there was no reason for it," Abigail continued. "I asked the parson to pray that cholera not take him, but our prayers went unanswered, even when offered by the revered parson himself. And certainly, no prayer could've done Ruth any different either. She did plenty to aid her demise, and she's already given up her little one, swallowing her pain with the accursed drink. And for what, the devil's vice? They call it firewater for good reason."

Elizabeth listened while reaching into a jar and pulling out a hard candy. "If that daughter of hers don't give her reason to be decent, nothing will, I'm afraid."

"Wouldn't it be nice not to care about anyone but yourself?" said Abigail. "Everything centered on me." She pressed her fingers to her chest and left them there.

"Couldn't agree more," said Susannah. "Marjorie claims Ruth suffers from consumption, but we know differently. Marg is just being kind; they are family, after all. But I assure you it's something far more sinister."

"If anyone were to bother consulting me, I'd say being hard-nosed is Ruth's only illness," said Elizabeth. "She knows perfectly well what corrections must be made for her to be considered with any decency. I wouldn't lay blame on Marjorie, though. She's obligated to defend a family member, as we all are."

"Myself, I expect no less of Marjorie. And, yes, ladies, one must defend family. We all must," Abigail said while each nodded in agreement, so impressed were they with their own compassionate natures and genuine concern.

"It'll be a miracle if Emily grows up to be worth a damn," said Susannah.

"Now, now," Abigail chastised. "We mustn't resort to cussing. But I couldn't agree more. And if Emily does grow up to be worth a damn—excuse my language—it won't be to her mama's credit, though it pains me to say it." Abigail fanned herself with her hand and looked to her cohorts for approval.

"You're right, Abby," said Elizabeth. "Her aunt Marjorie havin' to raise poor Emily. I heard Ruth abandoned her and even refused Albert and Marjorie's hospitality. They offered her a room without payment of board, no less."

That was the first Abigail heard of such an offer. It bothered her that she hadn't heard it first.

Elizabeth continued. "Who knows where she sleeps? A barn? The gutter? With a gentleman who is no gentleman at all?"

"Now, ladies, let's not judge," Abigail urged. "That belongs to God alone, and woe be unto her, for His judgment is far worse than we could ever levy. But as for guilt, it is not ours to decide." To the delight of Elizabeth and Susannah, the edge in Abigail's voice evaporated into the inauthentic perfume of social grace.

Abigail set her purchases on the counter, and Hyrum began the arithmetic, dipping his quill into the inkwell in front of him.

"Pardon me," he said, "but I couldn't help but overhear. If you're talking about poor Ms. Ruth—"

"What of it?" barked Abigail.

"It's just that . . ." Hyrum pretended to resume his calculating. "Well, the sheriff found her at the back of Ernie's Tavern this morning." He continued scratching the paper with his quill, not looking up.

"Nothing new," said Susannah. "I've walked past her there before. I would typically have offered assistance, but I thought better of it—if only to save her the embarrassment. Best leave her be until she regains her faculties. What Ruth needs—"

Hyrum didn't let her finish. "They found her dead."

Just then, the door opened and Hannah Burroughs, the parson's wife, entered the store. During her lifetime, the saintly woman had gathered years of joy, sorrow, and the resulting abundance of empathy. Her once-long brunette hair now sprinkled with gray was drawn up and tied at the back of her head. Disarming sapphire eyes softened by all she'd witnessed guided hands made rough in the service of others. The ladies glanced her way before Abigail quickly turned back to Hyrum. She had no interest in Hannah's sudden appearance. Where Hannah gave little audience to Abigail's carefully crafted conversations, Abigail returned the favor.

On the other hand, Elizabeth and Susannah appeared quite surprised and kept their attention on Hannah. She acknowledged them with a solemn nod, a gesture not in keeping with her usual, cheerful manner. But aside from it all, Hannah could sense their alarm, and only then did she speak, her voice solemn but kind. "It appears you've heard the sad news."

"Yes, just now, this minute," said Susannah.

With a weary heart, Hannah forced a smile. "Pardon me," she said as she excused herself. "I must see to proper preparations. My husband insists Ruth be paid respect no different from anyone else. It seems the torment of this life is over for her. Let us be gracious in her passing."

Elizabeth hurried to help Hannah gather the items on her list. "Will there be a funeral?"

"I don't believe so," said Hannah. "Albert and Marjorie requested that the services be discreet. We must honor their wishes."

"Yes, of course," said Abigail. "Spare the family the embarrassment." She turned away, shaking her head.

"Please be kind," Hannah tenderly urged. "One can die of a broken heart. Our prayers must now be that God takes her into His graces."

Hyrum piped up. "Of course, a broken heart. Poor Ms. Ruth. Unimaginable. All those years of never finding out what happened to her Jedediah."

Attempting to appear sympathetic, Abigail added, "I'd die a thousand deaths myself. I nearly did when the fever took Norbert from me, God rest his soul. Even the parson's prayers failed on his behalf."

Such words from Abigail allowed Susannah and Elizabeth to show their grief. But unfortunately, neither recognized the slight to Hannah, nor did they acknowledge their guilt in Ruth's demise. Instead, they kept up their torrent of vicious gossip, the likes of which had left Ruth face down and lifeless behind Ernie's tavern.

"Albert and Marjorie's home is a fine place for Emily to grow up," said Hannah. "They were indeed gracious to offer it and their love. It's on us now, ladies, to give Emily a chance. She shouldn't have to live in her mother's shadow."

"Of course, that goes without saying, now doesn't it?" Abigail rolled her eyes for all to see.

Hannah only shrugged, made her purchases, and politely excused herself as she exited the store.

Chapter 3

These aren't my hands, he thought, allowing himself to stop but for a moment. *I've lost mine, and these here—where did these come from?* He moved his fingers. In their place, other things moved. Furry things. He heard distant voices, menacing voices. *I can't stop. I must keep moving!*

The fire glowed hot from behind the latticework of pine branches that protected him from the eyes of those who would hunt him. Turning away, he willed himself onward as all he ever cared about ascended in flame and smoke. In front of him lay a brutal, unforgiving oblivion where no light could penetrate the blackness, a place of abandonment where the dire consequences of his transgression would be thrust upon him. But the wilderness was his only escape.

He started to cry but heard only the whimpering of a wounded animal. *Relax, it'll be all right,* he thought, doing his best to ignore the sense of impending doom overwhelming him. He screamed in agony, but what came from his lips did not sound right, did not sound human. It was a guttural howl of pain.

I deserve nothing less. It's all my fault. He could not break free from his self-condemnation. Under the strain of suffocating remorse, he fled. Everything was gone: his home, his family, his life. Whatever it was that pursued him had found a way into his head, painting his memories black. He had trouble remembering the simple things, the mundane bits of his life, his very self dissolving into nothingness.

He stopped again, panting. His gaze returned to what should have been hands and arms, but what was this? He did not have to see the rest to know what he was: the stuff of nightmares.

The only thing left to do was run. And so he ran. He ran into the darkness of the woods, hoping never to be seen again.

Had it been days or weeks? He couldn't be sure. He knew only that time had passed as he'd pushed deeper into the wilderness, convinced that someone or something pursued him. *I must keep going. I'm not safe.*

He strained to remember why they'd followed him, but his mind did not seem his own, at least not entirely.

There were men, angry men on horses. Yes, they gave chase. Are they still after me?

And what was this chaos inside his mind? It infected him like a parasite and erased his memories, replacing them with beastly urges.

Am I possessed? he wondered, then scrambled over more rocks, pushing branches out of his way.

A feeling of guilt came over him. He had done something, something terrible, something that made his fellow humans angry.

Fellow humans, he thought. *Am I human?* He looked at his naked body—the arms, torso, and legs covered with fur. His hands, now so large, ended in enormous claws.

He had no recollection of shedding his clothes. He remembered only the sensation of his body bursting at the seams, growing larger and more powerful each day. Even now, he felt the strain of transformation in his bones. He ran, clawing his way over rocks and through the underbrush, trying to ignore the hunger, the flesh, the fur, the fire, his mind slipping all the while.

Lightning flashed, and thunder rolled across the landscape. Purple clouds churned darkly above him, unleashing a torrent of rain.

The exhaustion of another day weighed upon him. He longed for shelter, a place to sleep.

He found an outcropping of rock rising from the dense foliage, the rock face slanted just enough for him to take cover from the storm. He ripped easily through the branches beneath the rock until they formed a nest around him, his strength no longer surprising him. Then, shielded from the rain, he curled into a fetal position, his breathing labored.

Behind this cloak of leaves, branches, and darkness, he felt, for the first time, a sense of calm. His heavy eyelids blinked, shedding droplets of rain. A bolt of lightning illuminated his makeshift abode, and, for a moment, he felt oddly small, like his enormous size, which nearly surpassed that of a grizzly bear, meant nothing.

When sleep finally overtook him, his dreams included a parade of angry faces, screams, fire, and the smell of gunpowder. He woke to realize they were but shadows lacking substance. What troubled him most now was this thing he felt stalking him, turning his urges from those of a man to those of a beast.

I must resist it, he thought, not sure how to articulate his struggle. He resolved to keep some part of himself, some thinking, knowing part of himself, alive and free from the malicious spirit taking possession of him. For if he still had a mind that could consider itself, then he still existed, was still human, or at least a part of him was. And if human, there remained a nagging, haunting question: Who was he?

Chapter 4

"Emmy!" Marjorie Hampshire called as she fussed about the kitchen, her portly figure pointing to years of sampling her recipes. "Set the table, would ya? And later, we must see to the curin'. The St. Clairs brought more pork. So come on, dear. Can't let the sunny day get away from us. Your mother, God rest her soul, wouldn't want you sulkin' forever."

Drying her hands on her apron, she adjusted her baby-blue cotton day cap over her long platinum hair and called to Emily a second time. "Dear, is Christian comin'? Of course, he's always welcome. He's gotta way of makin' ya feel better. Way I see it, it's about time we start setting the table for four. Life goes on, don't it?"

"Please forgive my dour mood, Auntie," Emily said as she entered the kitchen. "It was one thing when Mother left, but she's gone for good now, and even though I don't have to worry about where she is and whether she's all right, it still hurts."

"I know, dear. Better place. Better place. What about Christian? Is he comin'?"

"Should be on his way," Emily said as she brushed past her aunt.

Marjorie handed her a tablecloth and four plates. "Be a dear?"

"We've arranged to spend time together before afternoon dinner," said Emily while covering the table with the cloth.

"Well and good," said Marjorie. "After your time together, we'll share our meal and exchange pleasantries. Though I've got nothin' special tonight, dear. Just pork stew and potatoes. Christian, so thin that one, best bring his appetite. Either that or wastin' what's left to the compost." Marjorie handed Emily a handful of tomatoes. "Slice these for Albert, would ya? He loves his tomatoes." She washed her hands, untied her apron, and turned to leave. "I'll be in the—"

"Wait!" Emily interrupted. "You say he's thin?"

"Who, dear?" answered Marjorie, having already moved on from the topic of Christian.

"Christian. You just said it."

"Oh yes," said Marjorie. "So very—"

"Well, he tells me he's already had supper each time he comes by but you prepare him a plate regardless. 'What's your auntie fatting me up for?' he asks."

Marjorie wasted no time in answering. "For sickness or a long winter, you tell 'im."

"Yes," muttered Emily, more to herself than anyone else. She carefully set a bowl on each plate and a spoon next to each bowl. "'Who knows what God intends for us' is what you always say."

"That's right, dear. Such a good listener, you are. Must always be prepared, mustn't we?"

Having heard a word or two from the adjacent room, Albert entered, not wanting to be left out of the conversation. "Your boy, Christian—that's who we're discussing?" he asked.

"Of course, Albert. There's been no other," Marjorie said more sharply than intended.

"Yes, there has," said Albert.

"Who?" Marjorie looked at him in disbelief.

"For a time, I imagined it was the older boy, the other one."

"What other one?" Marjorie shook her head and looked at Emily. "Who is Albert talkin' about?"

Shrugging, Emily answered. "I have no idea. Uncle, who is it you are referring to?"

"Christian's older brother, the other one."

"Marco?" asked Marjorie.

"That's him," insisted Albert. "That one. I thought he was the one who captured our Emmy's interest."

"No, no, no," Marjorie insisted.

With that, they both turned and stared at Emily for validation.

Emily nodded. "Yes, Marco, when they first arrived here. We were so young, and he was so smart. I liked him, though he was so reserved. I never knew what he was thinking, dare I say it. But we shared a precious moment, and then . . ." Emily shrugged.

Intrigued, Marjorie asked, "And then what, dear?"

"Well, I'm far from certain as to what happened. Perhaps, I suppose, for reasons of shyness or disinterest, it never went anywhere. With Christian, however, and his near-daily pronouncements of affection, I'm never left to wonder. He makes his intentions toward me known, and I've never had reason to doubt or question. Eventually, my heart surrendered."

"The Salvatori boys are tall and handsome," Marjorie said. "Either one is fine with me, but Christian is the early bird. I suppose he gets the worm."

"Well then, it's Christian," said Albert. "Are things gettin' more serious? Is that the subject of this conversation? I mean, is it time we call upon the parson?"

Emily smiled and wrapped an arm around him. "It's nothing, Uncle," she insisted. "Just that auntie wants to plump him up, is all. But I think he's handsome as he is."

"Can't argue there," said Albert, "though he could sit a little longer in his father's barber chair."

Emily quickly came to Christian's defense. "Uncle! I adore his long hair. And how he tilts his head to one side. And his eyes . . . the way he looks at me . . ."

Albert smiled as his gaze drifted to Marjorie. "Our dear one's smitten."

"Don't tell me you're just now noticin', Albert," said Marjorie. "Our dear Emmy can't say his name without grinnin'. Understandable, though. He's a handsome sort."

Emily looked at both of them as if to say, *Hello, I'm standing right here!*

An awkward silence passed between them. Mostly, Marjorie and Albert stared at Emily, who stared back at them. Eventually, Emily spoke. "May I remind you," she said. "He hasn't asked me, and I haven't said yes." Then she began slicing tomatoes, hoping the topic of conversation changed.

"Well, well," said Marjorie. "Georgia tells me Walter's impressed with Christian. Since hiring him at the post office, it's worked out well for both of them."

Just then, there came a knock at the door. Emily's face lit up as she sprinted from the room.

Marjorie called after her. "Dear, do tell Christian to walk in from now on. No need knockin'. He's practically family."

A moment later, Christian followed Emily into the kitchen and greeted them. "Mr. Hampshire. Ma'am." He smiled exuberantly.

"Sit," Marjorie ordered. "You know where."

Christian looked to Albert.

Albert nodded. "Best do as she says."

"Yes, sir," he said, then turned to Marjorie. "Ma'am?" Marjorie pointed with her chin to the empty chair beside Emily's usual spot. He eagerly took a seat.

"How's Shears?" asked Albert. "I believe that's what they call your father, yes?"

"Yes, sir, Shears, on account of his trade. My father's given name is Tommaso, Thomas in English. But hardly anyone here in Harmony knows that."

"Well, how is he?"

Marjorie interrupted. "What my Albert is askin', dear boy, is how he's doin' since your mama . . . you know . . ."

"Oh," said Christian, "since she passed?"

"Yes. Since then," said Marjorie, leaning in to hear his answer.

Christian lowered his head. "It'll be a year this fall. Papa doesn't talk much, but I can tell it weighs on him, ma'am."

Marjorie attempted to lighten the mood. "Your mother, a lovely woman. I delighted in her talkin'. It was her accent I enjoyed most of all. And your brother—will he ever return to Harmony?"

Christian looked at Marjorie with eyebrows drawn. "Marco?" he asked.

"You've another?" Marjorie asked.

"No, ma'am," answered Christian. "My brother's coming home soon. He's finished with schooling is what his letters say."

"So, I understand he's a doctor now? That what he is?"

"Yes, ma'am. Marco was one to keep his nose in the books. He's very smart," Christian answered, then turned to Albert. "But I assure you, sir, I also have my ambition."

"I'm sure you do," Albert said. "New Harmony could use another doctor, but there are other occupations that serve as well—the post office, for one. Walter, your boss, he's our neighbor. He has fine things to say about you."

"I like it there, that's true. But I've heard it said the mayor intends to start a bank here in Harmony. We're large enough to have our own, and I'd like to find employment there if possible."

"Banking?" asked Albert.

"Yes, sir."

"And work for the mayor?"

"If he'll hire me, yes, sir."

"Might as well," said Albert. "Half the town is under his employment, and there'll be even more once he opens another mine near the one he closed. Plenty lost their jobs when he did, and so there's a need. Fault the mayor all you want, but he does provide industry."

"Wait, Uncle. Is the one he closed the one where Father worked?" asked Emily.

Albert nodded. "The very one."

"And yet another coal mine. Is it a good idea?" asked Emily. "Mother told me the mountain was unstable. She worried each time Father left the house, as if Erebus was a thing of evil, though she always insisted the mine was not the cause of Father's demise. And it didn't matter to her whether others believed her or not. She contended that closing the mine was a ruse. Regardless, the mountain may not be stable, and such an endeavor may be irresponsible."

"It may well be, Emmy," said Albert. "But it doesn't matter. Safe or not, there's more black gold in the mountain, and that means profit, especially with rumors regarding the discontent brewing in the Southern states, even talk of war. So, stable or unstable, what does the mayor care? With war comes opportunity, and the mayor has a snout for such things. He's going to dig all the same."

Christian took Emily by the hand and looked into her eyes. "If it comes to war, there'll be little chance my brother won't be goin'." He paused, then added, "Or me. But I figure such rumors are exaggerated. Surely—"

Marjorie interrupted him. "Come now. What good is it rufflin' our feathers? What tomorrow brings is in God's hands, war or no war."

"Of course, once again you are right, darling," said Albert. "Either way, there'll be more people movin' in, workin' for the mayor, and more opportunities. The town's growin', along with our need for a bank here in Harmony. It's about time for it. And the town could use another doctor as well." Albert turned his attention back to Christian. "Your brother—he does intend to practice here in town, does he?"

"It's what Papa says," said Christian. "Warren's meetin' him at the train station in Bloomington on Thursday and bringing him here. And with Mrs. Williams telling everyone—"

Marjorie interrupted, "You mean Abigail?"

"Yes, ma'am. Mrs. Williams and the other two ladies—the ones who are always with her."

"Yes, yes, the other two," said Marjorie, "Elizabeth and Susannah."

"Yeah, them. They're tellin' everyone Marco can't possibly be a doctor—maybe a horse doctor but nothing more. They said my papa, since he's only a barber, isn't smart enough to raise a boy to become a doctor. That station in life is reserved for a different class or something. So Marco already has a patient waiting for him—Barlow's sick horse. Mr. Barlow visited my papa at the shop. He requested that Papa send Marco to his farm as soon as he arrives. Marco loves animals, so I suspect he'll go."

"Gossip alive and well. Imagine that," said Albert.

"Anyway, Warren is bringing him here on Thursday."

Albert asked, "Warren Sowell?"

"Yes, sir. Since Warren brings the mail to the post office from Bloomington and delivers Hyrum's orders for the store, he offered Marco a ride."

"How convenient," remarked Albert.

"They're close friends," said Emily.

"Yes. Very convenient," agreed Christian. "Or I'd have to travel to Bloomington to get him. But he and Warren have been best friends forever. It was Warren who got me the position at the post office."

"Understandable." Albert nodded, but before he could say anything more, Marjorie interrupted him.

"Enough talk, Albert!" she insisted, then stood and busied herself, putting a hot bowl of pork stew on the table in front of their guest.

The mood in the room instantly warmed with the pleasant odor of steaming goodness filling the kitchen, and the cordial conversation resumed until Emily protested. "It's not nearly dinnertime," she said. "We intend to have our time together first. We agreed, Auntie, didn't we? Dinner at the usual hour?"

Ignoring Emily, her aunt said, "But it's hot now, dear. Let the boy eat."

"Auntie, please. Can't it wait?"

Christian watched as steam rose from the bowl. Then, leaning forward while keeping his hands in his lap, he inhaled. "Oh, my," he exclaimed. "Certainly better than mine or Papa's cooking. Reminds me of my mother. I'm afraid I'd nearly forgotten. I'd be content just sitting here smelling it." He smiled at Emily and then at Marjorie.

Right then, Marjorie knew. She looked over at Emily and saw the contented smile on her face. "I can see why ya fell for this one," she said. "Charming. Simply charming."

"Thank you, ma'am," said Christian.

"Eat," Emily conceded. "It's all right."

Marjorie watched the young man take the first spoonful, his eyes partially obscured by his long black hair. "Christian?" she said. "A little motherly advice . . ."

"Yes, ma'am."

"When someone trusts ya enough to place their heart in your hands, they gotta know you'll watch over them. A man and woman must keep each other from harm. The heart's a delicate thing. Ya won't disappoint, will ya?"

Emily spoke before Christian could answer. "All right now, Auntie," she said. "Let's not get too serious. No reason to cause him indigestion."

Christian looked up from the bowl under his nose, held her attention, and solemnly said, "There's nothing in this world more important to me than Emmy's heart. Nothing!"

The words stirred something deep within Emily, and her desire to be with him grew. Nonetheless, she resisted the urge to take hold of him, promising herself she would taste his lips before the evening ended.

Chapter 5

The beast moved through the bogs of the northern hunting ground, his breathing labored, more growl than air flowing through his windpipe. Ticks and fleas crawled through his matted fur, and a rank odor hovered around him.

He knew he was safe in the wilderness, though he couldn't remember exactly from what. It was as if he had left a trail of memories behind him. The days were a blur of hunger and hunting, then retreating to one of the many lean-tos he'd struggled to build even though his mind told him it should be a simple task. Instead, each one he fashioned looked more primitive than the one before, and each seemed more difficult a task than the last.

A rustling of leaves broke the silence. *Food?*

The beast sniffed the air for the familiar scent of prey. His gnarly snout, wet and cold, turned toward the sound, his dark eyes focusing on a possum caught in one of his carefully placed spring-loaded snares. The possum struggled and hissed as the beast lurched forward, his thick, brutish claw seizing the animal by the neck and crushing it. He raised the twitching animal, letting its blood drip onto his tongue.

I must make a fire to cook the meat, he suddenly thought. The possum dropped to the ground while the beast seized a crudely fashioned bow drill. Though his hands had grown enormous, he moved the bow to and fro to create friction until sparks danced about the dry kindling he'd gathered. He blew gently, and flames sprang up. In short order, a column of smoke rose from a crackling fire. The chilly night was upon him, and darkness set in, though his eyesight remained inhumanly keen.

The fire felt too hot for his bulky, fur-covered frame. Moreover, the light from it hurt his eyes, blinding him and conjuring a sort of primal fear.

Why did I make a fire? he pondered. He felt an irrepressible urge to back away, and so he did, taking the dead possum with him. He now felt more comfort in temperatures that once chilled him to the core. *There is no such thing as friendly fire,* he concluded while puzzling over the nature of his conclusion.

He gripped the dead possum tightly, his claws digging deep, his hands smeared with its blood. He enjoyed watching the blood drip into the dirt. An irrepressible desire to lick the wounded animal overcame him. The blood tasted sweet. Licking turned to chewing, and he easily tore flesh away from bone, the taste filling him with satisfaction and subduing his hunger, but just barely.

Blood dripped from his lips. *Such a little thing, a possum.* His mind turned to larger prey. He imagined devouring a deer or moose limb by limb. *Oh, how fulfilling that would be.*

Chapter 6

Emily woke to a soft rose color flooding her room and a delicious smell filling the air. "Cider cake. Oh, please, please tell me today is not my birthday." Emily rolled onto her stomach and groaned into her pillow. *I've no use for my birthday. I'd rather sleep and wake up tomorrow,* she thought. Through sleepy eyes, she peered around her room, which looked no different from the prior evening. The dresser stood in the corner, the lantern on the stand. Nothing had changed—exactly how she liked it, exactly how she wanted it.

Remembrances of birthdays past settled in her memory as she thought of her time living with her uncle and aunt. She loved them dearly, but each year while living under their roof, she faced one burden—her birthday.

Auntie must have been up for hours baking, she thought. *When will she leave well enough alone? She knows what happened on my birthday. Yet, once again, I must appear gracious.*

Inwardly, Emily was all tears. The haunting memory of her eighth birthday came flooding back, just as it did every birthday since the one that changed her life. Suddenly, she found herself in the toolshed, hiding in the darkness amongst the clutter of the cabinet, waiting for her father's return. Then came the crushing image of her mother wailing over her father's disappearance, her birthday in ruin and Emily too young to do anything about it.

Emily rolled onto her back and lay quietly, wishing not to alert anyone she was awake. *I must take some joy on my birthday,* she thought. At the very least, she should show courtesy and grace for her aunt's sake.

She forced herself out of bed and slipped into her corset. Was it too much to ask that today be no different from any other? Housedress in hand, she lumbered into the kitchen.

Upon seeing Emily, Marjorie smiled broadly, then spun her around to cinch her corset.

"Morning, dear." Marjorie pulled at the lacing with practiced hands.

"I know what you're up to, and I fear appearing ungrateful." Emily moaned. All the while, Marjorie ignored her.

With her corset secured, Emily fussed with her dress, pulling it over her head and down until it hung comfortably from her shoulders.

While Marjorie returned to her duties in the kitchen, Emily sat at the table, resting her head on her arms. "Christian asked if he could visit later today."

"Of course, dear. One day I imagine he'll be the one tightenin' that corset—when you're married, of course." Marjorie giggled, attempting to lighten the mood, but Emily remained somber.

"Forgive me, Auntie. I don't mean to be sullen. But, for a reason I can't explain, I both look forward to seeing Christian today and not seeing him." Emily sighed. "If only today would go away." Emily put her head down, avoiding her aunt's gaze.

"Oh, Emmy, whatever will I do with you?"

"I'm not ungrateful," Emily said, "if that's what you think. It's just that . . ." She struggled to avoid hurting her aunt's feelings. After a pause, she added, "It's about how people are supposed to live, at least here in Harmony. The sun rises, and they go about their business bathing, eating, talking, breathing, and the rest, like normal. Then, when the sun goes down, they sleep, only to do it all again the next morning, as it should be, exactly how *I* want it to be—every day just the same."

Marjorie expertly scooped the cider cake from the black cast-iron oven so as not to break the spongy disk in half. Then, addressing Emily, she said, "Don't get to choose, do we? Not always. But ya don't want that, my dear."

"I do!" Emily insisted. "Why wouldn't I?"

"Cause, in the end, when all this . . . this life thing . . . is over, you'll wonder what meaning there was. Life should be good *and* not-so-good. It means you're alive."

"I don't wish away the bad, at least not all of it—only the bad on my birthday, the day I lost my papa. That day. Only that day. It's why I was there, at Papa's work. He promised to leave work early and said I could ride home with him on his horse." Emily looked up to find Marjorie staring at her.

Marjorie wrapped the cake in a tea towel and set it on the table to cool. She then sat opposite Emily. They looked at each other, Marjorie's expression softening.

"Emmy, ya got no closure, dear. I'm aware, as is your uncle." She reached across the table and took Emily's hand in hers. "Sweetheart, I'm not bakin' your cake on my account. In truth, each year, I close my eyes and think of your mama. I ask her, here in my head," Marjorie raised her other hand and tapped her temple. "I say to your mama, 'What would ya do if you were here?' And all that comes to mind is your mama's recipe. When she left ya with us, she told me ya always asked for cider cake on your birthday. That was her one request, so important was it for her. Enough so, or she wouldn't have mentioned it otherwise. So the cake cooling here isn't from me." Marjorie looked deep into Emily's eyes. "Do ya understand, dear?"

Emily stared at the steam rising from the spongy cake in front of her. The same sweet smell had filled the house the night her father disappeared.

"Silly, I know," Emily admitted. "But I do understand. All to do about a cake, right? But it's more than that. To me, it is." Tears spilled onto her cheeks as she looked at the woman who'd picked up the pieces of her shattered life and desperately tried to put them back together. "I'm so very sorry, Auntie. I love you and Albert so dearly, but I can't do this . . . this here." She looked down at the cake. Can you possibly understand?" She paused at the sorrow on Marjorie's face. "I still miss them." Emily turned away to hide her tears.

She stood to leave, but Marjorie, still holding her hand, gripped it tighter. "Stay with me another moment, dear," she urged. "Please?"

Reluctantly, Emily sat down.

Marjorie let go of her hand, and with a flour-dusted kitchen towel, wiped a tear from Emily's cheek. "Have I shared with you the night you came into our lives, the night you were born, or, I should say, early morning? I'm certain I've told you."

Emily shook her head. "I would have remembered."

"Well then, as I said, 'twas nighttime when your father came for me and Barbara Folsom, our neighbor. The old house was a ways from town, and by the time we arrived, your mother was slipping in and out of consciousness. I kept a cold, damp cloth on her forehead and prayed in earnest. Ya see, her pregnancy hadn't been without incident, and your mother was frightened, even terrified, that you or she would not survive. But she wanted you so badly."

Emily's eyes grew wide. "I haven't heard this. But I want to hear. What happened?"

"She labored all night, your mother, her suffering and cries so palpable I told Albert to take your father into the adjacent room and shut the door. Hours passed, and when we thought we were certain to lose her, lose the both of you, then came the miracle." Marjorie tilted her head to one side. "Have I truly never told you this?"

Emily's eyes widened farther. "No, Auntie. Never."

"All right, where was I?"

"You thought we wouldn't survive. What was this miracle?"

"Oh yes, the miracle, Emmy, was that just before sunrise, we heard the song of a whippoorwill that came and perched on the windowsill. At first I was frightened. Ya know what it means when you hear the whippoorwill?"

"No, Auntie, tell me."

"Some say the whippoorwill can sense a person's soul departing and capture it as it leaves, delivering it safely to heaven, though it had the opposite effect on your mother. It brought us comfort to see your mother revived and gaining strength. You know how she loved the little birds, especially starlings. I always imagined that was why they lived farther from town, away from your uncle and me, so your mother could sit on her porch for hours and watch the starlings above the fields. Few things brought her more comfort. And that little bird in the window was all it took for her. You were born a perfect baby, and your hands—I remember your hands, how delicate. I couldn't help noticing as I counted your fingers and toes."

Marjorie gave a little gasp when Emily frowned. Clearly, the story did not have the effect she hoped for. "Are you all right, dear?"

"No, Auntie. I'm not all right."

"What troubles ya?"

"This talk . . . it serves mostly to remind me of my father gone missing. And what about my mother? How can I ever know what happened to her? I don't . . . I can't believe the sordid things people say. They judge her character flawed, but they don't know. They don't understand what happened. I promised my mother I would never tell, but can I now defend her?"

Marjorie lowered her eyes. "I wish I knew, child. I don't know what you promised your mother. I—"

"It's all right, Auntie. I'm grateful for everything. I truly am, though I'm not ready to celebrate. I don't know if I ever will be . . ." Emily's voice cracked as she tried to explain. "Cider cake," she said, "makes me believe Mama is still here with me when she's not. It brings her back when I can't have her. You understand?" The tears began to flow. "I can't have her. Now, will you please . . . please excuse me?"

Emily headed into her bedroom, where she closed the door.

A moment later, Albert entered the kitchen through the back door. Using the kitchen cloth, Marjorie wiped her tears away.

Albert inhaled, then smiled. The freshly baked aroma of cider cake had that effect on him. Then, noticing Marjorie's forlorn expression, he grew concerned. "What happened? Where is Emmy?"

"No cause for alarm, Albert. Give her a moment. Christian's on his way. The boy has a talent for healin' her heart like none other. She'll be right as rain as soon as he arrives."

Albert nodded, grabbed his hand planer, and exited through the front door. Marjorie took a fork from the table and sampled the cider cake. Then her eyes drifted to the kitchen window and the beam of light pouring in. In a quiet voice, she whispered, "I'll try again in a year."

Chapter 7

It was a typical day in most respects, temperate for a spring afternoon, with everyday conversations taking place around town. Suddenly, however, the azure sky over New Harmony dimmed. The citizens felt something strange in the air. Folks craned their necks and called to one another to come and see.

Transfixed, Albert set the planer aside and sat quietly, a heap of shavings at his feet. Slowly, he got up and looked skyward. Something blocked the sun. *A solar eclipse?* he wondered. *Imagine that. On Emmy's birthday, no less.* He'd seen one or two in his lifetime, but something about this one felt different. *Must be an omen—one of benevolence, I hope.*

As if God cloaked the sun and set the world in shadow, everything around Albert turned gray, the gloom seeming to soak through his surroundings. Then came pregnant clouds, dark and threatening, as if conjured into existence by some villainous source.

Albert shouted to his family. "Margie, Emmy, come see. Quickly now!" He crossed the street into Walter's yard, where Walter and Georgia sat on their porch, as they did most evenings. Barbara Folsom sat there too. The smell of onion soup wafting from the window would normally have whet their appetites, but the change in the air unsettled their stomachs. It was more than just the darkening sky on an otherwise sunny day. Something was coming. They could feel it. They joined Albert in the yard, necks bent, gazes upward.

As the solar eclipse reached its zenith, there came a thing beyond explanation. *What is that?* Albert thought. *Music?* So subtle was the sound that, at first, Albert could only wonder. He turned his head left and right, listening. But he couldn't discern the direction of the sound until he tilted his head to the north. Was it indeed music he heard? He closed his eyes and listened carefully. It was, and it played inside his head.

Opening his eyes, he looked around to see if anyone else heard it and he didn't experience some form of insanity. To his relief, the others appeared equally befuddled. They too seemed lost in the corridors of their minds, questioning what could be intruding upon such a private space.

Georgia spoke up first. "I do believe I hear something," she said, looking at the others. "Am I alone in hearing it?"

"Music?" asked Walter.

Georgia nodded hesitantly.

"I hear it as well," said Albert. He turned and looked back across the street. Marjorie and Emily had yet to come out of the house. He looked back to Walter, Georgia, and Barbara, who listened in silence.

Georgia tilted her head. "I don't like it. The sound is pretty enough, but it's not natural."

"Certainly not," agreed Albert.

The canopy of gloom hung heavily above them as the ethereal sound filled their heads. *So soft and soothing,* Albert thought. Had the heavens opened? Were they witnessing the accompaniment of angels? Or was it a matter of darkness that descended, something unwanted?

He searched the skies in vain. The music was soft enough that he could hear Walter's chickens fussing in their coop yet loud enough that each note rang clear. Each note traveled along a treble scale, combining with the others and creating complex cords that had an almost intoxicating effect. It wasn't the sound of harp, flute, or horsehair drawn across strings. No, the mysterious music sounded something like a medieval chant but less somber, like a choir of angels but more penetrating.

"The persistent darkness and whatever I hear in my head feel wrong," Georgia said as she turned and hurried back into the house, Barbara following.

They no sooner shut the door when a tumultuous north wind began pounding the earth, followed by a furious hailstorm that knocked Albert on his back and left Walter barely standing. Tree branches snapped, and trees toppled, their roots ripped from the ground, the dirt that bound them to the earth thrown into the air. Shingles flew from rooftops, and windows shattered. Then, as suddenly as it began, it stopped and everything went eerily silent—no twittering birds, no chirping crickets, no barking dogs. Even the peculiar music was gone. Only their worrisome thoughts remained.

Feeling nauseated, Walter looked at Albert on the ground. "You all right?" He extended his hand. "Let me help you up."

With Walter's help, Albert stood but remained bent over, catching his breath, before speaking. "My goodness! What was that? For heaven's sake, it knocked the wind out of me. And what about you? How do you feel? Are you all right?"

Walter's words tumbled out of him. "I'm fine, Albert," he said. "Dazed and a bit dizzy, but otherwise . . ."

They took a moment to look around at the debris.

Though it was early afternoon and the moon no longer eclipsed the sun, the darkness remained. In its wake, a stubborn shadow subdued the sun, diminishing its power to shine. Astonished, Albert and Walter stood, unable to move, their mouths agape.

Emily came running from the house. Christian followed and had yet to swallow a mouthful of cider cake. They stood in the yard, wide-eyed. Marjorie came out, stepping over branches, leaves, and splintered wood.

Just then, the schoolhouse bell sounded the emergency signal—its three distinct chimes calling volunteers to the town center.

Marjorie yelled, "Albert!" but he didn't hear. Instead, as if he'd gone deaf, he stared north toward Mount Erebus, the direction from whence the gale had come.

"Albert!" she yelled more loudly.

Half startled, he looked over at her. "Back inside!" he ordered. "Emmy, take your auntie into the house. Now!"

"No, Albert," said Marjorie. "I would rather go with ya. I don't want to stay here alone."

Albert shook his head. "Absolutely not," he insisted. "Walt and I will go. You won't be alone. Emmy will be with you. We'll go see what the mayor says, then come back."

Walter tugged on Albert's shirt. "Albert?"

Albert turned. "What?"

"They'll be organizing cleanup, is all. If you stay and watch over Georgia and the others, I'll—"

"No. You and I should both go. With that storm, there may be more need than simply cleaning up after." Albert looked at Christian. "You should come as well."

Christian nodded. "I will, Mr. Hampshire. But first I must see to my father. I'll meet you both after that."

"What about your brother? He's a doctor. Perhaps you can bring him as well."

Christian shrugged. "Trust me. Wherever he's needed, he's already there." Excusing himself, Christian set off at a run.

From the street, Albert heard Marjorie, now on the front porch of their home, calling to him as she wrapped a gray shawl around her shoulders, Emily at her side.

"We're heading to the church," she called out. "See what the parson has to say. Walter, would ya please ask if Georgia wants to go with us? Tell her we're goin' to the church."

Before Walter could answer, Georgia and Barbara appeared on their front porch. "We're coming," Georgia called.

Chapter 8

These damnable flies! The beast scratched his back with his massive claws. He again looked at his thick, furry arm and monstrous paw. *If anyone sees me, they'll kill me.* He blinked against the onslaught of insects and swatted at those that buzzed past his sensitive ears. He looked down at his body. What brought him to this? *I'm neither wolf nor bear, but beast only, not anything natural. I need a bath. That's what I need.*

Just then, his ears pricked. Something moved in the distance. An animal or a man?

The thought of being hunted sent him scurrying farther into the remoteness and away from the memory of the angry faces and men with torches. He could no longer recall who the men were, only that they wished him harm. His days and nights blurred together as time passed, and still he felt unsafe. He must find shelter, and soon.

How long? he wondered. Had it been weeks or months since he'd seen anything that might indicate a human? Not knowing calmed his nerves. He was, nonetheless, torn between the comfort of it and the loneliness. *I used to have people,* he thought, *people I no longer remember. And who am I, or, rather, what am I?*

Hunger stole his mind from his thoughts of isolation. His belly ached with a constant need to fill it. The empty feeling stirred thoughts of his pursuers; the more he contemplated, the more his rage grew. No more running. He would rip them apart, devour them.

He recoiled at this last thought. *No. Not humans. I'm not an animal.*

What shame he felt for his momentary desire to tear into human flesh, consuming it. In despair, he clutched his head, then scrubbed his paws over his new, horrible face, the protruding jaw packed with crushing teeth.

He roared into the wind while in his mind he screamed, *I'm cursed!* Then he crumpled to the ground in a heap. He could ignore the emptiness in his stomach more easily than the loneliness inside. His only relief came from imagining he did not exist. Sleep was the closest he came to that, deep and dreamless sleep. He'd almost closed his eyes when he noticed the sunlight dimming, and high above him, black birds riding on the wind, circling. He couldn't remember why it didn't surprise him, but it didn't. He half expected to see them, and although he had no way to be sure, he knew they'd followed him for days.

He looked toward where the sun floated like a gray disk in a cloudless sky. He looked at the sun directly for the first time in his memory with little discomfort, feeling no need to avert his eyes. *Such strangeness,* he thought. *It isn't night or day but a dismal stillness, like death.* He froze with fear. *Is this the end of me? Or the end of everything?*

Then, like the sound of a thousand horses charging to battle, a fierce wind crashed through the forest, ripping branches from their trunks and bending the trees lining the river, their leaves whipped away in the wind. Instinctively, the beast dug his claws into the earth, bracing himself against the force. A large tree anchored haphazardly on the riverbank, its roots exposed by the water chewing at the soil, collapsed into the river with a crack, sending a blinding spray of water into the wind.

Then, as suddenly as the wind began, it ceased, everything returning to the soft, gray stillness.

The beast remained motionless, his claws set like spikes in the ground, his back arched.

A beautiful musical sound unlike any he had ever heard pierced the silence.

This lullaby stirred within him emotions, calming him. He felt himself slipping out of consciousness, seduced by memories lost and a beautiful, most welcome dreamscape—a country garden. Suddenly, he was there. It seemed familiar, but he couldn't understand why or recall when or where. The garden consisted of a mixture of ornamental and edible plants. Flowers lined a white, wooden picket fence. All around him grew cabbages, radishes, turnips, and other vegetables best planted in early spring. The gate to the fence stood open. He cautiously approached and began to tremble. A young woman knelt, pulling turnips from the dirt and placing them in a wicker basket at her side. She wore a yellow dress, bright-red butterflies fluttering across the fabric. Her long brunette hair flowed down her back, swaying gently in the breeze.

His heart flooded with inexplicable joy.

Who was she? He felt certain he knew her, but how and from where? If only he could see her face.

A sudden memory stopped him.

Wait! I do recall some things! I believe I tried rescuing her. She was possibly sick or sleeping, but she needed me. Then what did I do? He sensed there was more.

The beast struggled, trying desperately to remember. Gradually, more of the memory surfaced. She had said he was a good man and begged him not to do something, but he'd done it anyway—to save her! But he'd ruined everything and lost her!

Cautiously, he approached, desperate to see her face and fill in the gaps in his memory. But when she turned to look at him, he recoiled. He shook his head violently but could not tear his eyes from the hideous face staring back at him. The hair and the dress he'd presumed belonged to another, someone once dear to him. But this?

In place of the woman from somewhere within his memory was an elderly, decrepit face with a bent nose and eyes that looked like coal.

Just then, the garden where he stood melted like boiling tar and was sucked into what could only be described as total and complete oblivion, though his conscience self remained. The lullaby transformed into something dark, a mindless cacophony, before going quiet. The yellow dress dissolved into black, the butterflies wilting as if dead. The only thing remaining was the face of the old, demonic woman, her lips curling into a smile. His horrified reaction pleased her.

"There you are," she hissed. "Remember me?"

The beast staggered backward, answering her in his mind. *No, get out of my head. I don't know you. Who are you? What are you?*

"We've met before. Yes, yes, dear beast. We're well acquainted. You could say we've had dealings."

His attempt to speak came out as a growl. He continued speaking with his mind. *Dealings? Was it you? Did you turn me into what I am? Tell me. And who are the men following me? Did you send them?* He grew more infuriated, his growling more intense.

Another haggard face appeared from behind the blackness, her withered lips also drawn up in a grin. From within his mind, he heard her say, "Found you!" an unrestrained glee peppering her ancient voice. "Thought you got away, did you? Never!"

Laughter filled his head when a third hag appeared, her deep-set eyes scrutinizing him through a face more rounded than the others'. Her eyebrows formed a thick, gray bristle above her crooked nose. She opened her mouth, and through rotted teeth came a whistling sound. "'Tis nothing but what the beast deserves," she slurred, speaking to the other disembodied faces that floated in and out of view. The trio of tormentors clearly delighted in his discomfort.

What have you done to me? At a sudden realization, he cried in anguish. *Whatever this is, I brought it upon myself. I know it now. For my sin, you've made me an animal, but I am no animal.*

They looked on in amusement. "Sure you are. Look at you. You're a beast," the first old woman replied, grinning. "You're much worse than an animal. You're a monster!"

Only because you made me one.

"Oh no, dear beast," said the most aged of the tormenting faces. "We couldn't have changed you into what you are. There's no one with that power. We simply turned you inside out, the ugliness inside you exposed. Only now are you seen for what you truly are—a monster, no longer able to hide your inhumanity. This is your curse."

I'm cursed, surely, but I'm not a beast.

"We admit it. We created you, but not without your help."

"Can't do it without your help," agreed the one with withered lips. "And you were helpful, yes, very accommodating."

Stop it! the beast cried. *Let me be!* With that, the beast wailed as he thought of the woman he'd lost, the one he'd somehow betrayed. He anguished for her and the loss of her and the transgression that tore them apart.

He opened his eyes, forcing his mind away from the nightmare. The aftermath of a storm met his gaze. In the physical world, the evergreens had fared best against a barrage of wind, while the river birch and elm trees, robbed of their leaves, no longer stood.

Feeling the need to hide, he got to his feet and retreated farther into the woods, slowly moving through the brush that led up bluffs covered with splintered branches and broken shrubs. Finally, he reached the edge of a ravine. At the bottom, a stream cut its way through the heavy vegetation. He climbed over the ridge and down to the rocky streambed, where he spotted a well-worn trail on the other side.

A game trail, he thought.

The trail followed the stream, banking left and running parallel to a thicket of leaf dogwood. This was more manageable.

The afternoon sun limped across the sky, so dim the beast could hardly see it. Leaving the trail, he broke through a crop of spear thistles and poison ivy, then traveled uphill until he arrived at the top of a bluff. A heavenly sight sprawled before him—a valley untouched by the wind that had pounded the forest behind him. Flanked by cattails and clumps of switchgrass, a clear stream wove its way through the valley like a ribbon, eventually emptying into a brilliant blue pond. A dazzling display of red, yellow, purple, and white wildflowers carpeted the valley. Best of all, nothing indicated the presence of humans.

But then, in the brush near a cluster of granite stones that looked to have broken off from the ridge above, he saw something that sent his heart pounding.

Had he finally found a home?

The beast's eyes narrowed on the dark opening at the base of the ridge. A cave! But was it deep enough for shelter?

Amidst his feelings of hope, a sense of nervousness washed over him. *Something's coming*, he thought as paranoia gripped his heart. Suddenly, a clap of thunder assaulted his sensitive ears, and he buried his face in his paws. Then, slowly lifting his head, he peered south, past the meadow, at the mountain, so grand and imposing he couldn't ignore it. His gaze moved to where the rocky face and towering cliffs rose into thin air until lost in dark, foreboding clouds that glistened amidst sporadic flashes of lightning.

Ominous and imposing, it stirred within him a sense of impending danger, like a serpent waiting to strike.

But he had not the time to consider whatever peril there might be. Nothing mattered more than exploring the cave.

Chapter 9

A chill breeze blew grass shavings and crumpled leaves across the road leading to the ranch house. A flock of starlings crossed the setting sun just as Martha Owen arrived, though she was less aware of the time owing to the pale-gray sky soaked in unrelenting dusk. Tall cottonwoods waved in the wind as she pulled back on the reins. "Whoa!" she hollered while stopping her carriage short of the house. A fallen tree blocked the road.

"Skinny!" she yelled.

Almost immediately, a man who was anything but skinny shuffled out of the stable. Hurrying toward her, he hiked up his pants and pulled his suspenders over his shoulders.

"Ma'am, you all right?" he asked, noticing her disheveled hair and dusty clothing. He'd never seen Mrs. Owen in any condition other than her usual well-fed, pampered self.

"Don't I look all right?" she snapped. She handed him a sizable bundle of soiled clothing. She always brought more fine dresses, bonnets, and women's personals whenever she returned from Bloomington. "Hand this off to the help," she insisted. "Tell them to launder it immediately, and I don't care how long it takes, no matter how late the hour. Just have them do it. And while you're at it, why is this tree blocking the road?" She swished her hand as if her stern command could brush away the fallen trunk and branches with no effort on her part. "Remove it."

"Beg your pardon, ma'am. I hadn't noticed it with the storm. There's been other things I . . ."

"Just do it!"

"Should I remove the tree first, ma'am? Before I . . ."

"Should've removed the tree already. Of course, you've been lazing around, I suppose. Is that it?"

Not allowing him to answer, she continued. "But never you mind that. Listen to me good," she demanded. "I had an unfortunate accident on my way here. Like a thief, a terrible storm stole my new dresses from Italy or France, one or the other. Does it matter? No! They blew away, and I had to stop the carriage and gather them up. Took most of an hour. And now, if it's all right with you, I'd rather they not be ruined further, so get the laundry started, then return for the tree by lantern if necessary. Is that clear?"

"Yes, ma'am."

"Robert—is he here?"

"He is, ma'am. Your husband's inside." Skinny bowed his head before rushing off, arms full of Mrs. Owen's laundry.

Martha brushed the dust off her skirt, trying to appear more presentable, then crossed the yard and entered the house through the front door. There, she called, "Robert!"

The house felt cold and empty.

"Back here, darling," he called. "It's warm here. They kept the fire burning for us."

She followed Robert's voice to where he sat, his boots drying next to the fire, his feet warming on the hearth. He appeared too comfortable and too unconcerned about her, enough so that he deserved a piece of her mind.

"Where were you?" she demanded.

"Whatever do you mean, darling?"

"You expected me back hours ago or more. Did you not think to look for me? By the looks of you lazing about, I suppose not. But I'll have you know I nearly ran off the road. The wind practically blew me out of the carriage. Only by the grace of God am I alive."

Robert groaned, eyes half closed. "Forgive me, dear. I've been at the office—town business, an emergency of sorts." He slowly stood and poured himself a glass of red wine, then peered over his shoulder at her. Only then did he notice her untidy appearance. He breathed deeply as he took in her tousled hair and dirty, wrinkled dress. "My, my," he said. "Looks like you could use a drink yourself." He handed her the one he'd poured for himself, pinched another glass between fingers, and overfilled it, spilling wine onto the polished floor.

"Of course, I was worried about you. It's just that . . ." He sat on the plush leather couch and tapped his fine crystal glass with his finger. "Perhaps you haven't noticed, but the entire town is in shambles because of that damn storm."

Martha stood stiffly, questioning whether she was still angry or not. Deciding on the latter, she sipped her wine and sat beside him.

"Did you do everything we agreed upon?" he asked.

"If you're asking whether I submitted an advertisement to the Bloomington newspaper, no, not yet. I already told you. I hired Emily Hampshire as we agreed. She hasn't started her first day of teaching, and you already want me to release her?"

"Who? Jedediah's daughter?"

"Yes, Robert. Emily. Where have you been?"

Puzzled, the mayor looked at her inquisitively. "Darling, I fear you are confused. I'm not referring to young Ms. Hampshire. Whatever concern she is of ours, there's one more troublesome."

Martha nodded. "Yes. The headmaster, Mr. Parrish, of course." She took another sip and added, "It's not that I've forgotten, dear, as you suppose. But I recall you mentioning that we had to wait on ridding ourselves of Parrish."

"That's right. I said we must wait until after the election. And?"

"But that's not for nearly a month, and yet you want an advertisement posted now? Won't doing so tip our hand?"

"Perhaps. I'm anxious, I suppose. Mr. Parrish always undermines me, questions me. I must always remind him he isn't the mayor, and it's damned annoying."

Martha set her near-empty glass on the table. "What do you mean?"

Robert sighed. "Why, just this afternoon, the sheriff rang the alarm after the storm. By the time I arrived, Bronson Parrish was already there, organizing everyone to check on their neighbors, as if he was the authority."

"I know, darling. I know. The man undermines actual authority at every turn. I've had to live with it for years."

Robert shook his head in disgust. "He supposes himself so damned important. Even in public, I need to remind him that he is not the mayor—that I am. Worse, I must commence doing what he was already doing. It's more than frustrating."

Martha couldn't agree more. "And that's why he does it, darling."

"Precisely why, all in an effort to undermine me. It's no wonder few showed up for my instructions. And adding insult to injury, everyone knows they must make their way to the town hall when the emergency bell rings. Yet, today, most people went straight to the church. I was left wondering—"

"Now there's another," Martha interrupted.

"Another what?"

"Another who supposes themselves the authority."

"Uh-huh, Parson Burroughs." Robert's jaw tightened. "Yes. Except he's not just an authority but the ultimate moral authority." Robert bent over his sizable belly, picked up a boot, and reached inside to see if it was dry. Sensing moisture, he threw it near the fire, leaned back, and rubbed his sore feet, sulking.

"Patience, darling," Martha urged. "There's no rush, and we've gotten rid of worse. It's only a matter of time. I'll find Mr. Parrish's replacement, but until then, as you say, we mustn't show our cards, remember? Not till after the election."

"Yes, sweet Martha. No cause for controversy. Not yet."

"Not yet," Martha agreed. "Not yet."

Chapter 10

After the events of the previous day, a calm would have settled over New Harmony except for the curious sound, inaudible to the human ear, that played softly in everyone's heads.

Marjorie closed her front door and turned to see Georgia across the street, sitting on her porch, knitting. She covered a yawn with one hand, then called, "Georgia, did ya hear it last night?"

Georgia Buchanan rubbed her swollen eyes. "I did. I hardly slept. And you?"

"Same," said Marjorie. "Kept Albert up as well."

"Any idea what it could be," asked Georgia, "or what's causing it?"

"No," said Marjorie. "It's not unpleasant but for the strangeness."

"Akin to music," agreed Georgia. "That's what we heard, Walt and I." Georgia looked behind her to see Walter come out of the house. "I'd be more worried if it were less agreeable."

"Me as well. Glad to know we're not the only ones to hear it," said Marjorie. "Lulled me pleasantly to sleep, then woke me tellin' me I was in danger or some such nonsense. Albert can sleep through anythin', but even he was disturbed until he gave in to its calming effect."

Georgia pointed at Walter, who quietly listened on the porch beside her. "I thought he was speaking to me during the night, but he was sound asleep. So then I feared someone had broken into our house. I must have woken Walt half a dozen times."

Walter smiled and waved before turning and disappearing into the house.

Marjorie continued their conversation. "I doubt we're the only ones hearin' it. We're headed to the church this morning. The parson said he'd have more to tell us today. Wanted to pray on it, he said. And who isn't curious to hear what answers he received?"

Georgia yawned and rubbed her neck. "We'll go together if it's all right with you. We had the same thought. I don't suppose we're the only ones. I imagine there are people there already. The church is the first place people run to when something awful happens, even the ones who can't find their way there on Sundays. They'll be there all the same."

Marjorie agreed. "We all seek words of comfort at times like these."

Georgia nodded. "Walt's not to open the post office this morning—mayor's orders. But since everywhere's closed, I suppose that will only add to the crowd waiting at the church. We best hurry."

"Albert's still gettin' dressed," said Marjorie. "Only be a moment." As she said it, she walked across the street and peered at the damage to Georgia's house. "Looks like the wind got the better of you. We'll come by after and help clean up. We were lucky. Not much damage."

Georgia brushed it off. "We'll be fine," she said. "Looks worse than it is." The screen door banged, and they both turned to see Walter reappear on the porch.

"Albert!" yelled Marjorie. "Let's not keep the Buchanans waiting!"

Albert came out of the house, and the two couples headed toward the church on Main Street. Turning the corner, they noticed the street wasn't as cluttered with storm damage as the neighborhoods. In the distance, they could see a large crowd gathered at the church.

Amelia Taylor and her husband, Old Man Taylor, greeted them when they arrived. The restless crowd was tightly packed together, spilling into the street.

Marjorie took Amelia's hand. "How long have ya been waitin'?"

"Less than an hour," said Amelia. "Parson's not here. Doors to the church are locked."

Just then, they noticed Barbara Folsom weaving her way toward them. "Parson's on his way," she hollered. "I'm told it won't be long now." She hugged the women and nodded at their husbands.

"How long ya been waitin'?" Marjorie asked.

"Believe it if you will," said Barbara, "but I was first to arrive, even before Abigail and her toadies. I've been milling around, listening. And get this . . . I've gathered that we're all experiencing the same thing. So very peculiar, and everyone has an opinion. I've heard some say the music is soothing, while others, which is mostly everyone else, are frightened by it. And why shouldn't they be? But everyone has their reasons. It's just that no one knows what to think. If anyone knows, the parson will." Suddenly, Barbara peered about curiously. "Emmy's not with you? I just heard Abigail saying Emmy's the new teacher with Woolhauser retiring. I wished to congratulate her."

Beaming, Marjorie answered, "She is. Starts Monday, first of the week."

"Still seeing Shear's boy?" Barbara asked.

Marjorie's grin widened. "Yes, Christian."

"That's the fellow."

"They've had eyes for each other for as long as I can remember," Georgia said.

"They have," admitted Marjorie. "Speaking of Emmy—I wonder what's keepin' her." Marjorie looked about, stretching her neck to look over the crowd. "Albert, you tell her where we'd be?"

"She's coming, though not without Christian. That's who she waited for."

"Might be here already somewhere," said Barbara. "Everyone in town is here." She tried peering over heads, but she was too short for it to do any good.

A whole foot taller than the ladies, Walter could see unobstructed. He began scanning the crowd, searching for Emily, and noticed the parson approaching. "Here he comes with Hannah!"

Bodies shifted and heads turned to look south, down the road, at the two figures approaching and holding hands. As they got closer, the parson stopped and whispered to his wife. She immediately left his side, disappearing into the crowd and heading to the church. Meanwhile, the parson greeted people while weaving his way to an empty wagon parked in front of the school on the other side of the street from the church. He coaxed his old bones up and into the wagon bed, then stood, silently waiting. A hush fell over the crowd.

Though aged, the parson was well-preserved in faith. His full, gray beard covered most of his face, and his gray-blue eyes appeared as if holy relics kept behind his round wire glasses. His expression, kind and unassuming, emanated the warmth of a saint. Raising his voice, he addressed the gathering.

"I call upon you, my brothers and sisters," he said, "neighbors and friends. Eclipses have long been suspected as signs from the heavens or forces of nature that foretell impending disaster and human suffering. But let me remind you: eclipses have been part of the human story from the beginning. Considered alone, they bode neither good nor evil. But it was what accompanied the eclipse yesterday that has sown discord and caused such great concern. The source of the sound we hear in our heads is, for the moment, unknown. However, let us not be careless. Have we not assurances that the Lord will sustain us? Rather, listen to the still, small voice in your hearts and not the voices that vie for your attention, especially voices that drown the conscience or stir fear."

The parson paused, looking out into the sea of faces. Upon noticing the longing in their expressions, he continued. "There are no answers; therefore, your worries are legitimate. Nonetheless, let us concern ourselves with repairing the damage. We must work together, neighbor helping neighbor. It is our good fortune the crops were planted. In seven days, New Harmony will celebrate the arrival of spring. We shall bond as we've always done by attending the Spring

Contra dance. If we wait for brighter days to be happy, we allow the darkness to dim our souls."

With that, he climbed down from the wagon and went to the church, where Hannah waited. She greeted him with a hug, and together they disappeared into the building. Once the doors closed, the people began to depart for their homes.

"Wait!" said a boisterous voice. "Listen to me, all of you!"

The crowd turned back in the direction of the wagon. There, just as the parson had, stood Abigail Williams. She boldly raised her hands skyward as if she had descended from heaven. "Listen to me," she shouted. "This is important." She waited until she had everyone's full attention, and when all could hear, she proceeded. "Last night, the heavenly voices we all hear—they spoke to me. The splendor and quality of their voices defy description."

Marjorie and those around her gasped in disbelief.

"It did!" she hollered. "I swear to it on the memory of my late husband."

As absurd as her claim was, who could resist listening? And so they did.

"The voices told me," she continued, "and I quote, 'Those who hearken to our warnings will find refuge from the coming storm. Beware the coming storm!'"

A sense of uneasiness stirred among the people, the gloom hanging heavily over the town seeming to intensify.

A voice rose from the crowd, that of a young man. "The parson advises otherwise!"

"Who speaks?" Abigail demanded as she looked in the direction of the voice.

A hand reached high above the crowd. "It was me," said Christian. "I said it."

With the eyes of a hawk, Abigail stared the young man down. Emily Hampshire stood at his side.

"Parson Burroughs is a man of God," Christian said, turning and addressing the crowd. "We're better off listening to him."

"You do that, young man," Abigail answered confidently. "But before you do, ask yourself this: Did the voices from heaven speak to the parson? Obviously not. He said so himself. You heard him. 'There are no answers,'" Abigail sneered. "The parson admits to having no answers because the voices don't speak to him. They've chosen me, and now I'm telling you. Beware the coming storm. Listen to the voices and save yourselves. I say no more. Consider yourselves warned."

Susannah Boyer and Elizabeth Howe climbed into the wagon and stood beside her. "I'd believe Abby if I were you!" screamed Susannah.

Elizabeth remained silent, peering wide-eyed and forebodingly into the crowd as if to accentuate the danger. Fear spread through the gathering, the peace of the parson's words vanishing.

Christian quickly led Emily away from the fear-stricken people who now panicked, pushing and bumping into each other.

From the safety of the wagon, Abigail, Susannah, and Elizabeth watched as the ruckus intensified. "I think we're done here, ladies," said Abigail, and the three climbed down from the wagon bed, disappearing into the crowd.

Chapter 11

Even before the Folsom's rooster crowed that Monday morning, the sound of clanging pots filled the Hampshire kitchen. Marjorie bustled about preparing sawmill gravy, flour biscuits, and fried eggs. She looked out the window to see another cloudy day. At first light, she hoped the sun would break through the gloom that had persisted since the eclipse, but the gray showed no signs of letting up. It was Emily's first day teaching, and Marjorie knew she would wake up soon, not wanting to be late.

As Emily staggered into the kitchen, Marjorie greeted her warmly. "Good mornin', dear. Sleep well, did you?"

Emily sighed. "Not very, I'm afraid." She stretched her back and yawned.

"Kept awake?" Marjorie asked. "Did you hear it during the night?" Marjorie anticipated her answer curiously.

"The music? If that's what it is."

"Of course, dear. It's what everyone is talkin' about."

"Yes, Auntie. I heard it. Once. Twice maybe, during the night. We might have to get used to it. It doesn't appear to be going away. But that wasn't the cause of my sleeplessness."

"What was it, dear?"

"Touch of nerves, I suppose. I'm accustomed to being a student, not a teacher. What if they don't like me?"

"Did I hear ya properly? Not like you? Slim chance of that."

"Your mouth to God's ear," said Emily. "I hope you're right. I suppose I'm still not all together, not with all that's happened."

"Of course I'm right," Marjorie assured her. "And things'll come back to normal."

Emily sighed. "What about you? Did you sleep well?"

"Mostly, havin' a lovely dream," Marjorie admitted, "floatin' down a river on a ferry boat with Jane, of all people."

"Jane?" Emily asked inquisitively. "Who is that?"

Marjorie giggled. "President Pierce's wife is who. She invited me to a ball at the capitol in Washington. I dreamed I was suddenly there." Marjorie grinned delightedly at the retelling. "I wore a beautiful green-and-blue silk dress with a mink fur collar—one of those fancy ones. And, oh, the music!" she said. "Lovely, lovely, so lovely the music." And then Marjorie grew silent, staring blankly off into the distance, lost in thought.

"Well, go on," urged Emily. "I'd like to hear more. It sounds wonderful."

Marjorie shrugged. "I awoke," she said.

"That's it?" asked Emily.

"It's not all," said her aunt with a puzzled look. "I awoke to the same sweet music playin' in my head, still hearin' it after I woke up. It orchestrated my dream like it planted everything I was dreamin', or at least it seemed to be. I . . . I don't know for what reason, but it makes me nervous, especially after what the parson said."

Emily nodded. "We all are, Auntie—nervous, that is. But I believe the parson. So does Christian."

"Well, I, for one, won't be givin' ear to Abigail. Not certain what to think of her, those things she said, but never mind that. Now, come here. Let me see to your corset."

Emily stepped forward and turned around, offering her back to her aunt for the tightening. "Neither am I nor Christian," Emily said. "Nor are we paying mind to the chanting or music or whatever it is. We don't care what voices there are or what they are telling us."

Marjorie pulled the lacing tight. "People say it's harmless. But harmless or not, it's unsettlin'." Marjorie finished by tying a bow, and Emily excused herself and left for her room. She reemerged a moment later, her dress on and ready. Under her arm, she carried teaching manuals and books wrapped with white ribbon. She kissed Marjorie's cheek before pouring herself a cup of coffee and sitting at the table.

Marjorie prepared Emily a plate as she spoke. "Couldn't help noticin' you were up awfully late. Your Christian can't bear partin' from ya, can he?"

"It was only eight o'clock," Emily lightly protested as her aunt set her breakfast in front of her.

"Just that it's your first day and ya must be tired, which reminds me—your uncle and I can't be prouder. You've grown up to be a fine young woman."

Marjorie's eyes smiled as she prepared a plate for herself. Suddenly lost in memory, she sat, tapping her fork on the table as the minutes from the past ticked away.

"Forgive me, dear," she said. "But I'm an old woman feeling a bit sentimental this mornin'. Just seein' ya all grown up can't help but put me to thinkin'. There's somethin' I'd like ya to know."

Emily waited for Marjorie to speak.

Quietly, Marjorie set her fork down and reached out to Emily. They held hands across the table, and Emily whispered, "I'm listening, Auntie."

Marjorie spoke pensively of days long gone but not lost to memory. "I wasn't able to have babies, not my own. After a while, your uncle and I, we stopped tryin'. We lost two to miscarry. We named 'em—though we can't bear to say their names out loud. I never held my babies, not alive, not alive and breathin'. Dreadful days those were." Marjorie sighed.

"Occurred to us it wasn't to be. The good Lord didn't will it, and losin' the babies—I, well . . ." She stared blankly out the kitchen window before continuing. "It was then that your papa went missin'. I thought I was to lose my Albert as well, so brokenhearted was he, losin' his brother an' all."

Marjorie's brow furrowed as raindrops beaded on the kitchen window, running like the tears she felt welling up in her heart. Shaking free of the distraction, she turned her attention back to Emily.

"Auntie, I'm certain you couldn't bear another loss. I can't begin to imagine."

"No. You're right. I couldn't. As it was, the day we lost your papa was when we lost your mama. We knew it, though it was hard to watch. She left us little by little—in her mind. The parson said, 'Ya either swallow pain or it swallows you.' Your mama—the pain just swallowed her whole. But I tell ya for certain, and I mean it. She'd be proud of ya now, seein' what you've become, what you've growed up to be. You made us proud, your uncle and me. But I'm left feelin' conflicted here." She lightly patted her chest. "I wonder, can a heart rejoice and mourn at the same time? What good comes from such sorrow and loss? Is it the price of a blessing? Is it? We got a child from the worst pain possible. From that, our greatest desire—you, my dear. We got you." Marjorie's eyes welled with tears. "How can we rejoice after everythin'? But we do, don't we?"

"There's no fault in it, Auntie. It's just life." Emily squeezed her aunt's hand more tightly. "What would I have done without you? How could you ever believe your prayers produced such pain? There must be a plan, one realized only in heaven perhaps. Things are meant to be."

"I know. I know. Albert says you saved us. You healed our pain."

Emily sensed the mixture of gratitude and heartache in her aunt's words. She understood perfectly. The sadness she'd felt at losing her parents had never squared itself with her genuine appreciation and love for her uncle and aunt—not entirely. It was easy to get lost in the what-ifs. But life was what it was, and above all, Emily felt grateful for the woman in front of her.

All Emily could do was embrace her aunt, and so she did. They held each other, neither wanting to let go. Then, finally, Marjorie retired to her sitting chair in the parlor, a cup of coffee in hand. She placed it on the end table and began mending a pair of Albert's stockings.

Quickly, Emily finished her meal, drank the last of her coffee, and grabbed her books. "Sorry," she called to her aunt. "In a rush. Can I wash these once I return?" She placed the plate, fork, cup, and saucer in the water bowl while looking over her shoulder at Marjorie.

"Don't bother yourself with that. You'll be late," Marjorie set down her needle and thread. She folded the pair of stockings. "Albert will be up soon enough, hungry for breakfast. I'll wash 'em together." She gave Emily a sideways grin. Emily returned the gesture with a gracious smile. "But I need ya to do somethin' for me, Emmy." She stood and walked into the kitchen.

"What's that?"

"Last night, Mrs. Folsom asked if I could loan her a cup of sugar." Marjorie handed her a cloth bag.

Emily took the sack and kissed her aunt's forehead. Marjorie's soft, wrinkled hand gently patted her cheek. The screen door slammed behind Emily as she hurried out into the drizzling rain. She dropped the bag across the street, then headed to the schoolhouse, jumping over puddles and holding a scarf around her head.

Emily quickened her pace as she turned left on Main Street. When the school came into view, she doubled her pace. It was her first day, and Mrs. Owen asked that she arrive well before eight to ring the morning bell precisely ten minutes before the hour.

Emily loved the old bell. She remembered the stories of how it came to be, cast decades ago in some Irish foundry. A distinctive sound resonated from the mixture of bronze and tin. Its tone felt like home to the residents of New Harmony. It not only announced the start of school but other events as well. Parson Burroughs rang the bell early Sunday mornings, calling parishioners to services at the New Harmony church directly across the street from the school.

The town's volunteer fire department rang the bell to summon volunteers for fire, flood, or any emergency requiring immediate attention. In such cases, the bell rang three times, paused a moment, and then rang three more times. That always brought people out of their homes to see what emergency had befallen New Harmony.

And yet, with all the reminiscences the old bell conjured, one memory brought about an ache Emily wished to forget.

Part 2

The Letter

Chapter 12

Emily peered through the school window at the regulator clock, taking note of the time. Because she arrived earlier than she thought, she sat alone, out of the rain on the steps under the eaves at the front of the school, waiting to ring the bell. She stared at the church across the street, remembering the stories her mother told of how the founders of New Harmony built the church in the center of town, and then the school, and then the town hall. They took immense pride in its construction: using redbrick rather than just lumber, pinkish granite for the foundation, and other materials meant to last.

Emily's first memories of the old bell marked one of the saddest days of her life—her father's funeral. How young she had been at only eight years of age. She tried to envision how the events of the day should have proceeded. After the service, those who attended would have followed her father's casket to the graveyard. The bell would have rung from the time the funeral carriage departed from the church until it arrived at the open grave. That was the custom, the way New Harmony honored its dead. Since her father went missing, however, there was no need for a casket or procession. But the bell rang regardless. It rang for the time it would have taken for her father's final journey to his resting place.

When Emily's mother died, they'd used an ordinary wagon from Hyrum's general store, not the shiny black funerary carriage drawn by an equally shiny black horse. Few accompanied the wagon to the cemetery, hardly a procession.

It was customary to show respect when death visited New Harmony, when the bell rang for the dead. People stopped what they were doing, gentlemen removed their hats, and everyone remained silent as the procession passed. Heads bowed, and even children stopped playing, but they'd extended no such courtesy to Emily's mother. The bell never rang for Ruth Hampshire. She'd become an embarrassment, and her behavior would neither be forgiven nor forgotten.

The hour arrived for Emily to ring the bell to signal the start of the school day. She gripped the rope and pulled hard. *I'm going to ring the bell for you, Mama.* The old bell rang loudly for all to hear. It rang in memory of her mother. Whether others knew it or not didn't matter to Emily. It rang for her all the same.

☾

Peering into her assigned classroom, Emily noticed someone seated in her chair. She stopped when she recognized Martha Owen.

"Good morning, Ms. Hampshire." Martha sat with impeccable posture as she motioned for Emily to enter.

Emily remained quiet as she stepped forward, stopping opposite Mrs. Owen on the other side of her desk. Mrs. Owen would not vacate Emily's chair until she was ready. Emily immediately recognized the position of power the simple gesture conveyed. It was Emily's first day as a new teacher, and her education in compliance had already begun.

"Good morning, Mrs. Owen," Emily finally said in greeting. "Can I help you?" Emily set her handbag on the desk, her voice cordial and measured. They were not strangers to each other. Although Emily's father, Jedediah, was a distant memory, her mother was not. She was that scarlet item of clothing that bled and tainted everything when washed with light colors. Unfortunately, Mrs. Owen had a talent for passively reminding others of such troubling things.

"Why, yes, you can—help me, that is." Martha stood and gestured for Emily to sit in the vacated chair. Emily walked around her desk and did as asked.

Students would soon be filing in, so Martha wasted no time. She strolled about, speaking as she went. "I remember the day your father abandoned you and your mother. What a horrible, horrible day, you poor dear. And then your poor mother—oh my. She couldn't quite cope, could she? But nobody blamed her, dear. Least of all me." Martha pressed both sets of fingertips to her heart. "Yet, had she only cared more about you . . ." She stressed the word *cared*. "I'm so sorry. I suppose it's unkind to speak of such unpleasantries." Her saccharine tone called into question any measure of sincerity. Emily remained silent, listening. "But your uncle and aunt are fine people, aren't they? Yes, exceptionally fine people. My husband, Robert, often asks, 'How's Ruth's little girl faring?' And when you got your teaching certificate, he insisted I give you a position. Isn't that interesting?"

Emily felt it best not to hesitate in responding. "Yes, thank you, Mrs. Owen. And would you please extend my gratitude to the mayor? I—"

Martha interrupted, continuing as if Emily had said nothing. "We all care about you. Not just my Robert, mind you." Martha twitched as if brushing the dust off her thoughts. "And, yes, since you asked, there is one thing you can do for me."

"Yes, of course."

"Keep an eye on Mr. Parrish. Would you?"

Emily's brow furrowed. "Mr. Parrish?" she asked.

"Yes, dear. Him. Sorry to say it, but Mr. Parrish hasn't the best intentions." She shuddered a bit and pursed her lips. Just speaking his name appeared difficult for Martha. "If you hear anything unseemly, unbecoming of someone entrusted with our children, please inform me immediately." Her eyes widened, and her eyebrows rose. "You do get my meaning, dear?" Emily nearly expected to be patted on the head.

"Yes. Certainly," Emily replied, but not without reservation. She'd never known Bronson Parrish to be anything but proper, the kindly headmaster never uttering so much as a swear word or statement of ill humor.

"Inappropriate," Martha stressed.

"Oh yes, of course," Emily answered while trying to mask the uncertainty in her voice. "But—"

"Lastly, my grandson Alexander is under your care. You are his assigned teacher. Special attention, mind you. He is a good boy. His papa? That is another matter altogether, a family matter. My son is not currently in my favor, but my grandson is all I have and care about. Keep that in mind, won't you?"

"You have my word."

Suddenly, the classroom door swung open and two young schoolgirls entered. They were lost in youthful conversation, unsuccessfully suppressing their giggles. However, as soon as they noticed Mrs. Owen, their expressions turned solemn and the conversation ended. The door remained open as more students filed in, they, too, quickly quieting and taking their seats.

Emily couldn't help but notice how unnatural their behavior seemed, their responses bringing back memories of her days as a student. No one need tell them a disciplinary note sent to their parents from Mrs. Owen carried the shame of the entire town.

Once the children settled into their seats, Martha said, "Good morning," her arms crossed in front of her.

"Good morning, Mrs. Owen," they answered in unison.

Martha snapped her fingers and sternly said, "Listen here, each of you. Treat Ms. Hampshire respectfully, as if I taught you." She forced the corners of her mouth upward in a smile that appeared more like a smirk.

An uncomfortable silence followed as Martha stared, waiting. Finally, in practiced unison, the students answered. "Yes, Mrs. Owen."

"Yes, Mrs. Owen, what?" asked Martha.

In the front row, Jenny raised her hand.

"Yes, you." Mrs. Owen pointed at the girl.

"Treat Ms. Hampshire with respect . . . as if she were you?"

"That's right, young lady. Now, the rest of you. I want you to repeat what she said."

In not-so-perfect uniformity, they answered, "Treat Ms. Hampshire with respect . . . as if she were you."

"That's correct." With that, Martha turned on her heels and left the classroom, the door behind her closing promptly at 8:03 a.m., the tension she brought with her dissipating like an unpleasant odor. Emily kept her head down, pretending not to notice when a moment later, Alexander Owen sneaked into the back of the classroom.

Eventually, she raised her eyes and addressed the class. "All right, students. Let's get started."

When the afternoon bell rang at three o'clock, the students put away their books and papers and charged the doors. Eventually, the clamor of voices and patter of footsteps faded, leaving Emily alone in the room. In the quiet solitude, she noticed the smell of chalk and the strange music in her head. *How long has the melody been playing?* she wondered. She walked out of her room to find Ms. Woolhauser monitoring the hall. Her eyes widened. "Ms. Woolhauser?"

Ms. Woolhauser had been a fixture at the school for as long as anyone could remember. Like everyone else, Emily assumed the woman would teach until her last breath. So it came as a surprise when she announced her retirement and suggested Headmaster Bronson Parrish hire Emily even a month before Emily received her credentials. Then Ms. Woolhauser stayed until Emily was ready to assume her position. Now that Emily was hired, she didn't expect to see Ms. Woolhauser.

"Emily Hampshire," said Ms. Woolhauser. "Have you seen a ghost? If so, tell me where so we may both run." She grinned.

"No, no, Ms. Woolhauser. You're flesh and blood. It's just that . . . I didn't expect—"

"Relax, young Emily. My time teaching is over. Mr. Parrish asked that I assist with the transition. A favor, he called it and made clear that I'd be unpaid. So a favor it is. But I'm more than pleased. It's wonderful to see you, young Emily."

Emily sighed. "Yes, so good to see you, even comforting." She recalled how only the students who cared about learning regarded Ms. Woolhauser favorably. The majority did not. As a teacher, she demanded respect and accepted no excuses. Emily had cared about learning, and as such, was fond of the older woman.

Ms. Woolhauser grinned. "How was it, your first day teaching? Have you any questions? Everything you thought it'd be?"

"Mostly," said Emily. "A little different, I suppose. There are enough students to fill three classrooms, but nearly half I expected didn't show."

Ms. Woolhauser appeared to brush it off. "Don't take it personally," she said. "Surely you remember. The farm children usually miss. Depending on the time of year, they've chores the other children know nothing about. Have patience with them. Right now, their parents must be worried about the crops."

"How so?"

"It's the rumor," said Ms. Woolhauser, shrugging, "but I believe it's true. Vernon—you know Vernon?"

"Mr. Davis?"

"Mm-hmm, Mr. Davis. He believes something unnatural's happening." Ms. Woolhauser imitated Vernon's male bravado. "'Feels like the end of days, Ms. Woolhauser.' Else why is the sun dimming? Best prepare. Some evil lies at the door.'"

Emily's head tilted at the thought. "End of days? That's what he believes?"

"Mm-hmm, and if he thinks so, so do the rest of the farmers." Ms. Woolhauser shook her head. "Is that even a sign? Where in the bible do you find that?" she wondered. "But then again, since the eclipse, no one has seen anything like it. Even when there is little or no cloud cover, the sun is hampered, and nobody knows how or why."

Emily's forehead wrinkled. "I've wondered myself. It doesn't seem typical for this time of year—or any other time."

Ms. Woolhauser nodded. "That's what has everyone wondering, that and the dreary, wet weather and cold—not kind to these old bones."

Emily nodded. "The strange music does little to quell their nerves and certainly adds to my concern."

"I hear people saying something inexplicable has befallen our town. Superstition, I would guess. Unfortunately, I've little time for that," said Ms. Woolhauser. "But until the next sunny day, I fear some parents will keep their children home. And until then, we must carry on. Speaking of that, do you know about the teacher meetings on Mondays?"

"Now? Today?"

"Yes, dear, it's Monday. We meet briefly after school."

"I'm sorry. I wasn't aware, but I can attend. Are you coming?"

"Wouldn't miss it." Ms. Woolhauser smiled and tipped her head toward Bronson's room, down the empty hallway. "Annette and Bronson will be anxious to welcome you. I'm certain of that."

"Should I get something to write with?"

"No need. This meeting is going to be fun."

Ms. Woolhauser locked arms with Emily, and together they walked down the darkened hallway where the afternoon sunlight beaming in from the windows above the classroom doors would have offered more light on a typical day. Unfortunately, the days following the eclipse were anything but typical.

Headmaster Parrish rubbed his bald head as Ms. Woolhauser entered his classroom. From beneath his bushy brows, his eyes fixed on Emily. She stood in the hallway outside his door as if waiting to be invited in. Sensing her apprehension, he enthusiastically called, "Come on in, Emily." He then paused and reconsidered, addressing her a second time. "Please come in, Ms. Hampshire." His voice stressed the *Ms. Hampshire* part. "You're one of us now." Smiling warmly, he pointed to a chair. In the wake of her encounter with Mrs. Owen, Emily appreciated the welcoming tenor of Mr. Parrish's voice. Emily's time as a student in his classroom remained one of her favorite memories. He'd always noted her achievements and seemed genuinely concerned with her welfare, especially in the days that followed the deaths of her parents. Emily sat at her old desk in the front row. It felt like an old friend. Annette St. Clair, one of the other teachers, was already there. She and Ms. Woolhauser sat on top of the students' desks, unwilling to sit at the desks like the students, but Emily didn't care.

The headmaster spoke first. "Welcome, Emily." Again, he hesitated, then quickly amended his greeting a second time. "Pardon me," he said. "Ms. Hampshire. Welcome. I must get used to that. How was your first day?" Each of the other teachers looked at her curiously, but none more so than Ms. Woolhauser.

"All was fine," said Emily. Ms. Woolhauser shot her an incredulous look, as did the others. Emily took notice. "Fine," she reassured them. "No problem." It appeared they assumed otherwise, though she had no idea why.

Ms. Woolhauser stared directly at her. "Has Mrs. Owen enlisted you to spy on Bronson yet?" Emily glanced nervously at the other teachers. Their inquisitive expressions suggested they all wanted to know. Emily hesitated, and her face turned rhubarb red. Then she looked over at Bronson, who stared back, equally as curious as the others.

Sensing her discomfort, he quickly interjected. "Don't worry, Ms. Hampshire. They've all been recruited." Legs crossed, he brushed the dust off his shoes. The others nodded, affirming that, indeed, they, too, had been recruited. Emily should have realized that Martha Owen's intentions were always intentionally overt.

"I'm a yellowjacket in her bustle, I suppose," Bronson admitted. "My grandfather left England years ago to rid himself of royalty, and I'm not about to curtsy to the likes of an Owen."

"Yellowjacket indeed," Ms. Woolhauser chimed in. "The rumor that you're considering running against the mayor must sting a bit." She smiled merrily to think she might be the source of the rumors, the guilty party. Nevertheless, the thought of another uncontested election soured her stomach, and she considered Bronson the perfect yellowjacket for the job.

Emily glanced over at Annette St. Clair, who taught the very young. Annette was only a few years older than Emily and had only started teaching the year before. She fidgeted as if mentioning Martha Owen could get them all dismissed. Annette was the nervous type, and if anyone could be counted on to keep her head down, it was Annette. Pale skin and petite in stature, she moved with constant apprehension. Even her voice was mousy.

Stuart, Annette's husband, had left his family's pig farm to find other means to support his family. The capable, stout man could outwork most men. He'd found a niche in carpentry, and it hadn't taken long before his talent was highly sought after. Only days earlier, Stuart confronted the mayor regarding fair payment. Unfortunately, the mayor considered his prized endorsement as compensation for Stuart's labor. Not to see the value of the mayor's recommendation of Stuart's work was an insult, or so he said. According to the mayor, it had been generous of him to offer to compensate Stuart for the materials. Her husband's labor should be a matter of his philanthropy.

In response to the payment demand, the mayor threatened to denounce Stuart's work as substandard, even shoddy. It didn't matter that Stuart spent months working on the mayor's ranch house, the mayor scrutinizing his every detail, or that Stuart had a wife and young ones to feed. That was reason enough for Annette to keep her head down. Her employment was a matter of survival. She already suspected Mrs. Owen would barge in at any moment and release her from her teaching position, so it seemed dangerously bold to support Bronson's aspirations for mayor.

Annette St. Clair timidly raised her hand, which wasn't necessary, but it did allow her to be seen and heard. She spoke quietly, and the room hushed. "I don't know any of the particulars, mind you, but I've heard Mrs. Owen was distraught over the handling of her grandson."

"Of course," Bronson assured her. "Comes as no surprise. That woman wouldn't let go of a cow pie, let alone a grudge. But Alexander is the royal grandson, so I'd expect nothing less." He held back a smirk, as did Ms. Woolhauser.

Emily looked curiously at Ms. Woolhauser and then at Bronson, hoping to hear more. But both remained silent. Finally, she ventured to ask the obvious. "So, what happened? Alexander is in my class. Something I should know about?" It became apparent Ms. Woolhauser knew the entire story and was eager for Bronson to retell it.

Bronson nodded. "Yes, yes, Ms. Hampshire," he said. "I'll have you know that disciplining Alex will not be tolerated, not by Grandmother. As a result, he has become something of a miscreant. He assumes to make his own rules. But it was Alexander's difficulty mingling with the commoners where the trouble began. When I heard—"

"May I?" interjected Ms. Woolhauser, eyes wide with excitement.

Bronson graciously obliged. "Go right ahead. You tell it better than I."

Ms. Woolhauser spoke mainly for the benefit of Annette and Emily. "If you dare to give Alexander a well-deserved low mark, he will undoubtedly threaten Grandma's wrath. Just be aware."

"The entirety of the situation is truly ridiculous," said Bronson.

"Truth be told, he's not kidding," said Ms. Woolhauser. "Grandma will hear his sad telling and always override the teacher's good sense. Every time! According to Mrs. Owen, any low marks on his test scores stem from his teachers' inability to educate him properly."

"Frustrating!" Bronson interjected. "Very frustrating. I could live with it since he only cheats himself. But when he bullied other students, those he supposed beneath him—that, I couldn't abide."

"Do go on," urged Ms. Woolhauser. She enjoyed the looks of shock on Annette's and Emily's faces.

"When I saw Sir Smart Aleck bullying Matthew, the Stewart boy, I initially hesitated to intervene. Boys will be boys, I figured, and I felt one shouldn't fight their battles for them. They had to learn to do that themselves. So, I waited. I waited until I noticed bruises, a black eye, and a swollen jaw. He bullied the Stewart boy several more times, and for what? Sir Smart Aleck didn't find Matthew suitable to breathe the same air. Either that or he just plain enjoyed hurting someone smaller than himself. To the Stewart boy's credit, he didn't squeal, for whatever reason.

Then, one day, after the bell rang a final time, he stayed after, worried about another beating, I assumed. But figuring he'd never ask, I resolved to offer advice."

"And that advice?" asked Emily.

"I told him I knew what was happening; no need to tattle. But if he was willing, I'd offer to help. He was more than willing. And so I told him, 'Next time, let him push you around. As he does, when he pushes, back up, but not enough where he won't come at you again. Let him do it several times. That way, he'll want to hit you. You'll see it in his eyes, in his gritted teeth. But before he swings, punch him in the gut, hard as you can.'"

The teachers' eyes widened, but Bronson hadn't finished.

"And when he bends over, and he will bend over, you hit him with an uppercut straight to the moon, like this." Bronson demonstrated a roundhouse punch that went all the way to the sky. "Aim right for the center of his smug little face." Bronson grinned. "Resulted in a well-earned bloodied and broken nose."

Bronson stopped when he noticed Emily's and Annette's jaws agape. "You, ladies, you're going to catch flies doing that." They quickly closed their mouths. Ms. Woolhauser looked positively gleeful.

"You're joking," said Emily. She could hardly believe what she just heard.

"Nope." He leaned back and folded his arms, beaming with pride.

Emily prodded further. "But don't you fear for the Stewarts? No telling what Mrs. Owen will do now."

"Yeah, feel bad about that," admitted Bronson. "Or what they'll do to me, remember? Why else have you been asked to spy on me if not to get rid of me? I assume Mrs. Owen heard that I may have had something to do with it. I was ordered to appear in front of the town council, and it was not a public meeting—closed door. Now, that was interesting. That's when I got the idea to run for mayor and put an end to the royal family."

"So, what happened at the council meeting?" Emily inquired.

"Yes. What happened?" asked Annette timidly. Ms. Woolhauser grinned, and they all stared inquisitively at Bronson, who stared back with a wry smile.

"I did admit to discussing the handling of bullies with the Stewart boy," he said. "But I stated honestly that he never implicated anyone. So I asked the council, 'How would I've known Alexander bullied him? I would never have imagined. He is such a dear boy.' That forced Mrs. Owen to close the meeting or admit her grandson was a bully. Of course, she closed the meeting, but not before making it clear the matter remained unresolved."

A silent admiration followed, yet Emily became more concerned with having Mrs. Owen's grandson in her class.

Her thoughts were interrupted by Bronson, whose demeanor became pensive. "Turns out," he said, "it was the appropriate correction for Alexander. Although, I must admit I still harbor my doubts. But, Ms. Hampshire, I don't believe he'll be unruly. He seems to have turned a corner, even respectable. His father met with me, apologized, and said Alexander would do the same and apologize in person. But for Grandmother, that wasn't enough, nor would it be. She's been recruiting anyone to rid herself of me ever since, and she'll eventually succeed, but I'm not worried, not for myself."

A smile crept over Ms. Woolhauser's face. "I believe you enjoy being a yellowjacket," she said. "You can't resign. Please tell me you won't even consider it."

"Don't intend to. Not yet," said Bronson. "Meantime, be careful, Ms. Hampshire. Watch yourself."

Annette agreed. In a near whisper, she said, "Mrs. Owen, she's . . . I haven't even words."

"It's all right. I already know," said Emily.

The meeting drew to a close, and the three departed after saying their goodbyes, leaving Emily to secure the building. First bell assignment and final lockup—a rite of passage for new teachers. Emily walked across the hall to her room, where she gathered test papers, then sat quietly as the faint light streaming through the window softened around her. When Emily learned the teaching position was hers, she'd hoped this would be her assigned room as it held special meaning. She stared at the desk in the front row, where she had sat years earlier.

I first saw Christian in this room, she recalled. She looked to the back of the room. *Back there—that's where he sat. His mother brought him and his brother.* She remembered his long black hair and sharp features. She remembered how handsome they were, he and Marco. And Caterina Salvatori, their mother, was the most naturally beautiful woman she'd ever seen, with black hair like Christian's, large brown eyes, and a face like one of the goddesses' in Emily's storybooks. Since that day, Emily's idle mind always swung back to Christian. It still did, to days of holding hands, playing in the schoolyard, and walking home together. He'd even asked if she'd allow him to come and walk her home after school today, but she thought it best to do so alone. She knew she had to lock up and was unsure how long it would take. She was sifting through her desk, looking for the answer sheet to grade test papers, when she noticed a sealed envelope, with her name written on the outside, placed squarely on her desk. She opened it and began to read.

> Ms. Hampshire,
>
> *Difficult to find words, so forgive me. This is not my first attempt at warning, but circumstances being what they are, forced my hand. These are harsh words, but no other option lies open to me. So I will be blunt. Your father was murdered, as was your mother. She was murdered to silence her. Those responsible are the very same who now worry. They are unsure of how much you remember and uncertain what threat you pose. Please remain quiet. Trust no one. They are watching. They intend to keep you close while staying in the shadows. Whatever you think you may remember, please keep it to yourself. There is nothing you can do and nothing they will not do. My greatest regret is not that I could not help you then, but that I'm powerless to help you now. At the very least, I am sending you this warning. Remember, keep silent. Trust no one.*

No signature followed. Emily held the letter with trembling hands, reading it repeatedly. Who wrote this? Who watched her? And why lack the courage to include their name? She placed her school papers in her handbag but kept hold of the letter. *Whoever penned this is determined to remain unknown, though it's evident by the contents they've complete knowledge of the crime. Or perhaps the murderer himself penned the letter, determined to frighten me into silence and serve notice that I am being watched. If I can discover who is responsible and who entered the school undetected, I may learn who took my parents from me. But at what cost, if I am truly in danger?*

Emily sat stunned as the letter's words filled the dark corners of her mind, confirming everything she had long suspected. A sense of vertigo overtook her, a feeling of spinning into a dark, hopeless place where her childhood fears threatened to consume her. The quiet of the room was closing in around her when she heard it—a soothing voice, like a melody, playing softly in her head.

"*Careful now, child. They are watching. 'Tis true. 'Tis true.*"

Emily turned and stared at the open door but saw no one. She hurried out into the hall, but it was empty. The ghostly voice continued inside her head. "*Dear one, oh, dear,*" it said. "*Unfairly enough, but an orphan are you. And unless you are careful, dark fate will ensue. 'Tis true. 'Tis true. What happened to them? Your parents are who. The very same fate will happen to you. 'Tis true. 'Tis True.*"

Like a children's rhyme, the words repeated in her head. She feared the source was now more than a benign, unnatural thing. It was aware of her and had singled her out. She felt like a rat in a bucket of water, splashing about, scratching at the sides, unable to climb out. *Why did I not ask Christian to walk me home? What a fool am I.*

Chapter 13

Stretched upward on his hind legs, the hulking beast stood on a grassy cliff that towered above the meadow. His keen eyes darted about in search of a way down the rocky slope, too steep for him to manage. At least that's what his thoughts told him until he remembered his powerful claws and the muscles that rippled underneath his fur-covered arms. *Cursed is what I am! A monster is what the creatures from the garden called me.* He shook his head in defiance of these thoughts. *No. I am something more, capable of much more.*

With surprising ease, he maneuvered down the treacherously steep, wet, rocky slope to the dark hole below, the strength of the limbs that carried his weight astonishing.

If I am cursed, these abilities are not gifts. And yet, so long as I have free will, don't I determine whether they be that—gifts or my damnation?

Suddenly, the rain intensified, washing away the thoughts that haunted him and causing him to focus on the task at hand. Standing in the mud, he contemplated what came next. He peered into the entrance, squinting at the dark void that filled the space beyond. His ears pricked forward, and he listened, hearing nothing above the breeze and pouring rain.

Then he heard a scuffling from deep inside the cave. He backed up carefully, his eyes on the opening.

Whatever it is, it knows I'm here, and it's not coming out. He had no choice but to go in and draw the thing out. He bent down and picked up a large stone with a sharp edge. A vague memory made that seem a reasonable thing to do.

Hunched over, he moved slowly. His immense form filled the entrance and blocked the already dim sunlight that would otherwise be streaming in. His eyes quickly adjusted to the quantity of light available.

Another gift, he realized. He peered deep into the recesses of the cave. Mindful of every move, every step, not wanting to make a sound, he ventured farther in. The damp odor of scat and the vile scent of rancid meat offended his senses.

Animals. Dirty, vile creatures.

With his heart pounding in his ears, he caught the faint sound of panting. He held his breath and froze, listening. Then he crept forward, sniffing. From the entrance came a hint of errant light, which was all the beast needed to see the outline of a large bear. He paused, contemplating how to lure the animal into the open. Being stealthy proved difficult as his massive weight crunched across the discarded bones beneath its feet. A jolt of anxiety coursed through him as a low growling filled the air. Ever so cautiously, he backed away, making no sudden moves.

Once outside, he moved farther back as carnal instincts rose within him. *I'll decide where the battle for the den will commence, where blood will spill.* Huffing and growling rang out from the dark opening. It didn't take long before the enormous black bear barged into the open. It stood erect on its hind legs, arching its head back as it roared in warning. Then it came down on all fours, pawing at the mud and splashing about. The bear continued roaring while baring its teeth, then made its intentions known with several charges, each time merely bluffing to ward off the intruder, but to no avail.

The beast was stunned but not by the bear's attempt to intimidate him. It was something else—a curiosity, a sudden realization.

I have no fear. None whatsoever. I'm about to fight a living, breathing bear! The beast dropped the heavy rock he'd picked up to use as a weapon. He didn't need it. And he watched as long, razor-sharp claws sprung from the hairy digits that were once his fingers.

Towering high above the bear now, he felt the hackles on his back rise. His lips curled, exposing massive canine incisor teeth stained yellow and sharp as knives. Hunger-induced saliva dripped from the fur that hugged his jaw. His eyes narrowed, and his breathing became rapid and excited.

He inhaled deeply, expanding his lungs to maximum capacity, and then emitted an ear-piercing roar. The bear recoiled and was backing away when something unexpected happened. Two furry cubs waddled into the faint light of day, unaware of the danger. The beast's eyes widened and then looked at the agitated sow.

She's protecting her yearlings.

The mother bear roared a warning to her cubs. One hurried back into the cave while the other found refuge among the boulders strewn about the entrance. It peeked out from around a granite stone and stared at its mother. She moved quickly, positioning herself between the intruder and her cubs.

Without warning, the sow made another charge, another bluff, but the beast didn't so much as flinch. Instead, it stepped aside ever so slowly, though not in retreat.

Go now and take your cubs. Moving farther away and lowering his head, the beast gave the sow and her cubs space to escape unharmed. He hoped she surrendered.

Care for your cubs, Mother, and live!

The beast waited, then waited some more, but surrender wasn't to be. The mother bear wasn't about to abandon her cubs or den. A battle was inevitable.

All right, then. So be it, thought the beast. An overwhelming sense of predatory ferocity erupted inside him, causing his chest, arm, and leg muscles to bulge and his heart to pound in anticipation. Now, the beast wanted this fight. His eyes widened with a keen awareness of the bear's every move.

The bear stretched its neck, opened its mouth, and bared its teeth. Then, suddenly, it charged, hurling itself at the beast. Anticipating the move, the beast met the charge and lunged at the sow, his claws gouging the left side of the bear's head, deflecting the bear's momentum before her jaws found their mark. Blood gushed from an open wound near the bear's mouth. It tumbled onto its side but quickly regained its footing and charged again. This time, the beast met the charge with his full weight. The claws on both his paws swung upward like blades, cutting deep into the bear's lower jaw. The blow lifted the animal into the air and threw her onto her back. Before she could right herself, the beast pounced, sinking his teeth into her neck. Thrashing about, he ripped into her flesh, her hot blood pouring down his throat.

The bear struggled, but the beast held her tight, sinking his claws into her belly and chest. Suddenly, a raspy voice howled from inside the beast's head. "*Finish it! Make the kill!*"

Like raw meat thrown to its bloodlust, the words conjured primal urges, and the beast bore down harder, his teeth sinking in deeper. Finally, the bear withered in a fury of helpless spasms, unable to defend herself. It was over, the victory won.

"*Take the kill!*" screeched another wretched voice.

His teeth firmly gripping the bear, the beast peered at the cave. There, he saw the two tiny cubs watching and whining. His jaw went slack, his teeth pulling back from the massive holes he'd created.

He lifted himself off the bear's prone body, which lay unmoving but for its shallow breaths. The one cub peered out from behind the boulder, watching, waiting for its mother to rise.

Slowly, the beast backed away, huffing and puffing—angry and not knowing why, not exactly. *You chose it! It's your fault!* The beast watched as the bear struggled to her feet, teetering back and forth, her fight gone, her eyes downward. Blood stained her fur in bold streaks. Her cubs bounced from their hiding places and ran to her. Defeated, the little family wandered slowly into the misty woods, never looking back.

She won't last the night, and her cubs will wander off and die without their mother. Not what I wanted.

A shrill voice sounded in its head. "*What a fool you are. That was supper! What? You think you make the rules? There are only nature's rules now, and nature is cruel. Do you intend to die of hunger? That meat was yours, and you let it escape for a morality that no longer applies. Sin doesn't exist. Not for you, monster. But you exist, predator. Accept it or see how cruel nature can be.*"

Quiet! the beast growled. *I am not your monster, and will not take orders from you. You tell me there is no sin, but yours are not the only voices I hear.*

The laughter that followed eventually grew quiet, fading into the pattering rain.

Chapter 14

A frightened Emily walked out into the rain, still clutching the letter. Lightning flashed, and the boom of thunder followed as another storm brewed in the north. She looked up and down the main street, occasionally peering over her shoulder, suspicious of who may be watching. The schoolyard felt abandoned under the gray sky, which grew darker by the minute as she headed home. Then, like a hot brand, the eerily seductive voices that had troubled New Harmony since the eclipse began to haunt her anew.

"*All you desired was an uneventful life. Remember?*" said a sickeningly sweet voice.

"*Be careful,*" another voice admonished in a tone more delicate than the first.

"*Lest your uneventful life end in embers like your father's and mother's,*" said yet another soft voice, dripping with concern.

"*Oh, dear Emmy,*" the voices crooned in false sympathy, "*why must you, so innocent and pure, have enemies? Why? Why must you, of all people, endure such cruelty?*"

Emily froze as the words repeated over and over. She couldn't deny that someone or something had singled her out and watched her. And whatever it was, it intruded on the most private part of her—her thoughts.

"Who are you?" screamed Emily. "And why concern yourselves with me?"

Emily waited, and when no answer followed, her stomach knotted, her heart pounded, and she suddenly felt light-headed. Sitting down in the wet grass, she looked at the weeping sky. With one hand, she held the letter to her breast, trying to keep it dry. With the other, she wiped the rain from her eyes and stared at the clouds that shrouded the valley.

The clouds don't move, she realized. *They defy the wind. It shouldn't be!*

She turned and looked north. The clouds were darker and more sinister there, as if they'd erupted from the peak of Mount Erebus and spread across the valley.

Why is this happening, and the eclipse on my birthday of all days? And now these voices in my head. Who are you? What am I to you?

Lowering her eyes, she stared at the letter confirming what she had long suspected—the murder of her parents. For years, Emily struggled to forget, so young was she when her father went missing. She'd found it easier to ignore than question what was real or imagined. But no matter how she'd tried to escape the memory, she suspected it would eventually catch up to her, and now that day was here. She squeezed her eyes shut and gritted her teeth, pushing against the onslaught of anxiety and melancholy.

Suddenly, amid the cold, pouring rain, there came a voice, not from inside her head. "Emily?" A moment later, she heard it again, this time more loudly. "Emily, is that you?"

She opened her eyes and listened.

"Emily!" She heard her name a third time and stood. From across the street, in the churchyard, Parson Burroughs stared back at her. Emily promptly righted herself, picking up her handbag and stuffing the letter inside.

"Come out of the rain!" he called.

Emily pressed her hand to her forehead, trying to stave off the dizziness as she staggered into the street.

Sensing her distress, the parson ran to her, took her hand, and helped her across. "Come in where it's dry," he urged.

They entered the church through the large walnut wood doors and moved into the warm, candlelit chapel. It was dark inside, like the cathedrals in her storybooks, but not nearly as spacious. Before Parson

Burroughs could inquire further about her state of mind, Emily burst into tears. Calmly, he led her to a seat in the aisle she and her uncle and aunt sat in every Sunday.

Emily sat, grateful to not be alone. She'd always considered the parson grandfatherly, his bushy beard and mustache reminding her of her father's. His deep voice calmed her, reassured her. What she loved most about the parson was his eyes—windows into a gentle soul.

"It's all right, Emily," he assured her. "Take your time. I've all the time you need."

"I'm so sorry," said Emily, sniffling.

"Why?" he asked. "People cry in the church all the time." A grin followed. "It's allowed."

"I suppose, Parson," she said, and her tears began to dry. She looked up and stared at the stained-glass window above the pulpit. Ever since she was a child, she had marveled at its beauty. The window depicted Peter halfway submerged in the waves and reaching up to Jesus, who stood on the water. Unfortunately, the light from outside was barely enough to make the image visible. The colors that shone brightly on a sunny day were now mostly hidden. In the failing light, she immediately sensed the void in Peter's faith, the bleakness of his situation, the dread he felt. Everything in New Harmony lay in shadow, and now the murky black had found her, even addressed her personally.

"Tell me what troubles you, Emily. Allow me to help, would you?" The parson's voice was soft, his eyes kind.

Emily reached into her bag and pulled out the letter. "Here." She held it out. "I hope you can read it. I should've taken better care. The ink might have smeared with the rain."

He took the letter, pulled his reading glasses from his pocket, set them on his nose, and looked at the paper. "I believe I can read it all right."

Emily nodded.

"All right, then," he said and began to read to himself. A moment later, he handed it back. Emily still sniffled, so he patiently waited while she wiped the last tears with her hands.

Together, they sat in the sanctuary, a place made sacred by the worship of believers. In the quiet, she reminisced about days gone by and listening to the pastor when she was a girl.

My feet barely reached the floor back then, she recalled. She looked down at her feet, flat on the floor, and felt the wood grain of the seat with her fingers. *This was our bench,* she remembered, *Mama, Papa, and me—before I was left alone, never to sit here together again. They're never coming back, gone forever, murdered.* Tears surfaced again, and the parson continued to wait.

Finally, Emily's eyes found the parson. "Did you see where it's written that my parents were murdered?"

"I did."

"Well then, what do I do?"

"Hmm. What is it you want to do?"

"I want to find whoever wrote it, whoever murdered my parents."

"Yes, I understand. This letter is not to be taken lightly. But then what?"

Emily thought. "I want to see them pay."

"'Vengeance is mine.' Thus saith the Lord."

"So I do nothing and allow such a crime to go unpunished? Is that how God intends for things to be?" She felt her anger swell, her heart beating rapidly. Her eyes dropped while she concentrated on her breathing until she got her emotions under control.

"You don't let them do anything. Listen to me carefully." The parson took her hand and waited until her eyes met his. "Their actions don't belong to you. They win for a season, but the dark cannot exist in sunlight, and the light always comes. The night always surrenders to the day. Winter eventually yields to spring. It may be dark now, but their day will come. In His time." The parson looked upward in recognition of the Almighty. "Hope brings light, light brings truth, and light always comes."

"In the meantime? I hear voices. But more than that, I've terrors, like dreams, and not only during the sleeping hours. It is as if someone pulls curtains in my mind, forcing me to remember things that belong to me but things I'd rather stay forgotten. However, the voices do not belong to me. And if it weren't for others expressing the same concerns, I would fear the implications."

"Be at peace. There's no reason for fear. I hear them as well, Emily. I suspect the whole town hears them. Several have come to confess, believing a sin they have committed is responsible, considering what they hear is somehow punishment. Yet they can't imagine what sin they might have committed. Nor can I. I don't have all the answers, Emily. But we all need to attend church and stay connected to what we know is right. Sadly, every Sunday, more go missing. One can only assume the voices are responsible. And now I worry how quickly good people normalize that which is abnormal and an abomination."

"So, what do I do?"

"Well, have I told you how I became your parson?"

"I heard pieces, things that happened to you many years ago. But other than that . . . I . . ."

"It's all right, you can say it. I was imprisoned."

Emily nodded. "But surely that has nothing to do with who you are now."

"Partly, but there's more. It so happens that we arrived in America when I was a child. Soon after, my father took sick and died, leaving my mother with my brothers, sister, and me. Though the oldest, I was still too young to work in any meaningful way but not too young to steal. I stole what I could—food, shoes, clothing, blankets, anything. At sixteen, they sent me to prison. Three years. They took my brothers and sister from my mother. I haven't seen them since. A sad story, true. But that's not why I'm telling you this. You see, I learned something there behind those prison walls. Emily, in the darkness of my incarceration, I recognized the light. Without the darkness, I might never have seen it—the light. Not ever."

"Why not?" Emily tipped her head inquisitively.

"Try and imagine the spiteful men, enraged at their incarceration, blaming the walls for their anger and saying it aloud. They claimed the guards made them hateful and bitter. They told me I was innocent, just as they were. They said it every day. They blamed everyone else—not themselves, not me.

I listened until I, too, blamed the guards, the policemen who arrested me, and the prison walls. I became angry and spiteful. Life became not only unfair but hostile. I became the victim of an unfair world.

Then, one bitterly cold night, as I slept on a hard bed of broken, flat, moldy straw, I had a thought, a spark of inspiration, an answer to an unsaid prayer. It occurred to me that whatever voices I heard did not matter. I could choose whether to listen to or ignore them. So I did just that. I paid no attention to the voices telling me how to think and feel. I let them all go. Me, I did that. And right then, as I did, I felt less cold, and my bed felt much softer. It was nothing short of a miracle."

"So I ignore the voices?" asked Emily. "When I hear them, I pretend they're not there?"

"That's right, Emily. Please understand that no one can rob you of your thoughts. They belong to you and no one else. The adversary knows that. Oh yes. The old liar, he knows. But he also realizes he can supplant thoughts, eventually, those tied to emotions of fear, ill will toward others, insecurity, and crippling guilt, to name a few, but you get the point. Such thoughts push yours out so deceptively it is nearly undetected. Over time, nothing remains of one's own thoughts, not even a sense of what was lost.

When Hannah and I first heard the music, we discovered that though the voices were the same, what we heard was tailored to us individually. I've concluded that the melody is the apple, the words the poison. It's not unlike the story told by the Brothers Grimm. Sadly, most people never realize they can ignore it. Hannah and I have decided not to listen. And now we won't even discuss it between us. Understand?"

"I believe I do, but how do you not hear it?" she asked.

"I still hear it, but just as quickly, I replace it with my thoughts. It takes practice and, I might add, vigilance."

"All right, Parson. I shall ignore the voices. But what about the letter? Do I do nothing?"

"You can do something, Emily."

"What?"

"Well, you have a purpose. Find it."

The parson saw her look of concern, her hope drowned in self-doubt.

Her eyes searched for more in the creases of his face, but she was left wanting. "What purpose? I'd like to know. I'm but a teacher and only recently appointed at that. There is still a child inside me, wondering why this is happening. Please tell me why. Can you be more specific?"

"I know my answer appears vague. But it is the answer. Really, now, what do you want to know? Why does darkness exist, or why does God allow it?"

Without a moment's hesitation, she answered, "Both."

"You can't know the light, not in its entirety, without being acquainted with the dark." He gripped her hand more tightly. "For me, it took the prison's darkness to see and understand things clearly, at last, to see the light with a brightness I would never have known." The parson's eyes drifted upward.

Again, she pondered his words and carefully formed her question. "But what if none of us survives the night? What then?" Her eyes looked into his with such sincere supplication his heart flooded with empathy.

"Emily, Emily," he said, trying to console her. "I understand you are frightened, and why wouldn't you be? I sense something worse on the horizon. Something is coming. The nation is tearing itself apart. Men's hearts have turned to stone, brother against brother, and civil conflict, and even war, lie at our doorstep. Luke tells us that men's hearts will fail them for fear. If we do not change course, there will be bloodshed. It will end, but how and when? You must be prepared. Something dark stalks New Harmony, and it is not of God. Some in town may become confused, but you must not be. Promise me."

Emily nodded that she understood. "I promise."

"That's good," he said. "But hear me now. Remember, and do not forget. I fear the time will soon come when you may be imprisoned, just as I was, by darkness so unyielding you'll be tempted to lose all hope, and for a moment, you may. But like me, surrounded by darkness, you will see the brilliance of God's light. And you will understand."

Emily stared into Parson Burrough's compassionate eyes. Then, while still struggling to understand, she asked, "How do you know this? Should I be worried?"

"I only know that I know. That's how it works sometimes. And when the time comes, you'll remember."

"And what if the darkness is too great? What if it swallows me? What if I die?"

"Whether we survive the night or perish is unimportant. One day, the morning light will shine for us, if only on the other side of this life. After Luke tells us that men's hearts will fail them for fear and that the powers of heaven shall be shaken, then shall they see the one who is the coming dawn. If we put our faith in God and fear not, our death will only happen at our appointed hour, not before. Until then, dear Emily, you have things left undone and a role to play, and with your faith, the darkness will reveal to you the light, and that light will be glorious."

The parson's words sunk deep into her heart, and she felt a surge of courage. "I can do that," she said. "I can ignore the music and voices. I can search for my purpose, but I remain unclear as to what to do about this." She held up the letter.

The parson cleared his throat. "I need you to tell me . . ."

"Yes, Parson?"

"Do you know who is responsible?"

"Who murdered my parents?"

"Yes, who, as you say, murdered your parents?"

Emily shook her head. "Can't be certain."

"Then have you an idea? Do you suspect anyone?"

"It was so very long ago, I'm afraid. It was my birthday. Did you know that? My father disappeared on my eighth birthday. My mother said things, things I suspected. I could never be certain, and it's not something I could go about accusing anyone of."

"Perhaps it's just as well. For now, tell no one. It could be dangerous if someone inadvertently overheard. It may put you and whomever you tell in peril. You'll know what to do when the time comes, and it very well may."

He let go of her hand and asked, "Do you recall the verse, 'Let not your heart be troubled neither let it be afraid'?"

"John 14. Yes, of course."

"Did you hear the word *let*? As in, don't *let* your heart become afraid. Fear is but one choice among many. God is telling you to choose not to be troubled or fearful, to trust Him."

Emily thought about her feet planted firmly on the floor, no longer swinging as when she was a child. The peace the parson wished for Emily radiated from within her. She placed the letter in her handbag.

"Hold on to it," Parson Burroughs told her. "This secret is ours. The time will come when you'll be called upon to confront the darkness. When that happens, listen for His voice. Listen to it and nothing else. Then you'll know what to do."

Chapter 15

The hour was late, the whale-oil lamp was out, and the fireplace had gone cold when a knocking disturbed the quiet of the Stewart home.

Still only half awake, Theodore hollered, "Hold on!" The pounding persisted as he pulled on his pants under his nightshirt.

Now awake and sitting up, the blankets bunched on her lap, Sarah whispered, "Who is it, darling?"

"Shhh, quiet."

The pounding continued while Theodore grabbed the rifle from near the chair in the corner.

"Just a minute!" he yelled as he quietly approached the front door. He didn't open it immediately; instead, he waited, his hand resting on the latch. Behind him, he heard his son's door squeak open and turned to see Matthew rubbing his eyes and staring at him.

"Papa?"

Behind him, Theodore heard the pattering of footsteps as his wife crossed the dark, moonlit room while hushing Matthew and sending him back to bed. Hearing his son's door close, he looked over his shoulder at Sarah, her face full of worry. It wasn't that they hadn't expected a visit, just not at this late hour. Sarah crept to his side only to have her husband move her back until she stood behind him.

Theodore called through the thin cracks in the doorframe where the light of a lantern seeped in. "Who is it?"

To their surprise, a woman's voice answered. "It's me, Martha Owen. We've things to discuss. I'm here with my husband. Now open up!"

"It's late! Come back tomorrow," Theodore shouted. "In the morning. We'll be here."

The muffled voice answered more harshly. "Listen up! We've come from town and need to speak—not tomorrow, not in the morning. Now! It's a matter of discretion that brings us so far and at such a late hour, so stop being rude and open this door!"

Theodore whispered to his wife. "Stay here. I'll send them on their way."

"No," Sarah insisted, still whispering. "Don't open it. Just tell 'em to go. I don't care what you tell 'em. Say anything. Just get 'em to leave."

Suddenly, Sarah jumped, startled when the butt of a rifle slammed into the door. Hearing the commotion from his bedroom, young Matthew cried, "Mama!"

"See to the boy," Theodore said reassuringly. "I'll handle this." Sarah nodded and reluctantly scurried off while Theodore slowly released the latch. He intended to open the door only slightly, keeping his rifle hidden from view.

But at the sound of the disengaged latch, the door flew open, throwing Theodore back as the sheriff barged in. He grabbed the rifle from Theodore's hands and pushed him against the far wall, the barrel of his revolver pressed hard against Theodore's gut. Screaming erupted from Matthew's room as Martha, followed by the mayor, entered the house, bringing in the chill night air.

"Don't come out!" screamed Theodore, but it was too late.

Sarah came out, shutting the door to Matthew's room behind her. Droplets of sweat ran down her face as cold fear coursed through her veins. She looked at Martha in the doorway. "Why are you doing this? What do you want?" she cried. "If this is about our boy and . . . and your grandson, Theo already spoke with Eugene. It's taken care of. It's all a misunderstanding, and they've already apologized to one another."

The mayor calmly sat in the rocking chair by the fireplace and set his lantern on the floor. He stomped his boots, leaving clumps of mud, and said, "That's not why we're here."

But Martha objected. "We certainly are here for that," she said threateningly. "And if your boy ever touches—"

"Martha!" the mayor barked, shaking his head and staring at her sternly.

"Just what, Robert?" she snapped. Her tight jaw and clenched fists left no doubt as to the cause of her anger. "What their boy did to our Alexander is unforgivable! I want to see them pay. You hear me, Robert? See that they pay!" Martha's eyes narrowed on Sarah.

"Go on home, dear. Take the carriage. The Stewarts are leaving New Harmony for good. They'll be gone by morning. Now, go home. They can't do any more harm. Just you—"

"All right, all right," she said, finally relenting. Turning to leave, she paused and slowly turned back around. "I don't want to see any of you ever again. Understood?"

Theodore finally found his voice. "We are not leaving, and you can't force us to. We've nowhere to go, and for what, an argument between children? Utterly ridiculous!"

But before Martha could say another word, the mayor interceded, mollifying her as best he could. "They're leaving tonight, dear. They're not your problem, not anymore. Go home."

Sheriff Weasley's grin assured her the Stewarts would be handled to her satisfaction, and she left without further argument.

"Mayor," Theodore pleaded, his voice calm yet filled with concern. "Can't we take this outside? My son can hear all this. He's frightened. You're a father. Please."

The mayor nodded to the sheriff, who stepped back, holstered his pistol, and, while holding Theodore's rifle, began pushing them out the front door.

Not a minute after stepping off the porch, the sheriff shouted, "Get down!"

Sarah knelt without protest while Theodore stood defiantly. A hard shove to his back with his own rifle and he joined his wife on his knees. They looked up to see the mayor step out into the night, holding the lantern. Behind them, a trigger cocked as the sheriff made ready to do the mayor's bidding.

The mayor paced back and forth, shaking his head. "Oh, what am I to do?" he said. "What am I to do with you two? This here is the part I truly can't help but regret, having to do what's necessary."

"But we told you, Mayor, sir," said Sarah. "Our boys, Matthew and your grandson, they are reconciled. Ask your son, Eugene. He'll tell you. All's been taken care of."

Theodore nodded enthusiastically. "It's true, sir. We spoke with Eugene and made things right. Our boys are fine. They will probably end up being friends after everything. There's no—"

"Shut your mouth!" hollered the mayor. "That's not the issue, not for me!" They watched as he pulled a letter from his shirt pocket. He held it in the faint light of his lantern. "Any idea what this is?"

Theodore and Sarah were stunned. They stared at the letter, then peered into the mayor's eyes. Theodore gulped. "Yes, that. I can explain, sir!"

Sarah cried, "Yes, w-we can explain."

"Of course you can," said the mayor, enjoying the fear that washed over their faces. "You know exactly what this is." He shook the letter in the air. "This is your letter to the governor." Then, putting it back in his pocket, he took another letter out and held it up for them to see. "And here's the governor's response. Shall I read it to you?" Smiling, he unfolded the paper and hooked his round spectacles over his ears, resting them on his nose.

"Says here, 'Dear Robert.'" The mayor peered over his spectacles. "I suppose you didn't know Governor Willard and I are friends, hmm?" Then, turning his attention back to the letter, he read.

Dear Robert,

Another letter and more accusations. You're either the devil himself or New Harmony is a wellspring of rumors and unfound accusations. There's even one from your parson. Perhaps you may want to be seen attending church more often. It is only suggestion, but I fear you may have neglected your reputation among the religious. Be careful, friend. They are well-versed in judging others while spreading rumors. As mayor, you must appease them most of all.

Now, Robert. Please grant me a favor. It would help if you put a stop to all this. I can't ignore their concerns forever. Charm them, appease them, do whatever you must. To help you, I've enclosed the more recent letters that found their way to my desk. See to it that I receive no such future correspondence. I haven't the time to waste, nor am I in good health. And I'm assuming you've heard of the trouble brewing. Only a rumor, perhaps. The Southern states are starting to ramble on about secession. That is true, and war may be imminent. God help us if it is true. So you see, my attention is needed elsewhere.

Please don't force me to pay you a visit. Our friendship is best served just the way it is.

The mayor peered over his spectacles. "Theo. Oh, Theo, Theo. You've made a dire miscalculation. Only by good fortune is the governor distracted and in poor health. But you see, I can't afford further false reports of my possible indiscretions."

With that, the mayor folded the governor's letter and returned it to his vest pocket only to resume his pacing and shaking his head.

Now trembling, Theodore spoke. "Sir, since you read our letter, you know well what concerns we addressed—mostly that of our boys. And it was only for fear of retribution that we sent it. And since our issue is resolved, I see no problem so long as you let us be. I'll write a letter confirming it. Tell me what to write, and I'll put it to paper."

Near tears, Sarah begged, "That's right, sir. Please, will you not consult Eugene? He'll tell you. We've been amicable as neighbors. He'll confirm it!"

"You will have no further concerns in our regard, sir," stressed Theodore.

"Hmm." The mayor stopped pacing, faced them broadly, and shook his head. "Truly unfortunate for you," he said, "but you wrote something more in your complaint to the governor than the issue with my grandson. Isn't that right?"

Theodore shook his head adamantly. "No, sir! Not that I recall."

"You forget I have your letter here." The mayor patted his vest pocket. "And I recall reading something about a rumor of a possible murder. Now, I ask both of you, how does such a vile rumor have anything to do with my grandson? Please tell me. I am curious!"

"Nothing, sir. Not exactly," said Theodore.

The mayor's eyes widened. "Not exactly? How not exactly? I'm listening."

Theodore slumped, head bowed, eyes averted so as not to look directly at the mayor. "They are just rumors. I'm sorry. I was angry when I wrote—"

"Who told you these things? Speak!" the mayor demanded.

"I don't remember. Lots of people, and they're quite convincing. I mean, look at you now. You've guns pointed at us. Why wouldn't we be frightened? Yes, I wrote the letter. I did it! Hold me responsible, but please, just, just . . . don't hurt my family! They are no threat to you."

The mayor took a deep breath, held it for a while, and then slowly exhaled. "Hmm . . ." he said. "Well, Sheriff, what do you think? Can we bet our fortune, our future, on this man's promises?"

Theodore and Sarah peered over their shoulders at the sheriff, still standing behind them. They watched as he shook his head. With a gruff voice, he answered, "Rather not."

"Yeah, I don't think so either."

Theodore and Sarah could hardly believe it. Beyond frightened, they turned and stared wide-eyed at the mayor.

Suddenly, a flash of light came from the north, followed by the rumbling of thunder, threatening to pour sheets of rain. The mayor turned to leave, wanting to get ahead of the storm. "You know what to do, Weasley!" he said.

He was about to mount his horse when Theodore screamed. "Wait! There's something you don't know!"

Before the sheriff lifted the rifle, the mayor raised a hand. "Hold it, Weasley." He closed his eyes as if irritated and sighed. "All right, Theodore, you have something to get off your conscience?"

Theodore suddenly became angry, and in a last-ditch effort to save his family, yelled as loud as he could. "Don't you think we figured this could happen? You have a dark heart, Mayor! You are a murderer, and Governor Willard will get another letter if you do this. I can promise you that! And that letter will confirm everything, exposing you for exactly what you are. And don't think for a minute this is a bluff! It's already arranged if anything happens to us."

The sheriff scoffed. "Huh. Lies. Tryin' to save your neck is all."

"Will you bet your life on it, Sheriff?" asked Theodore. "Go ahead. See what happens. You'll be found out no different than the mayor."

The sheriff suddenly quieted.

The mayor stepped toward Sarah and grabbed a handful of her sandy blonde hair. He cocked her head back so he could stare into her eyes. "Where's the letter? Who has it?"

"Why would I tell you?!" she scowled. "Best not hurt my son—or else!"

"Hmm," said the mayor. "So you do know who has it. Well, that certainly helps matters." The mayor looked up at the sheriff, motioned with his head in Theodore's direction, and said, "Kill him!"

A loud bang and the smell of black powder filled the night air. Theodore slumped forward, the ball having pierced his skull and planting his face in the mud.

"Nooo!" Sarah screamed as tears welled up in her eyes. "You . . . you murdering bastards!"

With his hand still gripping her hair, the mayor ordered the sheriff, "Go get the boy."

"No! Not him! Please . . ."

The mayor hesitated, as did the sheriff, who looked puzzled.

"Ya want me to go get 'im, right?"

"Just hold on, Weasley. I think Mrs. Stewart has something she wants to tell us." He tightened his grip on her hair, jerking her head farther back. "Now tell me. Who has the letter?"

"Promise me you won't hurt my son!"

The mayor shook her head violently and screamed, "Who has it?"

"Promise me!"

"Go get the boy!"

"Wait!" Sarah cried, her tears flowing uncontrollably.

"I'm listening. Who?"

"All right!" she relented, her voice growing hoarse as she struggled to speak. "The boy at the post office. He promised to send it if Theo stopped coming in. He's got it."

The mayor nodded. "Good thing you told me," he said.

"You promised you wouldn't hurt my son!"

The mayor scoffed. "I did no such thing." Then, without any prompting, the sheriff turned and headed into the house. "Don't stain the wood floor. Someone might notice. We've enough rumors to deal with," he shouted. "And remind me to put the parson on our list."

Sarah cried out, "Don't you touch him! Please! Please! I beg of you!"

A young boy's scream echoed through the night air, and then, for a moment, all was silent. Then, like tears from heaven came the pouring rain, mingling with the mud and blood.

Chapter 16

The bell above the barbershop door rang at dusk on another gloomy day in New Harmony. Hearing the sound of the wood floor creaking under the sizable mayor, Tommaso turned in time to see him sit in the barber chair, leaving a trail of mud behind him. He sat without so much as a greeting, only to say, "The usual, Shears," then leaned back, closed his eyes, and waited.

"Trim an' shave," said Tommaso as he dipped a towel in the pot of heated water on the parlor stove and then wrung it out.

"Do your best, Shears. Tonight's the spring dance, and I have assurances to gather. Must be in peak form with an upcoming election. I depend on you to take your time. Do me right, would you?"

"Certainly, sir," said Tommaso. He combed the thinning gray hair that crowned the mayor's head like a horseshoe.

"I do admit I am one for being pampered. And you should know, this is my favorite part of the week: a steamy, hot towel and the smell of Macassar. Why, even the sting of rubbing alcohol after my shave relaxes me. Interesting how one can derive pleasure from a little pain." Tommaso draped a hot towel over his face, and the mayor continued speaking while the steam softened his skin. "You don't say much, do you, Shears?"

"Hmm, sorry."

"That's all right. I'd be at Hyrum's store across the street if I wanted to hear the latest. That's where the cackling hens go on and on about this or that. I must endure my wife informing me of all that is trivial. Though I must say, the hens do lay a golden egg now and then."

"I only listen," said Tommaso. "I'm good at that."

"You certainly are. And a good man, Shears. You keep confidences, and I admire that. There's safety in that. But I've come here for more than just a trim."

Tommaso hesitated, setting the pot of hot water aside. "Sir?"

"One of your sons . . . not the doctor. That other one."

"My boy Christian?"

"He works at the post office?"

"He does."

"Well then, Christian. He has something that belongs to me."

"What?"

The mayor lowered the towel to watch the barber's reaction. Tommaso was quite obviously concerned over what his son might have done to draw the mayor's attention.

"Not to worry, Shears, not to worry. However, I do need to know . . . Where is he now?" The mayor draped the towel back over his face.

"I . . . I'm not certain. The post office?"

"Are you asking me?"

"No, no, sir. Mr. Buchanan, he closes at six. It's not quite that yet. So . . ."

Just then, the bell over the door rang, and the sheriff poked his head in. "Mayor?"

From underneath the towel, the mayor responded. "That you, Weasley?"

"It is, sir."

"Well, what is it?"

The sheriff paused and cautiously looked at Tommaso. "It's . . . uh . . ."

The mayor cut him short, sensing his apprehension. "It's all right. Say what you've come to say. Nobody else in here, and don't mind Shears. The man has the good sense never to repeat a word he hears. Isn't that true, Shears?"

"I mind my own business, sir. That's it."

"All right, Weasley. What is it?"

The sheriff removed his hat and stared hard at Tommaso. "I'm not sure I should—"

"What is it, Weasley?"

"Just that the Stewarts—"

The mayor quickly interrupted. "Careful now. What about them?"

"Got 'em all moved last night. Said they had a place back east?"

"Are you asking me?"

"No, sir. They, um, insisted no one knew where they were going. We used Hyrum's wagon. Moved 'em out."

Tommaso kept trimming, pretending not to listen.

"Well," said the mayor, "I hope they like their new home far away from New Harmony."

"Yes, I'm, um, sure they will." The sheriff put on his hat.

"Hey, Weasley?"

"Yes, Mayor?"

"Stop by the post office. The Stewarts requested that I deliver a letter they'd written to the governor. Theodore asked that I see to it personally. I promised I would. Shear's boy has it. Ask for . . ." The mayor paused, lowered the towel from one eye, and looked at Tommaso.

"Oh yes. Christian," said Tommaso.

"That's him. Ask for Christian. He's at the post office now. But hurry, it closes at six."

"Of course, sir," said the sheriff as the bell announced his departure.

"Never mind what you heard, Shears. Forget it. The Stewarts—they had their reasons for hightailin' it middle of the night—asked for my assistance in seeing to it, not wanting a soul to know. So, I must trust your discretion in the matter. But believe me, my responsibilities as mayor are not always to my liking. There are always unpleasant things, that's for certain."

Then, for a brief moment, the mayor fell silent, still relishing the sensation of the hot towel, though it started to cool.

Tommaso removed it from his face, a mirror already placed in front of him, ready for his inspection.

The mayor stared, admiring what he saw as he turned his head from side to side. "Well done, and right on schedule."

Tommaso pulled the apron off, shook it out, and began sweeping the floor when the mayor asked, "If I tell you something, will you keep it to yourself? Being mayor is a friendless responsibility. I've only parrots to deal with—no one with which to share matters of conscience."

Tommaso stopped sweeping and listened, not fully understanding. "Sorry. What are you asking?"

"I suppose I'm wondering whether you've ever done something necessary yet regretful. And I'm not certain how else to phrase it."

Tommaso thought hard as he tied the apron back on. He recalled a time while growing up, a life lesson his father taught him. "My papa," Tommaso said, "he always says to me, 'Tommaso, we are human. We have bellies to fill, ya know? At times we bite forbidden fruit. It's what we humans do.' But try not to bite, not to feed the hunger.' That's what Papa said."

"Hmm." The mayor smiled. "I suppose none of us are perfect. You may be a better man than I am." He pulled two coins from his pocket and dropped them into Tommaso's hand. "A little extra to thank you for your vote. You intend on voting?"

Tommaso nodded and dropped them into his apron pocket.

"Good." The mayor patted his shoulder. "Then I'll see you at the dance this evening. You are coming?"

"Since my Caterina departed, I've no song left in me."

The mayor nodded as though he understood. "Now and then, Shears. My advice? Take a bite of the forbidden fruit, as big a bite as you can manage. Somedays, satisfying your voracious hunger is the best thing you can do. Now, if you'll excuse me."

The mayor left while Tommaso continued sweeping. Once alone in his barbershop, Tommaso said to no one, "I'll try not to, mayor."

Chapter 17

Warren Sowell dumped a wheelbarrow full of manure near the fenced yard, preparing for the New Harmony spring contra dance. Once the floor was swept, the hay hauled to the back, and the horses herded far enough away so as to not taint the fresh air that blew through open doors, he sat on a hay bale to rest, his chores complete. Biting into a ripened apple, he peered into the drizzling rain, wondering how many would venture out in their Sunday best. It didn't surprise him when Old Man Taylor arrived first. Nothing would commence before he came. In his hand, he held a fiddle and bow, while inside the stable, more than twenty whale-oil lanterns hung from the rafters, inviting insects and people alike. Indeed, there were many more insects than people, but such pests were part of the fabric of life in New Harmony and, as such, were ignored. Not so easily dismissed were the town's busybodies. They were sure to attend, never allowing an opportunity to eavesdrop to pass them by. Before long, they and all the usuals were under the stable roof, mingling with one another, happy to be out of the rain.

Chief among the meddlers, Abigail Williams smoothed her thinning hair, which barely reached her shoulders. Her skin stretched over her skeletal frame like a tightly tucked bedsheet. Decked in a long black Victorian dress with a white bow tied high at the neck, she sat where everyone could see her, arms folded in her lap. As soon as the fiddler put bow to string and the dancing began, she watched the exuberant youth move back and forth, spinning and curtsying. Her days of frolicking were far behind her, leaving her abandoned to unbearable obsolescence, abandoned by youth and her dead husband. Now, she wore black in remembrance of days shared with Norbert. Widowhood did not suit her, but she'd broached the subject with the Almighty and clung to her resentment.

Next to Abigail sat Elizabeth Howe, a most willing accomplice. Elizabeth had a habit of brushing her fingers through her once-golden locks. She'd never had a reasonable suitor, and the season to entertain prospects never met her expectations. Such social occasions as Elizabeth found herself in had once brought bitterness. But now she'd found a new purpose, along with Abigail, in ensuring proper adherence to the norms of society. Elizabeth, too, wore black but wasn't altogether sure why. She did have white sleeves, though, and white ruffles around her neck.

Susannah Boyer, the youngest of the three prolific gossipers, sat beside Elizabeth. The royal-blue of her dress was much more daring, as was her neckline, which displayed an inch of cleavage, just barely within the range of decency. Her long brunette hair cascaded over her shoulders. If nothing else, she could still hope to attract a dance partner. She'd once been a wife and born a child, but fever left her a widow, and measles left her childless. Though she hoped to draw a man's attention, she nonetheless could not resist the chatter between Abigail and Elizabeth, the scandalous topics arousing her curiosity. The subjects of their conversations danced and swirled in front of them, conjuring all manner of lurid imaginings and enticing speculations.

Although the three women were quite different, one thing they had in common was the emptiness that needed filling with drama. Unfortunately, this too often involved the misfortunes of others, and it mattered little how much was blatant speculation so long as it perked ears and raised eyebrows.

Late to arrive, Parson Edward Burroughs entered with Hannah on his arm. As was the custom for contra dances, where opposites came together to dance, the women sat separate from the men. In keeping with custom, Hannah excused herself from Edward and made her way through the crowd to where Abigail, Susannah, and Elizabeth sat busying themselves in superficial chitchat. Hannah extended proper greetings before sitting next to Susannah. Afterward, she was ignored, their chatter continuing unabated.

"Evil premonitions," Abigail professed. "It's well known."

Susannah quickly glanced at Hannah and back at Abigail. "But what about the parson?"

"What about him?"

"The parson says eclipses are no such thing, not evil, but natural occurrences."

Before Hannah could respond, Abigail scoffed, "So now the parson's an astronomer? What does he know of such things when it's obvious we're witnessing not science but metaphysics—a realm he should stay clear of? I am more acquainted with the metaphysical, where my gifts lie. I'm telling you, the eclipse is an omen, as is the darkening sky. But evil does not come without hope, and I believe the music is a heavenly remedy to wickedness. I consider the voices a warning. They told me so, and I'm telling you. But first consider this before you form your opinions. Does hell inform us of impending evil? I think not."

Susannah quickly responded. "I must agree. I find the music and the voices rather angelic. Sort of. I know no evil that disguises itself in such a pleasant manner."

Hannah, though not given to argue, had heard enough. "Ladies, may I remind you? The enticement of sin can be pleasurable."

Susannah turned and addressed Hannah directly. "I, for one, sleep more soundly with the chanting. Where is the sin in that? Am I evil?"

Again, before Hannah could answer, Abigail interrupted, pretending Hannah wasn't there or at least not part of their conversation. "Have you asked the voices a question?" Abigail waited for the others to answer. When no one spoke, she continued. "How it works is that it doesn't answer right away, but eventually, sometimes in an appealing fashion, such as in poetic rhyme, for no good reason than to be pleasant."

The conversation attracted a gaggle of women who now eavesdropped, interested in what Elizabeth, Susannah, and especially Abigail had to say. Several women nodded that they'd experienced the same, though it was doubtful they were doing anything more than being agreeable.

"But what purpose is there that an accursed darkness descends upon us only to bless us with a sweet melody?" Elizabeth asked. "Am I the only one who does not understand?"

Susannah shook her head. "You are not alone. My sister believes sirens have descended upon us, but her husband finds that laughable. He suspects witches."

"Sirens? That's interesting," said Elizabeth. "What are sirens?"

"I'm not certain, to be honest," admitted Susannah.

Abigail rolled her eyes. "Sirens?" Then, taking a deep breath, she answered. "They are naughty women who lure sailors who haven't seen women in ages. They lure them to rocky shores, enticing them with their sensual voices, only to have them shipwreck."

"Well, the voices are enticing," said Elizabeth.

"I see," said Abigail. "But have you seen the ocean out your window?"

Elizabeth suddenly felt embarrassed, and both she and Susannah quieted.

Abigail cleared her throat. "To my reasoning, there's only one explanation," she said. "The darkness is a curse. Upon this we all agree. However, the singing could only mean one thing—angels."

"Angels?" asked Elizabeth.

"Yes, Eliza. Angels. Could be Michael, Raphael, Gabriel, or one of the others."

"But they sound like women's voices. Are there such things as female archangels?"

"Why not? And besides, did I say archangels? It doesn't matter. Either way, they are here for our benefit. And they have chosen me. I am their conduit. And I've another theory. I sense they, whatever *they* are, look down on us from Erebus. It all makes perfect sense. The blast of wind that accompanied the eclipse came from the mountain.

And, ever since, the dark clouds above us seem to be spilling from the top, perhaps shielding our mortal eyes."

"How interesting you mention that," someone behind them said. Abigail, Susannah, and Elizabeth turned to see a wide-eyed Delilah Thompson anxious to join the conversation. "Ladies," Delilah announced. "I have something to tell, but it's a secret, and you mustn't repeat it. Swear it." The secrecy requirement got everyone's attention, and all the women turned in her direction.

"Go on! You have our word," Abigail urged.

All eyes fixed on Delilah except for Hannah's. She stared at her husband on the other side of the stable, longing to be with him.

Delilah spoke quietly, as if sharing a dark secret. "So, my son, Virgil—he and the O'Conner boys climbed Erebus some time ago, before the eclipse. I thought it was a good idea at the time. Give 'em something to do . . ."

Irritated that the attention had shifted away from her, Abigail said, "What about it? Every boy in Harmony's been up there."

"Just that, the other day, they did it again. So, of course, I scolded Virgil as any mother would, not knowing what was up there. 'There could be demons!' I told 'em and made him swear never to do it again."

Abigail shook her head. "Demons, no less."

"Please, Abigail, allow me to finish." Delilah scanned her audience, looking at each of the women, measuring their sense of awe. They were utterly captivated.

Elizabeth blurted out, "What did they tell you?"

"Don't keep us waiting," Susannah added. "What's up there?"

"Here is what's so interesting," said Delilah. "Virgil said there wasn't anything up there but an old, dilapidated building or something."

"What's interesting about that?" Abigail asked. "It's simply the old lookout post. We all know it's up there."

Realizing that she was losing their interest, Delilah quickly insisted, "I'm not finished. There's more!" A moment later, her audience was back. "Virgil said he and the other boys heard a frightening voice. It boomed like thunder. He said the hair on his arms stood up straight. It could have been the charge from lightning, but I suspect from pure terror. The threatening voice told them to leave and never come back. They could hardly run fast enough down the mountain. Virgil could not stop shaking as he told me the story."

"Now that's interesting," Abigail agreed, speaking in an eerie fashion so as to invoke maximum intrigue. "And they all heard the same unearthly voice say the same unearthly thing?"

Delilah whispered for full effect. "Yes, that's right," and then looked around, relishing the captivation.

Finally, noticing Hannah sitting silently and looking off into the distance, Elizabeth asked, "Has the parson mentioned archangels?"

Anxiously, the women turned to Hannah, all except for Abigail.

Hannah anticipated the conversation would eventually turn to her. It so often did. She watched how they masked that the voices frightened them. She smiled reassuringly. "My husband says we are not to fear. Fear robs us of reason. Patience and prayer—that is what he prescribes. Patience and prayer."

Abigail dismissed the advice. "No fear? What if a snake happens by? Should we just pray and let it bite us?" A dismissive swish of her hand accompanied the slight.

"I wouldn't allow that. Who would? No one would," said Elizabeth.

"There's a darn good reason we're afraid of snakes," Abigail concluded. "There are things in this world that should frighten us."

The attention shifted back to Hannah, who looked at each pensively. "What kind of snake?"

"Excuse me?" said Abigail.

Hannah repeated, "What kind?"

"Just as well to be afraid of them all," said Abigail.

"Is it a garter snake, which eats rats and mice? They are no problem. The opposite, in fact. If, on the other hand, the snake is venomous, your fear may work against you. You may commit a sudden move, resulting in a bite. But if you act with reason, your chances improve."

Suddenly, Old Man Taylor's fiddle fell silent, and the dancing halted. Everyone looked to see Martha and the mayor arriving fashionably late as always, followed by the scent of her flowery perfume, a welcome distraction in the New Harmony stable. Mrs. Owen quickly made her way to where the women sat, and the fiddling and dancing resumed.

"Hello, Mrs. Owen," Susannah greeted. The others quickly added their greetings. They couldn't help but admire her affluence, made clear by the glow of her white, powdered skin. For Abigail, Elizabeth, and Susannah, it didn't matter that Martha barely acknowledged them. Elizabeth surrendered her seat. After all, she'd mistakenly sat in the center of the front row.

"Excuse me, ladies," Martha said, making herself the center of attention. "I suffered a terrible accident coming back from Bloomington. Yes, I'm all right," she answered before anyone could ask. "A bruise here and there, but I shall recover. Would one of you be so kind as to fetch me a cider drink?" Her request appeared as sweet as molasses. And, of course, they accommodated her every whim. The sweet Martha now spoke to them. They'd each had their own experience with the other Martha, the one who wasn't so cordial. The women quickly obliged, and several made the gesture of wanting to be the one to retrieve her beverage of choice.

Abigail patiently waited for a break in the fiddling, then spoke over the crowd's commotion. "Has your husband made any conclusions as to what is happening?"

"You mean the mayor, don't you?" was her response.

"Yes, that's what I meant to say. Forgive me." She restated her question. "What does the mayor think?"

Martha pretended not to hear Abigail for a moment before turning her attention to the hungry ears around her. Someone handed her a cup of cider. She peered into the anxious faces as she sipped, then lowered her cup. "Not much to know. Not yet. But I can assure you he'll get to the bottom of it soon enough. He's hard at work sorting it out."

Unsurprisingly, many women in town clung to her confidence since it felt reassuring, especially in such grim circumstances. Others harbored a quiet resentment but knew better than to cross her. After all, prosperity was often determined by association with those of influence. At least, that's how things worked in New Harmony. Martha's opinion alone could elevate or reduce one's social standing.

Chapter 18

Caught in the same recurring nightmare he'd been having since the eclipse weeks earlier, Robert tossed and turned. It was 3:33 in the morning, the middle of the witching hour. He dreamed of thieves and pillagers descending upon the ranch, whisking away his possessions, and demolishing everything in their path. But though he stood watching, he was unseen, and though he yelled for them to stop, he was powerless and unheard.

He watched a gaunt and shabbily dressed woman enter his house through the front door. Offended that someone so unremarkable would take such license, he couldn't resist chasing after her. With dirty bare feet, she strolled into the parlor as if she were the lady of the house. Robert followed. Most of the furnishings were missing. What remained was torn apart and in pieces. Even the floorboards were splintered, and shreds of expensive fabric littered the interior. Then, utterly dismayed, he noticed how she hesitated, her back silhouetted by the glow of the fireplace. Together, they stared at the ornately framed painting of the Owen family that hung over the mantel. Robert, Martha, and Eugene, their only child, were skillfully painted in bright colors. Robert stood prominently in the middle of the portrait, as he should, in a black, pin-striped business suit and black tie. Martha stood by his side in a long gray flannel dress and suit coat with a feminine cut and row of white pearl buttons from top to bottom. A young boy sat at their feet as if added to the painting as an afterthought.

The scavenger woman glared at the painting, as did Robert, who stood behind her. Then, suddenly, in a blatant disrespect, the woman pulled down the painting and tossed it into the fire.

"What right have you?" shouted Robert. He pushed her aside and reached for the painting. As he did so, the fire ran up his sleeves and he and the painting burst into flames. He thrashed about, screaming.

Robert woke with a start, his bed drenched in sweat. Liberated from his hellish dream, he opened his eyes to the darkness of the bedroom and cold ashes in the fireplace. He reached out and touched Martha, who still slept, breathing peacefully beside him. Then, suddenly, he sensed they were not alone. Something was in their bedroom with them. He could feel it. He lay quietly listening when he heard a sound barely loud enough to be more than the usual creaking. He stared into the darkness.

Marauders? Cowards! Come to steal in the cover of night. When he heard it again, he quietly reached for the long gun he kept under his bed. The unseen presence was more discernable this time, and, listening carefully, Robert heard rhythmical chanting, like the verse of a song he'd never heard. He recognized the strange phenomenon immediately—the sound they had all been listening to since the eclipse. The words mingled like imposters hiding among his thoughts, coming and going on a whim.

On this night, the singing had an ethereal quality, like the sound of gentle rain or ocean waves. It brought about a hypnotic trance, like a symphony conductor controlling the instruments to bring a musical score to life. In like manner, the bewitching music took hold of Robert's mind.

He listened intently to the lyrics woven into the melody. He had to focus through the mental fog to put the words together. The verse was as impressive as any angelic rendering imaginable. The chorus penetrated his mind, playing on repeat until the words took on a life of their own. Its theme: Come to Erebus.

We're here! So very fortunate for you.
A blackbird cawed what you desired.
We have the power to give it all.
An alliance is all that we require.

Come to Erebus. Come unarmed.
Superior men never hesitate.
Your wealth and power we will secure.
Tempus fugit, you mustn't wait.

Under a blood moon, precious time,
Venture alone through Erebus's gate.
By Hades's metal, you decide
What we conjure as your fate.

Come to Erebus. Ascend the throne.
No need your enemies to tolerate.
Blood moon summons when it's time.
Tick. Tick. Tick. We wait, we wait.

Once the words affixed themselves to his memory, the song faded. Robert lay on his back, his head heavy on his pillow. Finally, he tugged at his quilt, pulled it over his shoulders, and contemplated. *Come to Erebus? Hades's metal? Greek mythology? What's the meaning of this? Who bids me come to Erebus? Mythical creatures?*

Robert climbed Mount Erebus as a youngster to see the old guard post built during the Indian Wars as a lookout. He'd explored it, as had all the boys of New Harmony. But, as he recalled, there was not much to see, so he dismissed melody and verse as mere dreams. Yet, as sleep overcame him, the lyrics echoed in his mind, visions of a blood moon, ticking clock, and mythical gate tumbling over and over in his head.

Chapter 19

Emily awoke on Saturday morning, her first week of teaching not as she had hoped. The burden of the disturbing letter only added to the contentious atmosphere that accompanied all things concerning the Owen family. For now, she pushed those concerns aside.

I'm to see Christian today. That will lighten my mood, she thought. She sprang out of bed and began preparing. Brushing her long auburn hair, she thought of what the parson told her. It wasn't in her nature to keep secrets, especially from her beloved Christian, but there was wisdom in the parson's advice, if only to keep Christian safe. It was the right thing to do. Regardless, she couldn't help but feel guilty for keeping secrets from the man she loved.

The crisp morning air seeped in through the window's wooden seam. Emily pulled the drape aside to see a slight breeze pushing and pulling the branches of the elm tree in the yard. The leaves fluttered as if waving "good morning" in direct conflict with the gloom she felt upon awakening.

Please hurry, Christian. Why are you so late? She continued to stare out the window.

Suddenly, her face brightened, and she jumped up. Before Christian could knock, she opened the door. Emily grabbed his hand and pulled him into the kitchen. "Auntie gets you first. Then I have you all to myself."

Marjorie beamed as the two entered. A welcoming smell filled the kitchen as Christian greeted Aunt Marjorie, who was dusted in brown flour, having just baked bread.

"Good morning, ma'am."

"Good mornin' yourself. Now, sit down. Sit! Sit! Got a plate already for ya."

He and Emily sat and stared at each other across the table. Christian took a deep breath and held it, savoring the aroma. "Mrs. Hampshire, mmm, the smell." He winked at Emily.

"Call me Margie, dear boy, or better, Auntie. That's what ya call me, like Emmy does." Marjorie opened the back door and called for Albert to come in. "Poor man, worried about them tomatoes of his. Not growin' as well as hoped." They watched through the window as Albert crossed into the backyard.

Marjorie slid a plate in front of Christian, and without hesitation, he took a bite of fried egg. Emily waited impatiently, watching as he took another and then another. He'd barely finished his biscuits when she grabbed his hand and led him out the back door.

They sat together on the weathered steps of the back porch, the green paint chipped and peeling where footsteps had worn down the wood. Silence passed between them as Emily peered through the white fence slats to be sure they were alone. The air was humid, and she tapped her toes to the rhythm of the Folsom's chickens clucking next door.

"Something troubling you?" Christian asked.

There was something, but it wasn't a thing she dared share. "I'm all right," she said, then paused. Her eyes fluttered, and she sneezed.

"Sneezing's a sign you are not telling the truth." Christian smiled. "Either that or perhaps you are allergic to me. Now, which is it?"

"Oh no, it's just that . . ." she stammered in an attempt to regain her composure. "More that I sneeze when I'm nervous."

"So I make you nervous?"

She wiped the moisture from her eyes and smiled. "Oh no. Well, it's the good kind of nervous." She sweetly leaned her head against his shoulder.

Christian looked toward the garden. "Emmy, do you recall when we were picking strawberries and I asked you about the family we would have one day?"

She nodded and laughed. "Yes, I remember. I was but fourteen, a little premature to contemplate having babies, don't you think?"

"I only imagined the family we would have in the future, and you thought I wanted babies that very moment!" He let out a hearty laugh. "You looked at me like I was the most roguish of pirates! I'll never forget it."

Emily blushed. "I had to remind you I am a good girl and we *must* be married."

"You were panicked, waving your hands and insisting we be married before we even *thought* of having babies."

"Well, why not? You made me drop my strawberries."

Christian pulled a strand of her shiny hair from her cheek and tucked it behind her ear, his thumb gently caressing her skin. "I remember it every time I see your garden. I see you right over there, picking up those strawberries in the grass. You looked so beautiful. I never intended for us to marry so young, but had you insisted, I would have. I would've married you on the spot. In truth, I have an uncle in Florence who married at thirteen."

Just then, a dog barked, and a flock of startled blackbirds took flight, drawing Emily's attention. She watched as the birds circled high above, squawking.

After a moment, Emily said, "I'm sorry. Dear me. I lost myself for a moment. Now, what was it you were saying? What about your uncle?"

"Wasn't important," said Christian. "Only that I feel the same now as when we first walked this garden. I cannot imagine a future without you, Emmy."

Their lips gently touched, but before he could genuinely kiss her, she leaned back to stare into his eyes. "You realize teenage love isn't supposed to last," she whispered.

"Yet here we are," he said. "I suppose there are exceptions."

"Miracles?"

"Then let's call it that," said Christian.

Her eyebrows rose, and she chuckled. "Perhaps for you, my dear, but not for me. It is no miracle that I love you. It's just meant to be, is all."

"I beg to differ."

"What?" Emily giggled. "What do you mean?"

"It's a miracle you haven't married Weston by now."

She laughed even harder. "Weston? Why Weston?"

"Firstly, you've always held his interest—always. And besides, he owns a ranch, not like the Owen's, but considerable, and he's a town council member. But, of course, you wouldn't dare settle for a simple postman, would you?"

She replied coyly. "I might settle for a postman, a barber's son, or a banker. I would settle for a roguish pirate as long as it was you."

"Well then, I suppose I can admit it," he said.

"Admit what?" Emily pinched his arm. "Tell me!"

"Very well, I will," he said. "Do you remember when we were just thirteen, the bouquet you discovered on your desk on that first day of school?"

"You mean the bouquet you left for me? Of course, extremely sweet of you."

"What if I told you it wasn't from me?" Christian nervously waited for her reaction.

Emily's eyes widened. "Why are you telling me this, and if not you, then who? Who left them for me?"

"I'm confessing because we should never harbor secrets from one another."

"All right, then. Go on. I'm listening."

"The answer is Weston Riley. He is the one who left them for you. You'd yet to arrive that day, and I saw them on your desk. There was a card attached, but I lost it on purpose."

Her mouth hung open. "You're serious, aren't you?"

Christian grinned and nodded. "No secrets."

"Why, Weston never said a word about it."

"Possibly because you rudely ignored him." Christian grinned impishly. "I imagine he thought you knew it was him but said nothing, not even thank you. He must have imagined you'd chosen to ignore his advances."

She looked at him, shocked. "How awful."

"Yes, it was," Christian replied. "Appalling behavior. Such an arrogant, ungrateful girl."

Her eyes narrowed in mock scorn, but her smile remained. "You *are* a rascal and a rogue. You lied to me. You said those flowers were from you."

"I did no such a thing. I would never lie, not to you. You assumed, and I said nothing."

"A lie of omission, then."

"I admit I should've said something much earlier. I've struggled ever since. I wanted to tell you dozens of times, but the words failed me. Perhaps I was insecure. Is that awful?"

"I've given you no reason to feel insecure."

Christian lowered his head in shame. "You never really had to. Anyone could see you were the most beautiful girl in school. Look at you even now."

Her face beamed with amusement. "I see," she said playfully. "It's become clear to me now. You've been standing between Weston and me this entire time. Well," she paused and waited for Christian to look at her, "I can't thank you enough. Not that Weston is a bad choice; however—"

A wide smile appeared on Christian's face. "I hope you can forgive me, but I regret nothing." Christian flipped a lock of hair that had fallen over his eyes. "The rich brat threatened me that day. Luckily, my English was poor; otherwise, I may have been intimidated. He stabbed his finger at my chest, and his chipmunk face turned every shade of red. He did not want me anywhere near you. That much I understood. None of the boys wanted me around when you were there. Every boy in school wanted your attention."

She melted into him and kissed him without reservation. "Not everyone," she whispered.

"Tell me who, and I'll tell you you're wrong."

"Your brother, of course. I'm not sure even now whether he likes me."

"Of course he does. Marco likes everyone. He simply likes books more, is all."

"If you say so," said Emily. "It's just that he hardly looks at me. I can't help but wonder."

"That may be my fault," admitted Christian. "All I ever do is talk about you. He's certain to have grown weary of it by now."

"Well," said Emily. "He's your brother, and I wish him to be pleased with me."

"How can he not be?" Christian stood and held out his hand. "While the rain has stopped, I have something I want you to see. Come with me."

Emily eagerly accepted, and together they crossed the front yard, turning north. They walked past homes and gardens, jumping over puddles and an irrigation ditch. When they reached a barley field at the edge of town, Emily stopped and stared into the distance.

"What is it?" Christian asked.

"Over there." She pointed to where a dirt road led to an abandoned house, vacant and dilapidated. Parts of the roof and walls had crumbled to the ground. "That's where I lived before moving in with Auntie and Albert. I thought of returning, just for a peek, but I haven't. No sense in dredging up old memories. I have enough of those as it is. If I close my eyes, I can still remember every room, every corner of the floors I swept, and Tippy barking from behind the screen door, not to mention the memories of Mother and Father."

"I'm sorry, Emmy," said Christian.

"It's fine. I've mostly come to terms with it, though the aching in my heart will never completely disappear. Seeing the house in ruin makes me wish it had toppled and someone had buried it underground or, better, cared for it. As it is, it reminds me of my life in ruin, at least so it was, and a part of me even now. Unfortunately, it is a part of me I cannot wish away."

"I believe I understand," Christian said. He put his arm reassuringly around her shoulders. "After I lost my mother, I could hardly enter her room. Even still. It's not that we don't love them or want to remember them. On the contrary, it's the opposite."

"When you lost your mother," Emily recalled, "I saw myself in your pain. My mother was alive for a time but not really; she was more of a stranger, lost in her mind. I didn't know her anymore."

"That had to be worse."

Emily became quiet. A breeze from the north played with her hair, and the soft glow of a sun hidden behind the clouds glistened on her lips. A dragonfly flew between them and hovered there.

"It's a sign we belong together," said Emily. "Something my mother would say."

Christian grinned. "So I've heard. Dragonflies are the smartest of all God's creatures. They know things others don't."

They walked hand in hand before coming to a small crop of poplar trees alongside a freshwater creek that gave drink to the horses in the adjacent pasture and made everything greener along its banks. They removed their shoes and stockings and sat in the tall grass, letting their feet dangle in the cool water. A light wind sent ripples across the golden barley field, the waves of grain rolling all around them.

As they sat, their feet touched under the water. In that perfect moment, not a word passed between them. Emily could still see her old home off in the distance. She looked away to keep from slipping into the past. In the stillness, she heard the voices above the breeze passing through spring leaves and the gurgling of the stream. She looked at Christian, but he seemed unfazed.

"Christian? Do you hear it?"

"What?"

"The singing," she answered. "You don't hear it?"

Christian cocked his head. "No."

Still uncertain as to what she heard, she turned her head north and caught sight of her childhood home. Suddenly, her face filled with fear, as if something evil stalked her. Christian quickly rose, stood guard over her, and waited while words meant only for Emily called to her.

Emmy, dear Emmy, so innocent and naïve,
Unfathomable danger awaits you unless you believe.

Tooth and claw, sinewy jaw, points a vicious finger.
Wise to listen carefully. Best not to linger.

While Deimos and Phobos strike panic and terror,
Ignoring our warning is a most unfortunate error!

Eyes now watch you and ears do hear.
You've reason to worry. You've reason to fear.

Be mindful and watchful lest evil ensue.
Our warning is but a courtesy. 'Tis true. 'Tis true.

"Emmy? Emmy?" Full of concern Christian gently shook her. "Where were you?"

Emily blinked and stared back at him, unable to speak.

"We were conversing, and suddenly . . . your eyes—they were vacant!"

After a moment, she whispered, "I don't know what happened." She pressed her fingers to her temples. "I'm so sorry."

"I thought I lost you. Remember what you said about your mother, having lost her?"

"No, not the same," Emily assured him, her voice weak. "Not like her. I'm not like her."

"Then what was that? What caused you to drift? I only ask out of concern."

"I-I-I don't know. I can't say." Emily breathed in and out, suppressing the urge to run.

"All right, let's calm down," said Christian.

Emily nodded. "Yes. So, where were we?"

"Well," said Christian. "I was about to tell you something, but now I'm unsure."

"Please, Christian. Can we just forget what happened? I'm fine."

"All right," he said, shrugging it off. "You stay right here."

He gingerly walked across a patch of small pebbles to the trunk of a tree that would have shaded them if the sun ever decided to show itself. He disappeared behind it and brought out an ample bouquet of yellow and purple coneflowers sprinkled with reddish trumpet honeysuckle. Her face lit up, but only for a moment.

"Oh my," she said as he held them out.

"May I have full credit for these?" he asked. "Weston didn't pick a single one. I gathered and hid them all by myself before coming to get you."

"Fine, then. You're forgiven. The flowers are lovely," she said, but her thoughts drifted once again.

Christian approached, handing them to her, the worry he had seen earlier still evident on her face. "This isn't like you. There's something wrong, isn't there, something you won't tell me?"

"Please," begged Emily. "Can't we move on? I admit to being a little out of sorts, but otherwise, I'm fine," she said, somewhat less convincing.

"All right," said Christian. "Then I'd like to continue our conversation, the one we had while picking strawberries."

"Picking strawberries?"

"Yes, Emmy, when we were young. We just spoke of it, remember?"

"Of course, of course." Emily smiled, but her smile quickly faded. "Christian, I . . ."

"Emmy," he interrupted, "I may not have the means, not now but soon. What matters is that we desire to be together." He got down on one knee and lifted her chin. "Emily Ruth Hampshire, I love you, and you love me. Will you—" He stopped at the expression on her face.

"Christian, wait!" she urged as she thought about the letter and the parson's warning. *Tell no one,* she remembered. *If someone overheard, it may put both of you in danger. But you also said not to fear. So which is it, Parson?*

Christian froze, uncertain what to do. It seemed as if everything had gone still—even the bubbling stream and blowing blades of grass. Or was it that time had stopped? He watched as Emily's eyes drifted back to her childhood home. Each grueling second stretched into an eternity. He watched as tears formed in the corners of her eyes.

Finally, she cried, "My dear, I can and will marry you, but not now. Though I desire nothing more, just not now. Now is not the time."

"Then when?"

"I can't tell you. I'm sorry."

"Emmy, we're not schoolchildren. This is reasonable. It's what we both want. I know you love me, and you know I love you. Though my position in life is uncertain, it's only temporary. I'm full of aspirations and convinced I can properly care for you. So what reason do we have to wait?" His voice cracked, and his shoulders slumped.

"A reason I can't tell you. It's not a rejection. It's not," was all Emily could say.

His eyes lowered. "Feels like one," he said, holding up his hands. "Forgive me, Emmy, but I can't be here now." Hiding his tears, he turned and quickly ran away.

Emily dropped the flowers and covered her face with her hands. Tears rose from as deep a place as a human heart dared venture. *What have I done? The parson said not to listen, but I did, and now I'm frightened—not for myself but for Christian. I can only bring him pain when everyone I've ever loved ends up dead!*

Chapter 20

"Move aside!" Sheriff Graham Weasley pushed through the crowd gathered in front of the town hall, his thin frame weaving through it like a polecat, his pointed nose, sunken eyes, and protruding ears giving him a wolfish appearance. He appeared hungry, like a prowling scavenger searching for a dying animal. He tucked his long, blond, thinning hair under his wide-brimmed hat, then entered the building and peered into the mayor's office. "Sir, ya sent for me?"

"Come in, Weasley." The mayor looked up momentarily before he resumed scraping the gunk under his fingernails. A copy of *Ayer's American Almanac* lay on his desk, open to moon phases, the corner of the page dog-eared.

"Don't just stand there. Take a seat," he said as the sheriff entered. The mayor began picking at his teeth with his pinky finger. "Ms. Moser!" he called out. "Coffee for Weasley. Can you hear me?" he yelled louder. The mayor looked back at Weasley. "Hearing's not what it used to be. I yell, or she can't hear me."

From outside the office, they heard an older woman's voice. "I heard that! The problem is your patience, Robert. Give it a moment if you want it fresh."

"Slow as a tortoise on a Sunday stroll, but her coffee is worth the wait. So, what do you have to report, Weasley? What have you heard? Start with what's bothering those standing outside." His interest appeared to wane as usual. He half listened as the sheriff cut it as short as he dared. He knew the mayor asked as a mere formality.

"Well," Weasley hesitated. "Relative calm but for the farmers complainin' over nothin'. Wouldn't bother me if I were you."

The mayor stopped picking his teeth. "What this time?"

"Vern, out there, said he'd be fortunate to get half the harvest of the year previous. And that's if the sun breaks through, and soon. Before, they always whined about not enough rain, not enough! But now? They complain 'bout their crops drownin'. They want it to stop."

"Suspect a bit of exaggeration, do you?"

"Always, sir. But they're plenty worried, or so I've gathered, and not just Vern."

The mayor rested his head in his hands. "And now they're standing outside my office, wanting me to do exactly what? Somehow the sun is under my authority. But, seriously, what do they want me to do about it?"

The sheriff shrugged. "Can't tell."

"Listen here, Weasley, I have an idea. Suppose we refer them to the parson. He can lead them all in prayer." A satisfied smile crept over the mayor's face. "That'll do it. They can all pray together. The sun is certain to shine bright as ever, but have them take cover—we wouldn't want them to get sunburned."

The sheriff chuckled only after the mayor slapped his knee and burst out laughing.

The mayor sobered. "On a serious note," he said, "it's prudent for us to be careful. Things could unravel if people go hungry come winter."

The sheriff nodded.

"Timing's inopportune, for certain. With the election not far off, there's no telling what could happen. Until then, it's best the governor not receive another letter like the one from the Stewarts, but they can't be the only ones complaining. The governor alluded to there being more. If only I knew who. And what about Shear's boy? Did you get Theodore's letter from him at the post office?"

"I did."

"Well, where is it?"

The sheriff looked startled. "I burned it, sir!"

"Good," said the mayor. "Before burning it, did you check the seal on the envelope? Could anyone have read it?" Seeing the expression of concern on the sheriff's face, the mayor became angry. "Didn't occur to you, did it, Weasley?" The sheriff sheepishly shook his head as the mayor groaned. "Can't anyone else have a single morsel of common sense?"

"Apologies, sir. No, it didn't occur to me. Coulda been unsealed. I've no way of knowin'."

The mayor sighed. "All right. Fine. But now you best keep your ears open and an eye on the Shear boy. Add him to your list."

The sheriff nodded. "Anything further, sir?"

"Weasley! Have you forgotten? Beatrice is bringing you coffee. Relax. And while we're waiting, I want to hear what you decided we should do with the farmers."

Startled, the sheriff said, "Didn't you say to send 'em to the parson to let him deal with it?"

"And look unconcerned just before an election? No, Weasley. I must bow my head in humility, address the Almighty, and offer as a sacrifice my dignity so all will see me praying—as if that would do any good."

Just then, Beatrice Moser entered and set a cup of coffee on the desk for the sheriff. Steam rose, swirling upward and disappearing as it mixed with the cool air. She looked at the mayor, anticipating the question, the same she'd answered half a dozen times already that day.

"I told you, Robert," she said before he could ask again, "I'll be sure to let you know if he comes in."

"Thank you, Beatrice," said the mayor as Weasley blew on his drink.

As she left, the sheriff inquired, "Expecting someone?"

"I hope not. Only a rumor."

"What rumor?"

"Unfortunately, that damned Bronson Parrish feeds the gossipers, claiming he's running to replace me." The mayor yelled out the door and into the hallway. "Hey, Beatrice! If he comes in, you'll let me know?"

"Of course, Robert."

Weasley appeared shocked. "The teacher wouldn't dare." He smirked. "It's pure nonsense. The election will be uncontested. Always been an Owen sitting there at your desk—your papa before and grandpa before that."

"I appreciate that, Weasley, but Bronson's a threat I would be wise not to underestimate. And now, with sparse sunlight and crops drowning, it's just poor timing."

"The teacher ain't got nothin', sir," said Weasley. "Ain't nobody wants him. You'll always be mayor and your son after."

"I'm not so convinced anymore, Weasley. Times are uncertain. It's like time is running out for me. I once imagined becoming governor of Indiana, leaving this office to my son. Even so, my dream seems more distant every day. As for my son, regretfully, he's no Owen. He's nothing like me, or my father, or my grandfather. Unless Eugene comes to his senses, I fear I'm the last Mayor Owen."

"He will," said Sheriff Weasley. "Eugene will learn who butters his biscuit. Boy's never been hungry, has he?"

"No," said the mayor. "Too entitled, too ungrateful."

"I see why ya cut 'im off, sir. He'll straighten up once his stomach growls."

The mayor gave him a stern look. "What makes you think we cut him off?"

"Sorry. I, uh, assumed. It's just that . . . it wouldn't be New Harmony without a Mayor Owen. Never been anything but."

As the sheriff assured the mayor, his eyes peered over the cup, his tongue testing the coffee, checking the temperature. A long silence passed between them as he took his first sip.

"Shut the door, Weasley," ordered the mayor. "I need to tell you something." The sheriff quickly obliged, then returned to his seat. He took a second sip as the mayor spoke. "I require absolute confidence with what I'm about to tell you."

The sheriff looked straightway at the mayor. "You always have my confidence."

"I know," said the mayor. "Put down your cup and listen carefully. There's a blood moon tonight, Weasley. That is, I believe there will be."

The sheriff set his drink on the desk. "A blood moon?"

"It may not be an actual blood moon, not a real one. I'm not even certain what one is. But I believe the moon will appear red as blood, as a sign, and I need something from you. I'm not heading home this evening at the end of the day. Send word to Martha not to wait up. I have important business. Tell her not to worry, but nothing more. Understood? Not to worry, but nothing more. Repeat it."

"Not to worry, but nothing more. I got it. Of course, you haven't told me anything."

"And you don't want to know," said the mayor. "Believe me."

"I believe you," said the sheriff.

"Now, this here, Weasley, is most important of all. Are you listening?"

"Yes, sir."

"Tomorrow morning, I need you to check on me. If you can't find me here or at the ranch, I need you to come look for me."

"And where might that be?" Sheriff asked.

"Up Erebus."

"Mount Erebus? Should I be concerned for your safety?"

"What I'm doing, Weasley, what I'm doing requires an abundance of caution. That's it. You don't need to know anything further. Are we clear?"

"Got it," said the sheriff. "An abundance of caution."

"And?"

"And I'll go lookin' for ya," he said, "up the mountain if you're not around here."

"Good," said the mayor. "It's important, so don't forget."

"I won't."

"And come armed."

Chapter 21

Years earlier, Governor Harrison ordered the construction of a lookout post during the Battle of Tippecanoe. He required that it accommodate a small number of troops to watch the west ridge, from which Tecumseh and his Shawnee warriors might launch an attack. But it had served its purpose and fallen into disrepair, like the road leading up to it.

Boys considered the abandoned U.S. Calvary guard post a favorite adventure. As a teen, the mayor hiked to the peak and explored the ruins. Even then, nature had already reclaimed much, and nothing remained as it had once been. Rock walls mostly crumbled to the ground, and green moss blanketed those still standing. Wisteria framed what were once windows, and only a corner of the roof had survived. The stone chimney and fireplace inside, no longer functional, lay broken and scattered in the brush. As fate would have it, the mayor, now much older and potbellied, once again made his way up the mountain.

Candles were extinguished, windows dark, as he rode his horse, Buck, through the streets of New Harmony. Armed with only a lantern, he rode north toward Mount Erebus. It would not be easy to manage his horse and simultaneously hold on to his lantern given the steep incline of the trail. He hoped to leave the lantern behind, but that would require moonlight, which was unlikely with the persistent clouds over the valley. Then again, he recalled the song that called to him in the dark of night. *Look*, the lyrics told him, *look for a blood moon.*

Unfortunately, the almanac offered little information. Doubts crept into his thoughts. *How can I see if the moon is shaded in any color, whether bloodred, blue, or gray? Is this but a fool's errand? Do my imaginings run amuck?*

The truth, the very same he kept from himself, was that he, the mayor, feared what he might find at the end of the trail. Buck trotted along, his hooves matching the rhythm of the mayor's heartbeat and growing unease. *Why am I doing this? Why? Is it a choice I am making, or am I under a spell?* He pondered before concluding he was, no doubt, under a spell. He continued regardless.

He rode through the dark until he came to the mountain's base. Only then did he notice a moonbeam that shone down from the night sky, unlike anything he'd ever seen. A reddish glow lit the path before him as it broke free of the clouds, exposing a full blood moon. *What strange premonition, be it of heaven or hell, brought a blood moon?* he wondered. But what troubled him more than anything else was this. What force commanded the clouds above, and they, in turn, obeyed? The mayor couldn't deny his mounting fears, finding it more and more difficult to suppress the urge to turn and run.

As Buck turned onto the trail, the mayor noticed that a red, glimmering light guided his horse. All that was required of him now was to sit. As the clouds moved, Buck walked onward as if controlled by an unseen force. The mayor pulled back on the reins, signaling him to stop, but Buck kept his head low, irrepressibly drawn to the crimson light. Fear gripped the mayor, and he leaned back hard on the reins until Buck eventually stopped. The moment he relaxed his grip, however, Buck galloped toward the light, causing the mayor to lose his grip on the lantern, which blinked out the moment it hit the ground. As soon as they caught up to the moonlight, Buck slowed, then resumed his march, head down. The mayor considered jumping off and would have had it not been for the ledge that ran parallel to the trail. And, like it or not, he had an appointment with destiny, and skipping the appointment was no longer an option. From his saddle, he turned around and stared at the broken lantern disappearing in the moon's dim light.

I'll have to retrieve it later—unless there's no coming back.

As curious as was the beam of light leading them up the trail, it was not the only strange thing he noticed. The way before him appeared maintained and wide enough for a wagon, not what he remembered hiking to the peak as a boy. It wasn't the narrow trail with places where erosion made the way difficult, even on foot. Was he somehow lost?

A little before midnight, the mayor approached the ridge. As he turned onto the final switchback, a thick wall of smoke unfurled before him, rising as high as a tree and churning like a pot of gray stew. He pulled back hard on the reins, and the light that led Buck up the mountain paused. The horse stopped. The stench of death and decay lay heavy in the air. And although the smell was unbearable, there was no going around the strange barrier.

The moment he resigned himself to whatever fate lay beyond, the beam of moonlight moved, and once again, Buck obediently followed. Together, they approached the smoky curtain. When they came within a few feet of it, the mayor squeezed his eyes shut and pulled his shirt over his nose. Leaves from a branch brushed his face, and he pushed them aside.

Suddenly, a phenomenon difficult to describe beset the mayor. He felt pulled, as if he and his horse had traveled some distance, then pushed backward, and then twisted, like stockings sloshing in a wash bucket. His thoughts warped as long-forgotten images of his childhood splashed about in his head. It felt as if time had folded in on itself. Then things suddenly quieted.

He looked about, trying to orient himself. He still sat atop his horse, moving forward, as if nothing had happened. The clomping of hooves calmed his nerves. He turned back to look at the smoky barrier to confirm it lay behind him. It did, but something didn't feel right. A gust of frigid air rushed down upon him, and he rubbed the goose bumps on his arms. Looking ahead, he saw trees lining the trail.

Leaves and branches swirled in the breeze, blown in one direction and another simultaneously, their image splitting in two, then three, existing separately before coming back together as if the wind had never moved them. He marveled at the sight. He looked down to see Buck's head become two heads, then snap back together, only to split again. For a moment, he could not count Buck's ears as they disbanded, then came back together. He felt dizzy and squeezed his eyelids tight.

Holding fast to the saddle horn, he waited for his mind to clear. Buck moved unaffected past the trees, still following the mysterious light. A little farther up the trail, the guard post came into view. The mayor nearly tumbled to the ground when, without a kick to the flank or any prompting whatsoever, Buck charged forward. The mayor's heart raced as he pulled the reins to turn Buck around. But it was no use. Any effort to escape was now futile.

Suddenly, the horse stopped, the mayor thrown forward. Then Buck reared up, his nostrils blowing puffs of vapor, and dropped the mayor onto the ground. Everything went black.

How much time passed before the mayor stirred awake, he didn't know. It didn't seem to matter as time appeared relative anyway. At present, night ruled over day, forcing its will upon the sun, preventing its rising for as long as it cared to. He rolled onto his side and rubbed the bump on the back of his head. Though stinging, it wasn't his only discomfort. The bitter-cold wind penetrated his clothing, biting his skin and reddening his cheeks. He wrapped his arms around his torso, cursing himself for not bringing an overcoat.

After struggling to regain his footing, he noticed Buck nervously grinding his teeth while backing up.

It could be only one thing. Bathed in the light of the blood moon, the guard post stood before the mayor. The crumbling rock, splintered and rotted door, and roof sagging like a tired blanket no longer providing warmth were transformed into what he imagined the post must have looked like when it served the U.S. Calvary during the Indian Wars.

The mayor led Buck to a nearby tree and wrapped his reins around a crooked branch. Just then, the song he heard the night before played softly in his mind. There were, however, changes to the lyrics. He peered into the void behind the open door as he listened.

Summoned, were you? In shadow, we wait.
So state your purpose, your desire.
Grant it, we shall, ensuring good fate.
But first, an alliance is what we require.

Cast aside your foolish foreboding.
Superior men never hesitate.
Hitherto, see your influence eroding?
Tempus fugit, dear fool, you mustn't wait.

Blood moon, regretfully, 'tis an omen,
Tragic indeed. Blood will be shed.
Not ink but blood, so dip your quill.
Sign and see your enemies dead.

Impatient, are we? We shall not wait.
We'll submit to your every decree.
But first, come and ensure good fortune.
For you—the savior of New Harmony.

The mayor stood unmoving at the door to the old lookout post. A fire glowed dimly from within. Much too feeble to ward off the dark or offer comfort from the cold, the fire barely clung to life.

No good can come from this, he thought, *unless—*

Any illusion of an angelic presence blessing the town was ripped apart as a raspy voice issued from the blackness. "If you intend to be the savior of New Harmony, come in, come in."

Cautiously, he stepped inside. His heart felt weak, barely in rhythm with the flickering fire. Cold sweat beaded across his forehead.

He jumped as the door slammed shut behind him. The sickly fire blew out, leaving him in the dark.

Not even the crimson light of a blood moon dares enter here, he thought.

An ember flared from within the aged hearth, and by the light of the small flames that sprang up, the mayor began to see dark shapes moving in his peripheral vision. His stomach lurched at the stench of rot and death that suddenly permeated the room.

What is that?

After a moment of squeezing his eyes shut and clamping a hand over his nose, he risked a glance. His eyes having adjusted somewhat to the dark, he discerned a cast-iron pot hanging from a metal chain within the fireplace. Inside swirled a putrid stew.

What creatures are these that nourish themselves on such foulness?

Gathering his nerves, he looked into the near-pitch blackness, flinching when he saw three black, hooded figures, barely visible, in the corners of the room. Whether floating or grounded, he couldn't say. He could only slightly make out the space where their faces must be staring back at him. They appeared to move with unnatural ability, more than a mere illusion caused by the flickering light.

Witches! I'm in the company of witches! They're playing with me!

More than simply regretting his presence here, he now feared for his life. He looked for the door through which he'd entered, but he couldn't see it in the dark.

"Witches?" came a booming voice from somewhere in the inky blackness. "His thoughts are louder than his mouth."

And then another, more high-pitched voice shrieked, "He considers us witches!"

The mayor backed into a corner. "If you are something else, then tell me."

A dark figure appeared before him, its face obscured by its hood. He listened as the creature posed a question. "Do witches burn? Can you burn a witch?"

"There have been witches burned, so yes," answered the mayor.

The cloaked figure floated closer. Stunned, the mayor watched as a hand slithered out from a filthy linen sleeve, stopping inches from his face. Flames burst from the palm of the withered hand, which now glowed a fiery red. The voice from within the cloak said, "Turn a witch to ashes, but I you cannot. Care to explain?"

"I cannot."

"We are no such thing as witches. We are born of the fire of desire, not consumed by it."

"Then what are you? What do I call you?"

As if in answer, he heard the angelic voices in the chambers of his mind.

"Nero of Rome called us Parcae. We are Parcae, and we are not, only in the name given to us by mortals. Cleon, the Greek, considered us Moirai. We are Moirai, and we are not, though we are Spinner, Allotter, and the Inevitable. We are sisters. We are the source of your myths. We are the sisters of fate and fortune who grant you what you yearn for. We serve your appetites and ambitions. We are feared, sought after, and bartered with. We are the purveyors of destiny."

"You are not witches. Understood. But if not of this earth, whence have you come?"

There came a thundering answer. "Nowhere and everywhere!" The sound reverberated, now more devilish than angelic, from somewhere in the darkness of the fort, his ears burning as it assaulted him from every direction. Quietly and carefully, he hurried along the wall, away from the creatures, to where he imagined the door to be.

"So soon you are leaving?" came a voice to his left.

"You haven't stated your purpose. Why have you come?" Another unearthly inquirer hovered above him.

The mayor wasn't sure if only one of the shadowy figures spoke or if each took turns. Resigning himself to his plight, he steeled his nerves, turned, and addressed them all. "I heard singing. I—"

The mayor went quiet when the fire flared out from where it limped about in the fireplace, looking for unburned wood. For a fraction of a second, it filled the room. He began to fear being consumed when suddenly it was back in the hearth, barely burning. He patted his face, arms, and legs to find them unsinged. He strained his eyes until he could make out the dark figures, and though he couldn't see their faces, he knew they watched him closely.

"Waiting . . ." came the sickly voice. "Unwise to keep us waiting."

The mayor recognized the danger he'd placed himself in. Even so, he was encouraged to still be breathing. Finally, he said, "The song. I came because the song spoke of an alliance. I assumed it was you who called, you who summoned me." The mayor pursed his lips and looked about, wondering which entity would speak.

The eerie, dark apparitions circled him. "We did not call you, but your yearnings, your pleadings screamed for an alliance," said one.

"Quite right," said another.

"What you want, we grant," said a third gruff voice to his right.

"Small price for you to pay. Small but vital," came a voice from behind him. Before he could turn around, another spoke directly in front of him. He stepped back, felt a painful jab in his spine, and froze.

"Asking again," repeated one of the shadowy figures. "What is it you are not telling us?"

The mayor's anxiety threatened to undo him. "What am I not telling you?"

A deafening voice answered, "What you want!"

The mayor's words tumbled out of him. "The alliance. You contacted me, or I you. Doesn't matter. Tell me the terms and with whom I enter this agreement. What are you, if not witches or even human? And how is it you call yourselves sisters?"

"Because we are," said each.

"Are what?"

"Sisters," chorused the trio of voices.

"But then you must have a mother and father, yet you're not human? Explain."

The voices went quiet, and as he waited for their answer, he began to regret his line of questioning. Feeling cold sweat run down his face and feeling several sets of eyes staring at him, he attempted to apologize and explain his reservations.

"Forgive me," he pleaded, "but what am I to make of this? Are you fallen? Yes, fallen, from up there." The mayor pointed skyward. When the sisters remained silent, he continued. "I've dark thoughts. Yes, I have dark thoughts about all of this. If you are not human, are you the fallen as spoken of in sacred books? I must ask, for I am clueless as to your nature. Why are you silent? Why do you not speak?"

"The answer is incomprehensible to you."

Indignant, the mayor asked, "How is that possible?"

"Can an ant comprehend a human? Does an ant have words to describe a human? So different are they. Ever shed a tear for stepping on an ant?"

"No," the mayor admitted. "So you suggest I am but an ant?"

"Much more than that, you are. And we are not here to step on you but to grant you your wishes."

"I'm given to understand, then, that you are far greater than I, a human. And if that's true, why bother with me? For I pay little attention to an ant. Your logic begs the question, of what value am I to you?"

"More than you know," came voices. "And, fortunate for you, we can grant your desires. We heard you calling us across time, and here we are!"

"Then you're not evil?"

"Is it really a matter of good or evil, little ant? Of virtue or vice? No. It is a matter of fortune or misfortune, and the scale of fortune now tips in your favor. Fortune is a blessing for those on the weightier end of the scale, misfortune for those on the lighter end. Which do you prefer?"

"The weightier, of course, but what of the deal? What fortune can you grant me, and at what price? There's always a price."

Without warning, the dark presence drew close, their faces revealed. The mayor stumbled backward. "Why do you look so horrible?"

"Careful . . ." said the ungodly voices. "We appear as we choose. We can seduce with feminine charm, with irresistible allure, if you prefer, but good fortune does not come by deceit—only by choice. Seduction, like beauty, is fleeting. The terms we offer last forever."

The more ancient of the trio floated to within inches of his face, a fetid smell wafting about her, and he resisted the urge to vomit.

"Time is up. What do you want? Say it now."

His back pinned to the wall, the mayor closed his eyes. "I'll tell you. Patience, I beg you."

"Say it!"

"All right. The farmers are worried," said the mayor. "The sun doesn't shine, and the rain is drowning the seeds they've planted—ever since the eclipse, which, pardon me, accompanied your arrival, though I hesitate to cast aspersions. And now the harvest is at risk, and some may go hungry. Is this your doing, and if so, how may it be undone?"

A malicious voice answered. "Blocking the sun is but a courtesy, a courtesy not requested, neither earned, yet granted. Show gratitude. You and yours will always bloat your stomachs."

The old crones backed up and then swooped down again, the stench of death blasting him in the face. "Admit it," one said. "We already know. The scarcity of others feeds your desire. Powerful men understand this. A crisis demands cooperation, which requires compliance. Compliance grants control, and from control—power. The crisis of starvation is but a gift. And you, the powerful savior of New Harmony, are welcome whether you are grateful or not."

"Unless, that is," said another, "you are not a leader of men but a mouse."

One of the vile creatures moved to within inches of his face. He peered into the hooded darkness to see a pointed nose and tiny spots of light as the fire reflected off the specter's glossy, coal-black eyes. Her voice crackled in his ears. "We cannot grant what you want when you can't admit it."

Another sister took her place, staring into his face. "Admit it to yourself," the hag demanded.

Then the third whispered in his ear. "We grow impatient. Say it now or scurry away, little mouse!" The room turned icy cold.

"I've enemies," he said under his breath.

The creatures froze, waiting to hear more. "Go on . . ."

"I've enemies," said the mayor more forcibly.

"Listening," came the cacophony of craggy voices.

The mayor's shoulders slumped in defeat. "Well, there's an election."

The ancient crones urged him to continue. "Listening," they chanted. "Tell us. What cheese for you, little mouse?"

"I may lose an election, ending my political aspirations and delivering me to ruin."

"Our mouse is getting close, so very close to what he truly desires."

"I know what it is," he admitted.

"Then say it!" barked the sisters.

"Power," the mayor finally admitted, drawing his shoulders back and puffing his chest out. "I want power. But first I need the terms. Explain the meaning of the alliance, what you offer."

The figures moved away, revealing the door. It opened without the aid of hands, which no longer surprised the mayor. The light outside hinted at morning. He turned and peered into the coming day. How long had he been there?

"Hurry! Run home, or the way will close," said the voices in unison. "Soon. Very soon, we'll meet again. Ponder our words, savior of New Harmony."

A physical force pushed the mayor out the door, which slammed shut behind him.

All too willing to leave, he quickly untied Buck, pulled himself into the saddle, and headed back to town. He touched the still-painful lump on his head.

I'm alive! I'm alive, with only a bump on my head to show for it. But I may have found what I seek.

His heart filled with hope as he looked down into the valley from the ridge near the peak. Like a flour paste mixed with dirt, the dome of clouds still hung over New Harmony. Time again moved linearly for the mayor, and fatigue set in. He had been up all night. His eyes grew heavy, and he had to catch himself before he fell off Buck as they moved down the trail. Then, near the bottom, he noticed Weasley riding toward him, waving.

As he drew near, the mayor called out, "Weasley! You're a damn good sight to see."

The sheriff's horse halted short of the mayor. "Sir, you all right? What happened to ya?"

"No questions, Weasley."

Weasley nodded. "Headed to the office?"

"No," said the mayor. "I'm exhausted. Tell Beatrice I won't be coming in today."

"I'll do that, sir."

"And, Weasley . . ."

"Uh-huh?"

"Tell no one where I've been."

"No one, sir."

Chapter 22

As soon as the final bell rang, the clamor of boys hollering and girls chattering and giggling echoed through the hallway and spilled out into the schoolyard. Once the building emptied, things quieted and Emily gathered her papers. She walked into the yard and looked around, expecting to see someone. But the someone Emily sought had not come. With heavy heart, she realized that Christian wouldn't be walking her home. The gloomy patter of the unceasing rain only deepened the emptiness she felt. It didn't matter that she had chosen her solitude. She now feared it meant walking home alone each day. But it was worth it if the secret Emily harbored could put him in danger.

She'd do anything to keep him safe, even when it made her heart ache.

Emily looked across the street. The door to the church stood wide open, with no sign of Parson Burroughs. She looked up and down Main Street, but he was nowhere to be found. Emily's rose-colored bonnet grew sopping wet as she waited, wondering what to do. Finally, she crossed the street, stuck her head inside the church, and called, "Parson, are you in here?"

It was quiet. The lanterns and candles were unlit, the stained-glass window dark, and a dimly lit Peter still hoped to be pulled from the water. She walked passed the benches on each side and sat in the front row. The sound of the door closing and the tumblers in the lock clicking into place startled her.

"Wait!" She ran to the door and pounded on it, then listened for a response. A moment later, she heard the clicking of keys and the lock disengaging.

When the doors slowly opened, a surprised parson peered inside. "Why, Emily, I didn't see you enter. Dear Lord, forgive me!" He opened the doors wide. "What are you doing here?"

"It is I in need of forgiveness. I entered unannounced."

"Nonsense. You are always welcome." The parson's smile vanished. "My child, aside from being completely drenched, I sense something else troubles you. Tell me, my dear?"

"Trouble's me?" Emily lowered her head, uncertain where to begin. She looked up. "Everything, I suppose."

"Then your being here is meant to be. Besides, I've been worried about you. Please stay, and let's talk." He lit several candles and an oil lamp.

Emily looked past the parson in an attempt to deflect her sadness. "Auntie and Albert are doing fine. Everything is fine."

But the parson knew better. "Your uncle and aunt are not my worry. What concerns me is you. What is it, Emily?"

"I feel lost. I . . . I haven't the words."

"Yes, you have. And you can tell me. It's all right."

Minutes felt like hours until Emily finally said, "Only that Christian asked me to marry him."

The parson smiled broadly. "That's just perfect. Hannah will be so pleased. She's very accommodating when it comes to making arrangements." Just as suddenly as his smile returned, it disappeared when a tear rolled down Emily's cheek. "And yet you are distraught, pained by a thing I can't imagine. Why?"

"I said no."

The parson's expression turned to utter dismay. "Excuse me?"

"Parson, I said no."

"But why? You're inseparable."

Emily shook her head. "I dare not say." She looked up and stared at the tortured figure of Christ on the crucifix above the parson's office door.

Parson Burroughs nodded as if he understood, a practiced response to unburdening souls. "Would you like to talk about it?"

Emily sat silently, struggling not to flee or burst into sobbing. Christian was the only boy she'd ever truly loved.

"You have your reason, true. Will you share it with me? Perhaps I can help." His kindly eyes gazed at her as he waited patiently.

"Parson, can it be that I'm incapable of love? How can I love only to have those I care for most dearly taken from me? It is best I not love at all. In truth, I prefer that more than to lose another. And now the thought of putting Christian in danger . . . if anything were to happen, it would be my fault."

"Dear child, you are capable of more love than you know. But sometimes those who love most fear it most. They value it so deeply they fear losing it so completely. Do you understand?"

Emily stared at her hands clasped tightly in her lap. "I do love Christian, I swear it. I once loved my parents just as much. But it wasn't enough to keep them safe, and loving Christian may put him in danger without him knowing. I'm at an impasse, Parson. I can hardly breathe."

"Will you trust me? Please tell me what you fear, dear. Let's speak of it, holding nothing back."

Emily stared into his gentle eyes as he leaned in, then ever so softly said, "You are safe here, but whisper if you must. Sometimes it's easier. Think, Emily. What frightens you?"

Flashes of light from the storm outside deepened the shadows in the church's dark sanctuary as candles flickered, and the drumming of rain kept time with the rhythm of Emily's heart, now quickening. The church walls melted away, as did the wooden benches, pulpit, and stained-glass window above it.

☾

In the hidden corridors of Emily's mind, mingled among the silt and sediment of painful childhood memories, a young girl, only eight years of age, sat on a chair of splintered wood, staring out the dirty window of her father's work shed at the mine. Men on horses approached, a cloud of dust trailing behind them. One wore a wide-brimmed hat, his face hidden in shadow. The other wore a white shirt and black vest. The sun gleamed off his head, the brightness making it difficult to see the features of his face.

"Emmy! In here!"

She turned to see her father drop the broom he used to keep the place clean. Startled, Emily stared at her father, who now removed tools from the cabinet to make room for her.

He held the door open. "In here," he urged. "Now!"

Emily quickly got up and went to her father. He nudged her inside. But before closing the cabinet door, he said, "Whatever you hear, I need you to stay quiet. Don't come out. Can you do that?"

Young Emily nodded.

"I'll come for you when I can. Until then, stay quiet."

Tears welled up in Emily's eyes, and she began to whimper. He quickly pulled her from the cabinet and hugged her. "It'll be all right, Emmy. Don't be afraid. Please, dear, just do as I say." Then, just as quickly, he put her back inside, and she waited as everything turned dark.

The candlelight in the church pierced the darkness and the sound of rain once again filled Emily's ears. Under her breath, she whispered, "I know who I fear. I know who took my parents from me."

A gentle voice said, "I'm listening."

After a moment, a tearful Emily whispered, "I've never told anyone, mostly forgotten myself, but Mother made me promise not to tell."

"As any good mother would. She protected you when you were young. But you are no longer a child."

Again, the parson waited patiently, though he didn't have to wait long before he heard Emily whisper so quietly he could barely make out what she said.

"Sheriff Weasley. The sheriff and the mayor."

Parson Burroughs took a deep breath, let go of her hands, and leaned back. Upon seeing him relax, Emily's heartbeat slowed, as did her breathing, and she wiped away her tears.

He smiled reassuringly. "I understand," he said. "Weak men are the most dangerous when given power. Their insecurity turns to mischief and worse. Stay clear of them."

Emily nodded that she understood.

"Now, for the moment, let's put that aside, shall we?"

"I'd rather," Emily agreed.

"So, where to go from here?" The parson's voice was soft, and he took her hand once again and held it. "We always have reason for concern. Adversity and hardship may lie around any corner. But at any given time, we must consider what we choose. Your choice, as I see it, is whether to love or surrender to fear. So which is it? Which will you choose?" His question was filled with concern for her well-being. He continued. "Why not allow others to choose for themselves? We must all choose whether to love or surrender to fear. Why should Christian be any different? Besides, I believe he would choose you without reservation."

"I suppose," Emily conceded, "but I've another question regarding the consequences. If I am giving in to fear, as you say, if it keeps him safe, what then?" She looked at the parson, her eyes begging for resolution.

"Dear, child. You must choose whether to trust God. It is God's will how this ends, not ours, though we undoubtedly play a role. If we follow our conscience and do what we feel is right, His will prevails, and His will is far greater than ours, but He leaves it to us to decide whether we believe it. Whatever the outcome, the love you carry and the light you leave behind are eternal. Living without fear, the fear of loving without conditions, provides strength in the face of whatever earthly fate, tragic or otherwise, comes our way. We are all given a choice to love God and others or be ruled by fear."

"But I'm not strong like you. I didn't ask for the life I was given. I didn't ask for my parents to be murdered. I didn't ask for the fear that has been my constant companion."

The parson squeezed her hand. "Of course, but you're strong. You wouldn't be here after everything you've been through if you weren't. Please listen to me. Trust in God. Don't allow your fear to rule your life. That alone will make all the difference. Your choice is between happiness for whatever time you're given or isolation, loneliness, and regret. You must decide."

Emily looked into the parson's face and envied the strength she saw there. "I must leave," she said. "I've something I must do. I must make amends, see if I can salvage what I've done."

The parson patted her hand and then let go. "The door's unlocked, Emily. And would you do me a favor and keep it open? And your heart? Keep that open as well. And remember—let not your heart be troubled, dear one!"

"Nor let it be afraid," said Emily. "And, Parson . . ."

"Yes?"

"Thank you," she called as she passed through the doors and into the street.

Chapter 23

As a weakened sun limped across the dull sky, the lush meadow, though damp and cold, felt like home. The den now belonged to the beast. And so he no longer felt the urge to flee. Gone were the scat and gnawed shards of bone. He settled in, feeling safe in the dark recesses of the cave. Even so, he had much left to do.

Ever tapping at his thoughts was the need to gain weight, the instinct to feed never giving him a moment's rest, though winter was still months away. The primal voice within him craved fresh meat, warm and bloody. But each time he stilled a beating heart, he felt a pang of regret. He told himself that nature, not he, was cruel, and he tried hard to ignore that he was the dispenser of that cruelty.

Daylight faded as nighttime crept into the meadow. *It's nearly time*, he thought, no longer able to find an excuse to avoid traveling south around the mountain. So he headed out, following the stream, then crossing a small makeshift bridge before forging through the surrounding shrubbery. A dirt road appeared, the stream and road running parallel as they entered a gorge. The beast hesitated. The sparse vegetation on the sides of the stream and road gave him little opportunity to hide if he encountered humans. He held his breath and listened.

Hearing nothing out of the ordinary, he felt confident he could remain undetected if he encountered travelers, especially in the dark. He would see and smell them long before they ever detected him.

The beast sprinted on all fours, relishing the ability to move at inhuman speeds. An adrenaline-fueled exhilaration bolstered his confidence. He knew he could run faster still and willed his muscles to carry him farther, watching as the scenery flashed past him before he finally slowed to a stop.

Nothing can catch me, he thought. *Nothing can escape me. I've little reason to fear.* His chest swelled at his newly discovered ability.

The beast traveled some distance through the gorge skirting Mount Erebus until it eventually opened to the south. From there, the road dipped into a large valley. In the distance, he saw fields and pastures where cattle, sheep, goats, and horses grazed. It was humid and too dark to see color, but he recognized the patterns. He remained silent. His stomach growled at the sight of fenced livestock.

No need to hunt! he thought. *Meat for the taking.* And among the trees where the roads crisscrossed stood buildings with windows that twinkled in the night.

He sat on a rock, watching the cattle, anticipating the easy meal, but something troubled him, disturbing his thoughts.

Humans! This is what I feared!

His anxiety heightened as his hope of seeing endless wilderness fled. As he looked at the town in the distance, he felt something unexpected—a sense of loneliness. He longed for human interaction yet feared it all the same. What hurt most was something he hadn't considered until then. It was the thought that any hope of being human again was slipping away. He howled into the night.

I'm a foreigner in a world of words my tongue cannot form. I am a prisoner in a perversion of self not my own.

He stared at Mount Erebus, which loomed large in front of him. Near the inky blackness of the peak lived evil. He'd seen it in a dream, though dreaming was becoming less frequent. Rotting hags, not even human themselves, looked down on him. Somehow, he knew it. He snarled, then went quiet. Something called for his attention, voices and words mockingly calling to him, voices not his own, voices inside his head.

Discerning his thoughts, they knew exactly what to say, causing him maximum pain. "You'll never be human," they told him. "You are an animal, a monster. You might as well scatter your scat and litter your cave with bones. You suppose yourself better than a mere animal. You are not. You and the bear are equals!"

His lips curled back, exposing his razor-sharp teeth.

True, what you say. My tongue is wild, incapable of language. I'm no better than a deer, bear, or squirrel. The ability to speak would be wasted on such creatures, but not on me, though it doesn't matter.

Then he had an idea. *It wouldn't matter unless* . . . With eyes narrowing on the dark clouds that concealed the peak, he thought, *You come to me uninvited. Perhaps it's time I returned the favor. What's done can be undone.*

Chapter 24

Little Nicolas tapped his fingers on his desk as he and his classmates waited impatiently for the final bell. Ere long, the sound of chairs scuffing against the floor and footsteps rushing the door soon quieted, leaving Annette St. Clair alone at her desk that Friday afternoon. The silence lasted only a moment before she heard someone clear their throat. Looking up, she saw Mrs. Owen peering into her classroom with a loaded smile.

"Let's talk. Shall we?" Mrs. Owen didn't allow Annette to answer before barging in. There was purpose in the hurried way she closed the distance, and Annette feared what that purpose might be. Without taking a seat, Mrs. Owen made herself comfortable. She set her handbag and a piece of paper on Annette's desk and removed her fine-milled pink cardigan, slinging it over her arm. "Yes, indeed, you and I, we must speak."

This was not good, thought Annette, though she dared not say a word. Annette set aside what she was doing and gave the woman her attention.

Mrs. Owen could smell the fear. An involuntary smile creased her lips.

Armed with bait and setting a trap for the frightened little mouse, Mrs. Owen proceeded. "Oh, dear, it has come to my attention only recently, mind you, that my Robert forgot to compensate your husband a considerable amount of money, money we owe him for his excellent work on our home. Your Stuart has become quite an artisan, hasn't he?" She did not wait for a reply. "Robert and I would like to compensate him for our unintentional oversight. How does that sound, dear?" She poured it on so thick, Annette thought of the cold grease she had scraped from the bottom of her frying pan earlier that morning.

"I will write you a promissory note to pay our debt. In full. With interest. You can exchange it for dollars with Beatrice Moser at town hall, in her office." Martha reached over and picked up the quill on Annette's desk. She dipped it into the inkwell, tapped it several times, and set to work writing the note. As she did so, she continued their one-way conversation. "However, there is something you can do for us." She paused, allowing her words and the ink to soak in. She blew on the paper, drying the ink.

She returned to writing and talking. "Have you anything for me on Mr. Parrish?" She set down the quill and blew gently on the note a second time. Annette was silent. Martha moved to the door, shut it, and returned to face Annette. Then she got right to the point, holding the promissory note so Annette could see the dollar amount.

"Now, Mrs. St. Clair. Do you know whether Mr. Parrish knew my grandson would be attacked so viciously when he assisted the little tyrant, the Stewart boy?"

Little time passed before the door to Annette's classroom swung open and Mrs. Owen exited. As the school was mostly empty, there was nothing to drown out the distinctive sound of her heavy steps on the wooden floor. They echoed off the bare walls of the hallway, alerting all the teachers that something was about to happen. That something usually wasn't good. She went immediately to Mr. Parrish's classroom and barged in.

"Gather your things, Mr. Parrish. You've been terminated."

Chapter 25

Beatrice Moser stared at the clock, eager for her weekend to begin. It had been a busy day made busier by the mayor's absence. She was about to lock up and go home when the door to her office opened.

She'd already extinguished the iron stove and tied her rose-colored bonnet under her chin when Bronson entered. She greeted him with some alarm. "Mr. Parrish! It's you!"

"Well, yes, Ms. Moser, were you expecting me?"

"No, well, sort of, but not really. I'm sorry. Good afternoon."

He returned her greeting. "Yes, I suppose," he said, "if not for the constant rain."

She noticed the box under his arm, filled with personal items: a ceramic drinking mug, books, papers, and an inkwell. He was an odd sight.

"What brings you in? Dare I ask?"

"Hmm," he said. "I suppose you have an idea." He approached her desk and set the box on the floor. "I'm here to enter my name in the upcoming election. What forms are there for me?"

Beatrice took a deep breath, considering how to discourage him without seeming unkind. She stared at him, wondering. *Does he understand what he's in for—the problems this could cause him?*

"Mr. Parrish," she said finally. "Pardon me, but I must ask. Your intentions here, are they beyond reconsideration?"

"Far beyond."

"But why? Why would you consider this a suitable course of action?"

"For one, Ms. Moser, I just lost my position at the school and need to find another. Mrs. Owen herself is my inspiration."

"Mrs. Owen?"

"Yes. The charming Mrs. Owen. She terminated me, eager for me to do something else, so I stand before you, ready for what's next."

"But she cannot do that, not without the council's consent. Though I know she does things and later seeks their approval."

"And always gets it," Bronson added.

"Yes, always."

"Always. Now, if you please, may I see the forms I need?"

Beatrice leaned over and opened the drawer. She took the upcoming council agenda from it and placed it on her desk. "Here, let's consider other options. I'm placing your request for reinstatement as headmaster on the agenda for the council meeting. If there is no resolution, then maybe, and only then, should you consider the other." She looked at Bronson with an encouraging smile.

"I'm sorry," he said. "I'm resolute in my intention here. I'm tired of being ruled over, and I figure I'm not alone in my thinking. Free of my teaching position, I've nothing but time and nothing to lose. Now, the proper paperwork, if you please."

Reluctantly, she took a separate sheet of paper from the drawer and set it on her desk. With ink pen in hand, she recorded Bronson Parrish's name under the printed words, "Letter of Intent for Public Office."

"Complete the form. Pay the fee. But I wouldn't advise it." She handed him the pen and slid the ink well across the desk.

Where there was a blank space, he wrote, *I, Bronson Parrish*.

Beatrice read from the town charter. "Having qualified as outlined within the Common Law of Indiana statutes, I declare my intention to run for mayor in the township of New Harmony, within the county of Posey."

Beatrice stopped. Bronson wrote the rest and looked up. "Now, sign and date," she said. She shook her head disapprovingly. Bronson noticed but paid no attention. Instead, he signed and dated the document.

"Hey, Beatrice, can you put an item on the agenda for the meeting? Is there still time?"

"Tomorrow's meeting?" she asked curiously.

"Yes. Is it too late?"

"It is, but . . ." Beatrice considered and realized an exception was in order. Elated, she said, "Wonderful idea! I'll put the reinstatement of your position on the agenda, and let's forget that other thing. I believe once the mayor hears of your intentions to run against him, he may encourage the council to restore your position effective immediately." She looked up at him, relieved to have found a solution.

"No," said Bronson. "It's not what you think. I am running for mayor regardless. The item I wish to add to the council meeting has nothing to do with my position at the school. Here. Write this down on the meeting agenda. "I submit a proposal to change the name of New Harmony Township to Owenton Township."

"You what!" Beatrice looked up at him. "I-I can't write that!" She begged him to reconsider.

Bronson shrugged, "Why not?"

"You're teasing me. You can't be serious!"

"I'm very serious."

"But, Mr. Parrish, do you know what you're doing? Do you realize no one can remove it once I write it down? Not even you, until after a vote in front of the town council and everybody." She looked at him, wide-eyed and full of concern.

"I'm counting on it," he said. "One more thing, then I'll leave you alone. Can you get the last of my money from the safe as well as the deed to my house?"

Chapter 26

The eclipse, ensuing darkness, constant rain, and strange chanting ensured the much-anticipated council meeting had a record attendance. Carriages and wagons arrived early, and all but one of the council members had already come. People were desperate for answers, and the rumor mill churned out any number of conspiracies. Most concerning were the dreary days that beset the town and the possible evil that threatened the approaching harvest. A desperate feeling permeated the air. Something dark had come to New Harmony, and nobody knew what it was or why.

The strange voices warning of a pending cataclysm only added to the unease that swept the town. Many assumed the voices to be of benefit, a means of avoiding the catastrophe of which they foretold. And although the general population was easily given to conspiracy, they didn't consider themselves conspiratorial. The few in town who questioned or applied simple critical thinking were considered naive and silenced or ignored.

The most conspiratorial among them had the loudest voices, especially Abigail, who believed the guardian spirits had selected her to warn the people. At her side were Elizabeth and Susannah, and no one in town was surprised by their early arrival at the town hall.

From their Sunday carriage with walnut-brown-tanned leather upholstery and stylish brass lanterns, Mayor Owen and his wife, Martha, stared out the windows of their passenger compartment as they turned the corner. People spilled out onto Main Street from both sides in the drizzling rain. Unfortunately, the town hall was too small to accommodate the entire town.

"Pull to the rear!" shouted the mayor.

In the driver's seat, Skinny turned the horses toward the back of the building. Before their carriage stopped, the mayor spied Vernon and Old Man Taylor in the crowd. He looked at Martha as she stared out the window.

"The farmers," he said, "they worry me most, fussing about their crops. It doesn't matter that I don't control the weather. They'll hold me responsible regardless. Damn unfair! Hopefully, there won't be a need for an election."

"What's upsetting them?" asked Martha. "There's been plenty of rain. Nothing but. So, what's the problem?"

The mayor shook his head, staring out the window. "Look at them. They're all scared. Darling, the rain *is* the problem. The eclipse occurred only days after seeding the fields, and there has been constant rain ever since. Some of their seeds washed away, and puddles drown much of what's left. Haven't you noticed that even our fields are yellow from overwatering? If it continues . . ."

"And when aren't they panicky?" asked Martha. "Any one of them could cause us any number of problems. That's what I worry about. Look at their faces out there, frightened children. They're nothing but problems."

Something caught his eye before he could respond. He cocked his head, peering out the window. Three large birds, black as a moonless night, soared high above them. They swooped down, flying just above the crowd, and circled the building. Finally, the carriage came to a stop at the back entrance. Skinny jumped down and opened the passenger door.

"We're here, sir, Mrs. Owen," said Skinny. The mayor and Martha ignored him.

"Robert, not that it's necessary to ask, but are you prepared? Do you know what you'll say?"

"As always," he assured her.

"You're certain?"

"Turn the meeting over to me. You'll see."

As Robert stepped out and extended a hand to Martha, the three blackbirds perched themselves on the eavestrough. He noticed them as he helped Martha down from the carriage and as they walked to the back door. The most prominent blackbird turned its head sideways, its black eye fixed on him, eliciting a rush of apprehension. The mayor shook his head. *No. Can't be. They're mere blackbirds and nothing more*, he thought.

Inside, the council members sat at the front of the room, each occupying a small desk. As always, they'd reserved the first row of chairs facing them for the mayor and Beatrice. Sheriff Weasley always sat next to the mayor and opposite Beatrice. Flanking them on the front row were townspeople who sought to resolve civil disputes or address items they'd added to the agenda.

According to the town charter, the mayor was not a council member. They, the council, were the legislative body and he the executive. He could, however, endorse or veto any of their proclamations. Therefore, he always sat in the front row, in full view of the council, preferring eye contact whenever votes were taken. Behind the first row, the chairs that generally filled the council room had been removed. There would be standing room only for this meeting.

As usual, Martha, the last council member to arrive, entered the back of the building with the mayor in tow. The two headed down the hall to the side door leading into the chamber, where Beatrice waited.

"Robert," Beatrice called out, running toward him in the hallway. "May I have a word? It's important."

"Not now, Beatrice. We're already late."

Martha shook her head, nudging her husband. "Let's not keep them waiting."

The mayor brushed Beatrice aside, and he and Martha entered the chamber, Beatrice following. All heads turned as they entered, and the council members greeted them eagerly. Now, the meeting could begin.

Martha and the mayor took their seats. The crowd hushed as Beatrice read the minutes from the last meeting. The council members, along with the crowd assembled inside and outside the building, remained silent.

Once the minutes were read, Martha addressed those assembled. "All right, let's begin."

The chamber erupted as questions flew at them from every direction.

"Quiet, everyone!" Martha yelled. She gave the gavel one solitary bang and then set it back down. "We haven't all night. I know many of you have concerns, and we will address them, but we need your cooperation."

The council members peered nervously into the crowd, hoping no one would call upon them.

The council included five members: Martha Owen, the senior member, and four others. She sat front and center with two council members on either side. To her right sat Ernest Hays and Weston Riley.

Ernest, or Ernie, was a short, potbellied man with an unkempt mop of chestnut-brown hair and a handlebar mustache. The foghorn voice of the large man clashed with his short stature. He now co-owned Ernie's Tavern, having once been its sole owner. After establishing his business, he'd taken on a partner—the mayor. Rumor had it that the transaction between the two involved a licensing issue. Regardless, Ernie ran the day-to-day operations, and the mayor shared in the profits.

Next to Ernie sat young Weston Riley, short and stocky but muscular and ruggedly handsome. You'd have never guessed he was Irish but for his flat cap. Right out of school, Weston became the mayor's favorite, his future promising. He raised horses, sheared his sheep, milked his goats, and when someone in town needed a pinewood casket or fence mended, they called upon Weston.

To Martha Owen's left sat Jonas Becker and Hyrum Blaylock. Jonas was a shy man who waddled when he walked due to one leg being slightly shorter than the other. His short, blond hair was thinning, his doughy white skin untouched by the sun. His complexion matched his occupation perfectly since he owned the bakery and worked early mornings so the town could enjoy his freshly baked bread at sunrise. He'd found his way onto the council by keeping his head down. He always did as he was told, never making a fuss.

Hyrum sat next to Jonas, a short, stout brick of a man who spoke with a hint of a Scottish accent. Completely bald but for his facial hair, he sported a thick walrus mustache, black as coal. Folks recognized for his white apron, which he was never without. Like Ernie, Hyrum co-owned the general store with the mayor, and, like Ernie, he operated the business but shared the profit with Robert Owen.

Whatever profit the mayor skimmed, though sizable, Ernie and Hyrum recuperated from their salaries on the council. It was an unspoken arrangement. The mayor was most interested in their dependence on him, and dependent they were, all of them.

Once the chamber settled, Mrs. Owen looked to Beatrice. "How many items are on the agenda?" she asked.

"Only one. It has been proposed—"

Martha cut her short. "I suppose everyone here must have the same concern. Indeed, something inexplicable is happening, and the mayor would like to address it." The council members sighed in relief.

The mayor stood and faced the people. "Can everyone hear me?" A consensus of yeses echoed around the chamber. Then, outside the council room, someone yelled, "No!"

"My apologies," said the mayor. "I know some are beyond the reach of my voice. Those who can hear, share what you can with those who cannot. We'll remedy this situation in the future. For now, let's just do what we can."

"Speak louder!" came another voice from outside the chamber.

The mayor spoke as loudly as he could. "We're going to get through this," he hollered.

Someone in the crowd shouted, "Why the singing, the verses, the voices? What's causing it?"

From within the chamber, Susannah Boyer called, "From whence come the voices? Are there sirens on our mountain?"

That's when Amanda Taylor attempted to intervene. "The parson said not to listen." She turned toward the mayor. "Is that what we should do, not listen?"

Abigail yelled over her shoulder at the people behind her. "I wouldn't listen to the parson if I were any of you. He only pretends to know when he knows nothing!"

Vern yelled, "Never mind all that! What are you all fussing about? No one cares! If my crops don't start growing, and yours, too, Merle, we'll all be in trouble. There'll be hunger the likes of which we've never seen."

Merle and the farmers near him nodded in agreement.

The mayor shouted, "Quiet! Your yelling solves nothing. I'm still looking into the matter, though I haven't any answers, but does anyone?"

Abigail began to respond but fell silent when the mayor shot a stern glance at her.

He continued. "This, whatever it is, is unprecedented, and we must keep our heads about us."

A murmur rippled through the crowd.

"Settle down and listen!" the mayor insisted. "I've heard all the rumors: spirits, sirens, demons, even Mount Erebus being a volcano, for heaven's sake. It seems like nonsense, but what do we know? Heavenly manifestation? Let us pray so. Whatever it may be, we'll face it together. So I join the parson in prayer. We've no other alternative."

Albert and Marjorie stood near the back of the chamber, squeezed behind Walter. They each attended church regularly and welcomed the parson's message of faith. However, that didn't mean they weren't concerned, hoping for answers to assuage their insecurities.

Walter spoke up. "Mayor?"

Hushing the crowd, the mayor motioned to Walter. "One at a time."

Walter raised his voice so the others could hear. "The singing—could it be coming from the mountain? Something strange is happening up there, and I'm not alone in noticing. Shouldn't someone investigate what—"

The mayor cut him off. "No one is to go up there. Does everyone hear me? Please spread the word that nobody, and I mean nobody, is to go up there. We must first assess the risks. I don't want anyone to do anything until we know more about what we're dealing with." He looked down at the sheriff. "No one goes up there," he repeated. The sheriff nodded, and the room went quiet. The mayor softened his tone yet spoke louder still. "Has anyone been hurt?" he asked. "Has anyone come to harm from the chanting, or singing, or whatever you want to call it?" The silence of the crowd persisted.

"It warns us!" screamed Abigail. "What is the nature of benevolence but to warn of danger?"

"Good folks," the mayor called out. "Abigail's right. We should leave well enough alone for now. This thing that's happening is for *us* to investigate. Not any of you. If you see or hear of anyone taking matters into their own hands, report it to the sheriff immediately. We'll inform you once we've investigated the matter." The mayor closed without further questions and turned the meeting back to Martha.

Martha smiled at her husband and readied to close the meeting. She looked to Beatrice to confirm that nothing else remained, assuming she could pound the gavel and declare the meeting over.

"Mrs. Owen," Beatrice interrupted, sputtering. "There is one unaddressed item."

"We've addressed it. Weren't you listening?" Martha raised the gavel.

"I'm afraid what was discussed was not the item in question."

"Don't waste our time. What is it?"

Beatrice read so all could hear. "It is proposed that New Harmony, the township thereof, be renamed. The new name proposed for the consideration of the council is . . ."

Everyone in the room waited to hear what came next. Nervously, Beatrice looked into the myriad faces staring back at her. Feeling as if she were having a tooth pulled, she swallowed hard, nearly choking on the word. "Owenton."

"What?" Martha's jaw dropped. She glanced at Robert, who sat there, just as dumbfounded. Quietly, hoping not to be noticed, she mouthed, "Did you?"

Robert shook his head adamantly.

She looked at the other council members, who seemed just as bewildered. "Well, it appears that we can ignore this item of business as utter nonsense. Since, it seems, nobody admits to having proposed."

Just as she prepared to pound the desk, someone in the crowd just outside the council chamber yelled, "It was I who did it!" A chill settled over the room as Bronson Parrish pushed into the chamber, excusing himself as he did so. He continued through the crowd until he stood in the middle of the room. Before Mrs. Owen could protest, he called out. "Vote on it! That's the rule."

Through gritted teeth, Martha snapped, "Don't waste our time, Mr. Parrish." Again, she attempted to dismiss the item, gavel raised.

But Bronson would have none of it. "Hear me, everyone!" he called out. "I will not withdraw my proposal. Instead, I demand a vote." Determined, he stood like the old oak in front of the town hall. The crowd looked anxiously at Martha as she quietly calculated her next move.

Finally conceding, she set down the gavel. "Well then, Mr. Parrish, you shall have your vote. As the principal member of the *New Harmony* town council, I vote no." She looked at the other council members while shaking her head, letting them know what she expected. She had no reason to believe they wouldn't follow suit. They could always be relied on so to do.

But unfortunately for her, as diverse as they were, there was one thing they all had in common: an unbreakable umbilical cord attached to her and her husband. So conditioned were they to vote for the benefit of the Owens that each hesitated, staring desperately at the mayor in the front row. Each was keenly aware their position required complete compliance, and prior council members learned the importance of discerning the mayor's covert intentions the hard way. It was challenging and dangerous to decipher what course of action the mayor and Martha required when they sometimes publicly professed the opposite. And this smelled as if it were the exact thing the mayor wanted—to rename New Harmony in his honor. Yet, it appeared Martha opposed what would immortalize her husband and herself. They were confused. This agenda item was, after all, an honor the mayor couldn't rightfully self-apply. Being blissfully unaware of any conflict between Bronson Parrish and the Owens, the council assumed the mayor had surreptitiously arranged the proposal by means of coercion, as was the norm. And, of course, the Owens would act as if it were the last thing they wanted.

Still uncertain, Weston and Ernie stared at Mrs. Owen, hoping to see a wink or nod. Martha waited. Finally, she looked to her left, where Jonas and Hyrum squirmed in their seats, staring at her, then at the mayor, and back at her. Weston slowly raised his hand in the affirmative. At this, Ernie quickly followed. Jonas and Hyrum looked as if they stared down the barrel of a rifle. They promptly raised their hands.

"Imbeciles!" Martha said aloud, though she'd intended to keep the sentiment to herself. "Oh, come now," she growled, addressing the crowd. "Look, I was forced to release Mr. Parrish from his teaching responsibilities yesterday. He's just trying to cause a commotion, that's all. He failed to protect our children, those entrusted to his care, and we, the council, couldn't allow that." The council members looked at each other, dumbfounded. It was the first they'd heard of Bronson's removal.

All attention shifted back to Bronson, who addressed the crowd as much as he did Mrs. Owen. "Instructing the Stewart boy on how not to be bullied and beaten by your grandson—if that is not protecting children, I'm at odds to know what is."

"And that is precisely my point, Mr. Parrish. You are incompetently unaware of what is required. It was your responsibility to ensure a safe environment and to stop such bullying by any means other than violence, and you failed. That'll be enough—"

Bronson interrupted, an offense no one dared commit against an Owen, certainly never in public. The crowd gasped. "Yes, I'm guilty, but otherwise, I am a superb educator. I taught the Stewart boy a valuable life lesson. And he taught your grandson that being a bully can have consequences, also a valuable lesson." He paused before adding, "Well, only if you ask me."

"And who is asking, Mr. Parrish? No one is who. We've all heard enough. Allow me to put an end to your antics. Ms. Moser," she peered over at Beatrice, "would you please hand me Mr. Parrish's foolish proposal?" Beatrice approached and handed it to her. She held it up and, in a grand display, ripped it in two. "Thank you, Ms. Moser," she said. "That concludes our meeting." She pounded the gavel.

"Not exactly," said Bronson, holding up a piece of paper. "This is my intent to run for mayor!" he shouted. "My copy." The crowd gasped again. "It's time for much-needed change. I taught the Stewart boy how not to be bullied. Maybe I can teach the rest of you. You all witnessed how the council just kowtowed to the Owens regarding my proposal."

The mayor watched as the people in the room became increasingly disorderly, and he sensed a growing discontent. The sheriff started to stand, but the mayor rested his hand on his knee. "Not now," he whispered.

It was then the mayor heard a velvety voice. He had to listen carefully to make sure it called to him. "*Robert! Oh, Robert! The sun will shine. Tell them you will make it so. In seven days, no less, New Harmony will no longer be cast in shadow. Tell them that seven days from now, the sun will shine.*"

The agitation in the room reached a fever pitch. Distracted, the mayor didn't know who'd spoken to him. His eyes darted about only to realize the voice was disembodied. It did not come from within the room, so all could hear, but from inside his head. He marveled at how he understood it so perfectly over the commotion.

It came again. "What are you waiting for? In seven days, they will see. Then the sun will shine, your crops will grow, and you will be the savior of New Harmony." The mayor broke free of the trance to hear Bronson's voice.

"So, if you want something better," Bronson continued, "people who look to you when a vote is called, not to an Owen, then do something. I withdraw my proposal for our town to be named Owenton, but it makes no difference. We all live in Owenton no matter what we call it. Until we, the people of New Harmony, have had enough, it will never be our town. But I'll leave that up to each of you."

"That's enough!" Martha yelled while motioning to the sheriff, but Bronson was already leaving the chamber, disappearing into the crowd.

"Meeting adjourned!" she screamed as she lifted the gavel.

The mayor slowly rose to his feet. "Wait! Everyone quiet down." He turned and faced the crowd.

Calls for quiet came from inside the chamber and echoed into the halls. Martha continued to pound the gavel until she'd brought about some semblance of order.

While the mayor waited for the crowd to settle, he heard the voice again. "Promise them!"

Abigail, Elizabeth, and Susannah were captivated. They couldn't have hoped for a more eventful meeting, and, grinning, they joined the crowd calling for quiet. They needed to hear every word.

Suddenly, the mayor called as loudly as he could. Although he knew what he would say, he was, nonetheless, as much a spectator as those listening. He felt as if someone else spoke on his behalf.

"The sun will shine. I'll make it so. Crops will not be drowned but will have sunshine and grow. Listen to me. In seven days, the darkness will end. Mark my words. I will make it happen."

A stunned silence filled the room. Not an eye blinked. Abigail's face lit up in blissful surprise, while Elizabeth and Susannah looked at her to confirm what they'd heard.

The mayor shook under the weight of his promise. His knees became weak, and he sat down, head low, shoulders slumped. *What have I done?* he wondered, caught between exhilaration and remorse for having made a promise he could not keep. His head lay on the guillotine, and the witches, or whatever they were, held the rope.

A high-pitched scream pierced the room. "Adjourned! This meeting is adjourned!" Mrs. Owen pounded her gavel five times before turning her attention to Beatrice. "You and me, right now!"

As the attendees filed out, so did the town council. Mrs. Owen was standing in the hallway at the door to the recorder's office by the time Beatrice exited the chamber. She held the door open, and she and Beatrice disappeared inside.

Temper flaring, Mrs. Owen demanded, "Why did you not inform us that Mr. Parrish put that ridiculous proposal on the agenda?"

"Well, I—"

Mrs. Owen did not allow Beatrice to finish. "And why did you not inform us that Mr. Parrish submitted his intent to run for mayor?"

This time, Mrs. Owen waited for a response.

"Mr. Parrish came yesterday, moments before closing. Robert was absent all day. There was no opportunity to inform you, so I tried telling you before the meeting, but you were distracted and arrived late. Remember? I had something important to tell you, but you dismissed me."

"Gather your things. I'm dismissing you. Give me your key. We won't be needing your services moving forward." Martha looked down, avoiding eye contact.

"You can't! Not without the approval of the council." Beatrice knew the charter better than anyone.

"What were you thinking?" Martha's veins bulged, and her face turned beet red. Then, finally, she yelled loudly enough that everyone in the building could hear. "I am the town council!"

Chapter 27

Walter arrived at work the following day to find the door unlocked. He'd anticipated the usual cheery greeting from Christian, but instead, a gloomy young man sat behind the counter. Informing him the mail was sorted was as much as Christian could muster.

"Hmm, no 'Good morning, Mr. Buchanan'?"

"Forgive me, sir. I've been out of sorts, and I don't know what to do with the Stewart's mail. Nothing more will fit in their box."

Giving it little thought, Walter said, "Put the rest in the drawer behind the counter. Theo will eventually send a forwarding address. The sheriff said they left in a hurry."

"Which reminds me," said Christian. "When the sheriff came for the letter, the one Mr. Stewart entrusted to me, I felt wrong giving it to him."

"Why?"

"It's just that when Mr. Stewart handed it to me, he seemed worried, even scared. I was supposed to mail it if he didn't return for it himself."

"Hmm," said Walter. "There was trouble between his boy and the mayor's grandson. They spoke of it at the meeting last night. No wonder Theo left under cover of night."

"Mr. Buchanan, you think that's what it is? You think that's why they left like that?"

"They wouldn't be the first. I've heard threats, even folks running off. But what an unpleasant subject. On a more cheerful note, I may have a cure for your mood. What if you haven't sorted all the mail? What would you say?"

Christian looked at him curiously. "Have I missed something, sir?"

Walter held up a letter and waved it in the air. "Might you have forgotten this?"

"No, sir. Unless I didn't see it, but I swear it wasn't in Warren's delivery."

"Well, I don't know how you could have missed it, but here," Walter teased while handing him the letter.

Christian examined the handwriting. "It's from her. It's for me."

"As it was, a handsome young lady crossed the street this very morning, handed it to me, and made me promise to deliver it first thing. Open it."

Christian sat on the stool behind the counter and read.

My Dear Christian,

Will you ever forgive me? When you asked for my hand in marriage, I was frightened. I've lost enough of those I loved and was afraid of losing you. I still am. But by my rejection, I will undoubtedly lose you in the worst conceivable way. I cannot find happiness in this life unless I'm at your side. I know it to be true. So, if you feel the same, I ask for another chance. I have decided that come what may, I won't let myself be afraid. If your offer has not yet expired and you do not now feel otherwise, I would gladly accept your proposal and pray I will earn your love every day if you allow me the honor of being your wife. I await your reply.

Love, Emily

Hoping for the best, Walter watched as Christian read the letter. A moment later, the young man's face glowed as if freed from untold misery. "Young love, hmm. I do remember. I suppose you could do with the rest of the day off?"

Christian nodded enthusiastically.

"See you tomorrow morning, and don't be late!"

Without a word, Christian rushed toward the front door.

"Hold on, youngster."

Christian stopped and looked back.

"Tomorrow morning, I expect something different from you. 'Good morning, Mr. Buchanan.' That would be much better."

"Mr. Buchanan. I thank you, my heart thanks you, everything about me, all of me, and the entirety of the universe thanks you. All of it, sir."

"Well, that's certainly enough. But a simple good morning will do."

The bell on the door chimed as Christian ran out into the drizzling rain.

Emily patiently waited as her students opened their books.

"What page?" asked Victoria, a precocious girl who sat in the desk Emily once preferred.

"Page 22. You won't find the answer to the next question in your book, but we have discussed it." Emily waited for pages to stop turning. "What is the name of the president of the United States of America? Say it together, please."

"Franklin Pierce," the majority shouted.

"Not anymore, and there was another even after him. So, who is the president now?"

Victoria spoke, offering a guess. "Abraham Lincoln?"

"Very good. And what branch of the government does Mr. Lincoln represent? You'll find that answer on page 22." Emily waited for Rudy, who seemed distracted by whatever lay beyond the window. She repeated the question. "Which branch of government does the president belong to?"

Before anyone could answer, Rudy said, "Oh! Oh!"

Emily's brow furrowed as Rudy stretched his hand as high as it would go, nearly jumping out of his chair.

"What is it, Rudy?"

"Ms. Hampshire, your friend, he's right there!" He pointed.

She walked to the window to see a face pressed against the glass. "Christian!" Quickly, she opened the window.

With hair and clothes soaking wet, Christian waved at the students. All the girls and a few of the boys waved back. "Ms. Emily Ruth Hampshire. Will you marry me?"

Emily's heart raced, overcome with joy enough to tear up in front of her students. "Your answer is yes! I will marry you, sir!" Her students clapped and cheered.

"May I walk you home after class?"

"It would be an honor."

The girls squealed as if they might never see anything so romantic for the rest of their lives.

"All right, then. I'll be waiting."

"All right, then," said Emily, who shut the window. "Now, back to our lesson. Who is the current president?"

"Ms. Hampshire," Victoria had her hand in the air.

"Yes, Victoria. I know you already know the answer."

"But I've another question."

"That is?"

"If you are married, what will we call you?"

Emily grinned. She breathed in deeply, taking control of her emotions, and answered. "Our president is Abraham Lincoln. And yes, you may soon call me Mrs. Salvatori."

Chapter 28

The breeze whistled through cattails in the damp morning air, clearing the stench from the beast's cave. Venturing out, he drank from the stream and looked south to the mountain looming large under a gray sky. Setting his course, he concealed himself as best he could in the daylight, staying in the thick trees along the stream that led to the mountain. When he arrived, he didn't hesitate.

Up there are my answers, up there where they watch me.

Scaling jagged rock and graveled ledges, he jumped from one rocky shelf to another and scrambled up a steep grade to a protruding ridge. There, he squeezed through a fissure in the rock, clawed his way up the sheer mountain face, and rested on a ledge barely wide enough to keep him from plummeting to the depths below. Inspecting each hold, each rocky shelf, assuring himself it could hold his weight, he slowly ascended.

By late afternoon, he was only halfway to the peak. A cold front threatened from the east, and lightning flashed in the distance, heading toward him. Frigid air bit at his nose, ears, and wherever his fur offered little protection. High above the meadow, he labored to breathe in the thinning air. He felt the stinging of a claw that bled each time he used it, and he began to favor his other paw.

Much of the day slipped past, and finally, the peak lay within reach. He stopped to rest, gasping for air, watching the blood drip from his injured paw. He licked it, cleaning the blood.

At the sudden rumbling of thunder, he looked east, from whence the storm approached, but this was not where the thunder originated.

No, the sky directly above the peak churned with dark clouds. Another peal of thunder caused a sharp pain in his ears. He hid his eyes from the accompanying flash, his fur standing straight in the statically charged air.

He stared at the depths below, a primal fear flooding his mind.

What force of nature pits itself against me? If struck, I'll plunge to my death!

In desperation, he looked to the heavens when, suddenly, hail the size of small rocks began to pelt him through his fur. His grip weakened, but he clung to the mountain, the pain from his wounded paw now throbbing fiercely. Blinded by another flash of lightning, he paused to wait for his vision to return.

I must turn back.

His heart groaned against the defeat.

Even so, I may die all the same.

With no other choice, he headed down, his descent made even more dangerous by the ferocity of the storm. Water poured from everywhere, making the rock even more slippery and judging where to grip more uncertain.

His arms had begun to shake, his eyelids drooping from fatigue, when he heard the familiar, grating voice from within the confines of his weary mind—or did it come from above?

Did he hear something or just imagine it?

Steadying himself, he pressed his back against the rock face high above the meadow and listened until he heard it again.

"Giving up, are you? How disappointing for my sisters and me." The voice grated on his ears. The tone seemed far more amused than disappointed.

Another voice taunted. "Why? Why leave so soon? You're practically here. Just a little farther. Don't you want answers? You said you did. And we have the answers, don't we, sisters?"

The crones answered, "Yes, we do. Like who was the woman in the garden we showed you, the one on her knees, pulling turnips from the ground?"

The beast's roar nearly shook the mountain. He thrashed about in the pouring rain, almost losing his balance and tumbling down.

Who was she? Tell me! I beg you. You left me nothing of her memory but that I loved her.

A third voice, more sympathetic, answered. "And she loved you. Sadly, you killed her."

"Yesss," the crones chorused. "You are a monster, a beast, a killer of women and children. Better that you don't remember! Erasing your memory was a kindness you didn't deserve."

The beast's tears mixed with the rain as he slumped over, suffocating in self-condemnation as shards of truth pierced his heart.

Why torment me so? Whatever sin I committed is behind me. Though cursed for it, I am no murderer. I know it.

His eyes closed as the cold, uncaring rain poured down his face.

"Oh, monster," said the more ancient voice, feigning sympathy. "You insist you're a man, but no matter how hard you try, your hunger grows. As your instincts become more beastly, the animal within you will eventually feed. On the other side of this mountain is a town, and that, my dear monster, will be your hunting ground."

The beast issued a gut-wrenching roar that echoed down the mountain. *I will not surrender to the beast.* He groaned. *I cannot. But they're right. The beast inside knows where to find human prey. Eventually, the unrelenting hunger will drive me south. It is only a matter of time before I lose my grip and commit the unthinkable.*

While teetering over the ledge and peering into the darkness below, he thought, *I must stop this.*

He looked down at his brutish paws and hairy forearms. *It's time I come to terms with what I am—a monster. Time grows short. Soon there'll be nothing left of me.*

He continued staring into the void. The fall would be but a moment, and he'd be free. He closed his eyes. He would keep them shut on the way down, never to open again. He took what he hoped would be his last breath. He would hold it on the way down, never to breathe again.

Standing upright, like a man, he thought for the last time, *I'm cursed. There's nothing left for me in this world.*

As if their victory over him wasn't enough, the same voices that tormented him now urged him to commit the final deed.

"No more pain for you, monster. Let the maggots do their work."

He moved closer to the edge. With eyes shut and breath held, he thought, *Just a little farther.* He'd leaned almost to the point of no return when suddenly he heard a familiar voice, a woman's voice—kind, loving, and long forgotten. The timing and moment of need proved it had not come by chance. What she said next sent tremors through his core.

Jonathan.

He opened his eyes and took another breath.

Jonathan! he heard her say again.

If only he could see her, he knew he would recognize her!

Tears welled up in his eyes as feelings of hope coursed through him. He stepped away from the cliff and clung to the mountain.

My name is Jonathan.

He stood tall as the downpour diminished to a drizzle and the thunder grew silent. He felt invigorated. With no ability to speak, his words existing only in his head, he filled his lungs and in his mind screamed, *My name is Jonathan!*

His next roar echoed through the meadow and rose to the height of the mountain peak. He slowly descended, careful not to plummet into the darkness below.

Chapter 29

Skinny waited with lantern in hand as Robert rode into the stable, looking back at the yellow candlelight in the kitchen window.

"Where's my wife?"

Skinny pointed with his chin to the ranch house, then tended to the horse and carriage. Robert slowly made his way to the back door. Everything was quiet, which could only mean one thing.

Martha's awake and probably waiting for me.

As he entered, the house felt empty, absent the usual greeting. Instead, there was only silence. Avoiding the kitchen, Robert went straight to the bedroom and prepared to retire for the evening. He heard the hinges squeak but kept his back to the door, pretending not to notice.

"Are you going to talk to me?" Martha asked from the doorway. "I have your supper waiting. I kept the help up late so it'd be ready when you arrived." She turned and walked back to the kitchen.

Now's as good a time as ever, Robert thought as he followed her.

The clock ticked away the restless minutes until he entered the kitchen and sat down at the table. Martha slid a bowl of onion stew with chunks of pork loin in front of him. She grabbed a spoon and placed it next to the bowl. Robert sat, staring at the food, not reaching for the spoon.

"We'll talk eventually, so why not now?" Martha sat down, the ticking of the clock growing loud as she waited.

"You didn't tell me you terminated Parrish."

The candle on the table was about to expire. Martha pulled a fresh stick from her apron pocket and touched the wicks. Then she licked her fingers and doused the spent candle.

Robert looked up, eyes fixed on his wife in the flickering light. "I told you. We agreed to terminate Mr. Parrish only after the election. Not before!" A furious Robert kicked off his boots and threw them across the room.

Unflinching, Martha stared back at him with equal determination. "You're angry about Beatrice, aren't you?" They both knew she hedged as neither cared about Beatrice Moser.

Robert rolled his eyes.

"All right!" she said. "What do you want me to say? I got angry and terminated him. So what? All those teachers knew Parrish intended for that boy to hurt our grandson. They all knew and kept it from me, and you did nothing!"

Robert's expression turned to one of rage, his eyes digging into her. "Nothing?"

"You're shouting."

"I did nothing? Is that what you said?" He slammed his fist onto the table, spilling the soup.

Martha jumped.

"Please don't ask me what happened to the Stewart family, where they are, or why they didn't tell anyone they were leaving. Don't you dare ask! I did something, Martha. I protect you. Damn it all! I protect this family!"

"What? Are you saying you got rid of them?" She stared across the table, mouth agape.

Robert instantly regretted having said anything, never intending for her to know the gruesome details, unsure of her reaction. He exhaled, and his muscles went slack as his eyes fell to the ground. He could sense that she stared at him as the ticking of the clock banged loudly in his head.

Finally, she said, "Robert?"

"What?"

"It's just that I—"

"Just that what, Martha?"

She hesitated, then reached out, took Robert's hands, and, while peering into his eyes, said, "Just that, well, you're the man I fell in love with. I can trust you to do whatever needful thing, and . . ."

"Yeah?"

"I've never been so attracted to you. I never wanted you more." She sprang from her chair, taking Robert by the hand and leading him into the bedroom. His food sat uneaten on the table. A common housefly landed on the rim of his bowl, slurped the onion stew, and rubbed its front legs as if in gratitude. The clock ticked on, but no one could hear it as the fire in the bedroom burned hot.

In the dead of night, a melody stirred Robert awake. It was the witching hour, and the song repeated so only he could hear it, as before. But this time, Robert knew the source, the sweetness and purity of the singing masking the true nature of the hideous creatures from whence it sprang. Little could be trusted. Reality seemed to slip and weave to trap anyone who gave them audience.

Am I awake, or . . . ? He continued to listen, regardless, as the verse repeated in his head.

> *Blackbird cawed a fortunate omen.*
> *Your world crumbles as you grow weak.*
> *To the north, something wicked,*
> *Tempest fugit, soon we speak.*
>
> *What you seek, the gate is open,*
> *A pathway, though you cannot see.*
> *To the north—something wicked.*
> *Mustn't run while others flee.*
>
> *Be watchful. Yes, watchful.*
> *The time for you is not yet.*

Who? Who comes against you?
Soon. Soon. Pose no threat.

Without us, your world crumbles,
In the balance, what you desire.
By our alliance, your enemies topple.
You will light their funeral pyre.

Patience, patience, ashes, ashes,
See you swirling in our stew.
An alliance, yes! But not yet.
Come when called. You! You!

The song faded and he heard the beating of wings as a blackbird outside his window took flight. He sat up, wondering if he still dreamed.

So vivid, it's all too real to be the stuff of dreams.

He could remember every word, every detail—the tempo, the rhythm—the words lingering in some dark corner. He looked over at Martha, still asleep, undisturbed. He pushed the curtain back and looked out into the night. A harvest moon shone brightly, bathing the ranch, barn, stable, and carriages in brilliant, orange-tinted glow.

There has hardly been a moon visible since the eclipse. So what is this?

Suddenly, all that lay within his view burst into flame, the world outside his bedroom window disintegrating to ashes, the entirety of his belongings burned to the ground. The smoke rose high, turning the moon a crimson red. Horses ran from their burning stables, dogs barked, and the granaries glowed like torches against the night sky.

He woke with beads of sweat trickling down his forehead, his chest pounding. Overcome with panic, he collapsed to the floor. He crawled back into bed and slid under the covers.

I must have been sleepwalking.

As much as he tried calming himself, he didn't sleep a wink the rest of the night. And when another overcast day dawned on New Harmony, the message was clear. The creatures on Mount Erebus wanted him to be aware of all he stood to lose.

Part 3

BITE OF THE FORBIDDEN

Chapter 30

Christian paced back and forth, occasionally peering through the large front window of the postal office. The drizzling rain kept people shut away in their homes, waiting for better weather. Yet, the gloom that permeated the town could not dampen Christian's youthful exuberance as he thought of a life with Emily.

Tonight will be wonderful.

Walter called from the back, "Let's sweep up before Warren makes his delivery. Fetch the broom while I open the door."

Prying his eyes from the window, Christian rounded the counter and returned with the broom. "I welcome the distraction, sir." Broom in hand, he went quickly to work, sweeping the dust out the door.

"I was young once, way back when," said Walter. "Ages ago now, but I tell you, staring out that window won't hurry time along. At my age, you wish for time to move more slowly. But, unfortunately, the older one gets, time moves faster still. Cruel joke, if you ask me. But, eventually, we all must make room for somebody else."

"I suppose, Mr. Buchanan," said Christian, only half listening. "And where's Warren? He's late." He stopped sweeping and looked out the window to the corner near Hyrum's store, where Warren would come. "Mr. Buchanan?"

"Hmm?"

"After sorting, may I please deliver the parcels? Could push time along."

"We'll see what Warren and the weather bring us. It's better if we wait a day than have damaged parcels."

"Yes, but the rain never lets up." Christian resumed sweeping. "Mr. Buchanan? May I inquire as to a personal matter?"

"Hmm?"

"I'm wondering if, or how often, you confess your love to Mrs. Buchanan. Often?" Christian finished sweeping and quickly shut the door.

"Not often enough."

"Why?"

"Why do you ask?"

"It's just that Emmy's so pretty. I'll tell her every day for a hundred—no, a thousand years!"

Before Walter could give Christian's question much thought, the bell above the door rang and Warren walked in, a Colt revolver strapped to his hip. His boots clomped as he walked to the counter, leaving a mud trail on the wooden floor Christian had just swept. Warren tipped his hat before setting his leather satchel on the floor.

"Not much today," he said. "Road's a muddy mess. I had to travel by wagon. Slowed me down, in case you were wonderin'. With all the broken window glass after the storm, I had to bring a load packed in straw. Made the goin' slow—slow and easy."

Walter nodded. "Hold on." He quickly draped some sackcloth over the countertop.

"Sorry. Bag's wet."

"Bag's not the worry," said Walter. "Wet ink stains the wood."

"Right," said Warren. He dumped the contents of his satchel onto the sackcloth. "Nice and dry."

Anxiously, Christian asked, "Any parcels?"

"Only one," said Warren. He exited the post office and returned a moment later. "Kept it under my seat," he said. "Should be dry." He turned it over in his hands and read. "Mayor Robert Owen. New Harmony Town Hall. 100 Main." He tossed it to Christian and waved before leaving. "Gotta go. It's best not to keep Hyrum waiting. Every few days, he asks, 'Where's my glass?'" The bell sounded again, signaling Warren's departure.

Parcel in hand, Christian looked up at Walter.

There was no need to ask. Walter already knew what he was thinking.

"Tell you what," said Walter. "I'll do the sorting while you deliver the parcel. After that, you can head home, but I can only pay half a day."

"Done," said Christian. He took hold of the parcel. "Town hall. Deliver it there?"

"Where's it from?"

Christian read, "*Scioto Gazette,* Chillicothe."

"That one there goes to the Owen ranch. The mayor insisted I keep an eye out for it. Wrap it in wax paper. It's important. You mustn't allow it to get wet."

Though he'd never been to the mayor's home, Christian had heard the rumors about the lavish extravagance there. He hoped to get a peek. He covered the parcel in wax paper, tied it with cotton twine, then wrapped it in cloth for good measure. "Thank you, Mr. Buchanan. Tonight's a special night, a secret I trust you'll keep. Emmy and I are making the announcement, making it official." Christian beamed with excitement.

"Then allow me to be the first to congratulate you. And, of course, you have my confidence. After that, however, I might tell my wife, but only after I confess my love, thanks to you. But we'll keep it to ourselves."

"For the half day, Mr. Buchanan, thank you. I'll make up the time, I promise."

The bell jingled as Christian took his leave.

Chapter 31

Christian ran south down Main, then turned east, his feet splashing through puddles as he went. He held the parcel under his right arm, wrapped in his coat. There was no way he would let it get wet. As he neared the edge of town, he stopped to catch his breath. Harmony Creek lay just ahead and to the right. It quenched the thirst of many farms, the mayor's chief among them. The rain eased, and he heard a wagon approaching from behind him. Nearing him, the horses came to a halt. From atop the wagon, Mr. Carver, a man rarely seen in town, peered down at Christian.

Folks knew Moses Carver as a recluse. Years earlier, he'd found his way to New Harmony from down south, far south. Without companion or kin, he'd escaped from Georgia with the help of abolitionists. But nobody knew more than that. He wasn't one to share, wanting little more than to be left alone. People suspected it was the color of his skin that kept him apart. Or perhaps it was because he was the only one of his kind in New Harmony.

"Where ya headed?" he asked in a dreary voice.

"I've a delivery for the mayor, sir," said Christian, "It's important." Christian briefly looked up, wiping the water from his face with his sleeve.

"Climb in," Carver said. Christian approached the wagon to settle into the seat next to the burly man.

"No! Back der." He motioned with his chin to the bed of the wagon. Christian walked around back and climbed in. They rode silently for half a mile until the Owen ranch came into view. Before coming to a stop, the horses began to fuss, neighing and shuffling their hooves. Carver yelled, "Easy now!" then backed up the horses and stopped.

Christian lowered himself from the wagon bed, package in hand. Carver looked back over his shoulder, his dark eyes hidden under his black, felt, wide-brimmed hat. "Best ya stay away from da man," he said, "if'n ya can help it."

"Who, sir?"

Moses's eyes were focused on the Owen property beyond the gate. "Mayor's who," he said before grunting and snapping the reins.

"Thank you, Mr. Carver!" Christian called as the wagon faded into the mist. He saw Moses raise a hand in farewell before the wagon completely disappeared.

In the weeds that grew alongside the road, Christian saw what had spooked the horses—a cottonmouth, its muscles rippling under its black-and-olive scales. In its grip was a meal, an unsuspecting mouse that had happened along only minutes earlier. The mouse's tail and small foot twitched in the throes of death. Giving it a wide berth, Christian moved past only to nearly step on another snake hidden in the grass. Christian stumbled as he jumped back, the parcel dropping to the ground and ripping open. Luckily, the contents hadn't touch the wet ground.

He secured the parcel as best he could and hurried toward the ranch. Walking alongside the elegant stone wall surrounding the Owen property, he came to a large, wrought-iron entrance gate much taller than the stone walls. The words "Owen Ranch" had been inscribed across the top of the gate. He opened it and slipped inside, shutting it behind him.

The road continued beyond the entrance for some distance through a grove of cedars. Eventually, Christian arrived at a cluster of buildings, including a freshly painted, gleaming white stable; a bloodred barn; and the regal, sprawling home of the mayor and his wife.

All was quiet as Christian ascended the steps to the front porch, which, he calculated, could comfortably accommodate more than forty people. Someone had carefully placed a large table, rocking chairs, and gas lamps down its length. And set against the house and around the table and chairs, potted plants and Medici urns gave the place a palatial feel, more so than he could have imagined, and he hadn't even seen the inside. It reminded him of his childhood in Italy. It felt as if the mayor's insatiable desire for unique and beautiful objects poured from the house for lack of space.

The door, an elegant display of artisanship, had eagles and stars carved along the hinge panels and "Owen" boldly emblazoned above. It opened before he knocked. Mrs. Owen stood in the doorway, looking him up and down. Christian's long, wet hair clung to his face, his clothing was soaked, his knees and feet were covered in mud. She wore a look of disapproval. Then she noticed the parcel.

"Ma'am, Mr. Buchanan sent me, said the mayor requested that I deliver this." Christian held out the package, and she took it without a word. She'd turned to leave when the mayor appeared and took the parcel from her, allowing her to withdraw.

"You Shear's boy?" asked the mayor, though Christian couldn't tell if it was a question or statement.

"Yes, sir. He's my papa."

"Helping Walt over at the post office?"

Again, he couldn't tell if it was a question or a comment. He answered regardless. "Yes, Mr. Mayor, sir. I am."

The mayor looked at the partially unwrapped package and back at Christian. "Are you in the habit of opening letters or parcels not belonging to you?"

"Sorry, sir. I tripped and fell on the way here. I didn't mean for it to be . . ."

"Opened?" asked the mayor.

"That's right, sir."

"So you're not curious about things, are you? Enough to violate another's privacy?"

"No! I . . ."

The mayor studied him carefully, then relaxed. "All right, then. Come in. I require your service." Not expecting to be invited inside, Christian stomped his feet so as not to muddy their floor.

"Don't worry," said the mayor. "We've maids for that, and our wood floors have lacquer."

"What's that, sir?"

"Something new, comes from far away as Europe. I had it shipped here. It makes cleaning more manageable. Now, follow me."

As the mayor led him into the house, Christian's eyes went wide, having never seen anything so remarkable. The English chestnut wooden floors in the front parlor were shiny as glass. The air smelled of fresh-cut flowers. The leather furniture was stained red and studded with brass rivets. An entire library of leather-bound books with gold and silver lettering graced the walls, and the stone hearth ran practically the entire length of the main room.

As they ventured farther in, Christian stared at all the other beautiful things, like the stone fireplace in a room meant for nothing more than simply sitting. Next, they passed through another room with no apparent purpose. This one had maple-wood paneling; stained, cherrywood balusters leading upstairs; doors framed with molding; a multitude of ornate furnishings; and velvety red drapery. Christian didn't have the words to describe such opulence.

The sound of paper ripping drew Christian's attention as the mayor withdrew the contents from the package. He held a small stack of sheets printed on newspaper, along with several posters. He unrolled several of the posters, spreading them flat on the table. Christian leaned in for a peek.

"Your impressions, young man?" The mayor held one up so Christian could inspect it more carefully, expecting the young man to be nothing less than impressed.

Christian shook his head, not quite understanding. "I'm sorry, sir. I—"

"Well, what do you think?" asked the mayor, wiggling the paper to draw attention. Printed was a regal drawing of the mayor, obviously rendered in his youth. The lettering on the posters read "Mayor Robert Owen III—Continued Tradition of Leadership for New Harmony" but failed to list any qualifications or a platform.

"Very nice, sir," Christian agreed.

Next to the wrapping paper and twine lay a stack of printed slips of paper. Dividing them in half, the mayor handed one stack to Christian and put the rest aside. "Here's what I need from you," he said. "Put one of these in each post-office box. Do that for me?"

Christian took the stack to see "Ballot" printed at the top.

"Count them. You should have at least four hundred, one for each household, enough for each box at the post office. If there are extra, discard them."

"There are 411 boxes, Mayor, 412 before the Stewarts left town."

Surprised, the mayor asked, "You know that for certain?"

"I count each time I sort."

"Well then, here." The mayor took more ballots from the side stack and handed them to Christian along with the wax paper and twine. "I trust you'll discard the rest."

"I will, sir," said Christian, wrapping them. "Mayor, may I ask something, sir?"

"What? What is it you want to know?"

"What about those?" Christian pointed to the stack the mayor had set aside.

"Curious boy." The mayor said, his manner suggesting it was none of Christian's business. "I ordered more on purpose. I hadn't time to count the boxes, so I ordered more to ensure I had plenty. I'll discard these, and you worry about those." The irritation in his voice was unmistakable.

"Sir, I'm sorry if—"

Just then, Mrs. Owen entered the room, the smell of her fancy perfume trailing her. "Are we done here?"

"Yes, darling. Shear's boy—" The mayor cut short his sentence and looked at Christian. "What's your name?"

"Christian, sir."

"Yes, well," said the mayor, "Christian was just leaving."

Any pretense of courtesy vanished, and the room went cold.

"Excuse me, but I sense I may have offended. If so, I do apologize. It's just that tonight, I'll be officially engaged to marry." He hoped that would offer an acceptable excuse for whatever misdemeanor he may have committed.

Mrs. Owen appeared to compose herself. "Congratulations, young man, and think nothing of it. Ms. Emily Hampshire, so I'm told?" She forced a smile.

"Yes, ma'am."

"Lovely young lady. As you are well aware, she is one of my teachers."

"Yes. Thank you again, ma'am. You too, Mayor, sir," Christian said with a bow, eager to be excused. He quickly showed himself to the door. He stopped midstride and turned to face the mayor and Mrs. Owen. "Mayor?" he asked.

"Yes, boy. What is it? And please be quick about it."

"Well," said Christian. "I'm not saying it's true or not," his words faltered. "I mean, maybe it's true, and maybe it isn't . . ." he said, hemming and hawing.

"Just say it, son." demanded the mayor. "What is it?"

"Rumor has it you intend to open a bank here in Harmony. If that's true, I'd be grateful if you'd consider my working for you."

The mayor nodded but offered no encouragement, courtesy, or farewell. Instead, he and his wife stared at Christian as he awkwardly saw himself out.

Chapter 32

"Hold her still!" said Marco. Warren did his best to steady the mare while Marco examined her mouth, looking for changes in the color of the mucous membranes. "As I suspected. Hay-induced colic. It'll pass. Check your source. Some bales might have been tied wet or gotten wet. You have mold in a few of them."

"That's all?" asked Warren.

Marco nodded. "I think so, with this weather."

Marco was lean like his brother Christian, with shorter hair, but other than that, they looked similar, as brothers often did. He wore a young man's mustache, thin but dark enough to be noticeable. Marco patted the horse. "All those hours in medical school and I end up in a stable."

Warren laughed. "At least horses don't moan and cry, and they hardly complain."

"They hardly pay either," said Marco. "But who's complaining?"

Marco heard someone coming in from the rain and looked up to see his brother kicking the mud from his boots, a package in his arms.

"Give me a minute, Christian. This old girl isn't feeling well."

Christian rubbed his nose on his sleeve and waited. Hay always made it itch.

When Marco finished, he patted the horse. "You can put her away now," he said. "She'll be fine." Warren led the horse into a stall while Marco sat on a hay bale and looked at Christian. "Not at work?"

"No, I have the afternoon off."

"Hmm. That's good." Marco then turned and called to Warren. "Any others feeling sick?"

"Don't believe so," said Warren. "But I'm checking."

Christian peered over his shoulder at the open doors, noting that the rain had stopped. He set the package on the dry, hard dirt in the stable, removed his coat, and shook off the extra moisture. "Brother, do me a favor. Tell Papa not to be late tonight. I'm bringing Emmy home. We've got an announcement. Could you make sure he's there when we arrive?"

"Yeah." Marco showed no curiosity, which surprised Christian.

Then he heard Warren holler from a stall farther back, "Is it what I think it is?"

Christian's face beamed with excitement. "It is! Though I can hardly believe it myself." He then looked at Marco, who stared blankly out the stable doors at the gloomy day. "Brother?"

Marco stared in silence as if alone in his thoughts.

Less enthused than when he arrived, Christian picked up his package and quietly left.

There was no way Christian could have known that such an announcement would bring his brother any measure of unhappiness. But it did. The engagement was inevitable, yet it pained Marco all the same. Marco was no different than any of the other boys back in school, secretly harboring feelings for Emily. Yet his plight was much worse. He had to conceal his affection from his brother, and his grief now overshadowed the joy he felt for Christian.

He knew well why Christian loved her. Marco liked for her for the very same reasons—her soft, milky skin; her feminine touch; her school-girl giggle; and her long, flowing auburn-red hair. But other things caused his heart to long for her even more, like her independence, intelligence, and quick wit. The thought of forever having to keep her at length, never to hold her tight, pained him deeply. He would never confess such yearnings to Emily or his younger brother. Christian must never suspect. Marco loved his younger brother more than anyone except for the one person he could never have.

A moment later, Warren left without saying a word, and Marco was left with the horses and his misery.

Chapter 33

With a bounce in his step, Christian dropped off the ballots and went straight to the school, sure Emily would be just as excited as he was. He stomped his boots on the mat outside the front door and entered the school. Bursting to profess his love, Christian wanted everyone in the school to know, but he found the hallway vacant. He peeked into her room only to find it empty.

Where was everyone?

He heard voices coming from down the hall. He moved cautiously to avoid squeaking the floorboards. Approached Annette's room, he found the door cracked open. Inside, he could see Ms. Woolhauser's profile and a sliver of Annette's back. He heard Emily's voice among the others and quietly listened, something about the conversation giving him pause. Thinking it best not to interrupt, he waited patiently. His back slid down the wall until he sat soundly on the hallway floor. Their voices were loud enough that he couldn't help but listen.

Ms. Woolhauser spoke loudly, clearly. "Until told otherwise, I'll provide instruction for his students. Hopefully, Mrs. Owen considered our imposition before she released Mr. Parrish and his replacement has already been arranged. But let's not count on it."

Emily voiced her opinion, clearly upset with how Mrs. Owen released Bronson. "You'd think Mrs. Owen, at the very least, would have offered guidance in the meantime. After all, she scrutinizes everything else."

"Heaven forbid that any of us bring it up with her. No telling who she'll target next," Ms. Woolhauser said, "so be careful."

Just then, Christian became distracted by the opening of the school's front door. He glimpsed over his shoulder to see Mrs. Owen, and he quickly crawled into Annette's classroom. Emily and the other teachers went silent, wondering what on earth he was doing on his hands and knees.

He stood while pressing a finger to his lips. Then, nodding toward the door, he indicated that someone approached. They all recognized the sound of Mrs. Owen's footsteps, hurried and aggressive, hesitating at each door until she eventually found them.

"Here you are," she said matter-of-factly. "I see you're all present—even you, Ms. Woolhauser. Good. It saves me time." Mrs. Owen unbuttoned her pink cape and set it on the desk closest to her. Upon seeing Christian in the corner, her nose wrinkled, and her upper lip curled. He'd been in her home just that day, and yet she ignored him. "You ladies all know Mr. Parrish will no longer perform duties here. Tomorrow, I have a replacement for him. Constance Madison arrived yesterday afternoon from Bloomington. She will stay with me at the ranch until suitable housing is arranged. I can assure you that her priority will be that of the children. The shenanigans of the past are squarely in the past. Is that understood?" Before she received an answer, she turned to Christian. "Are you a teacher here?"

"No, ma'am. I'm here to see Emmy."

"Well then, please excuse us. You can wait in the hallway. Shut the door on your way out."

"Yes, ma'am." Christian quickly slipped out and shut the door.

"Thankfully," she continued, "one of you had the courage to protect our children, and to that person alone, I express my gratitude." She purposefully glanced at Annette and forced a smile. "Because of the courage of this individual, everything will be much better now. I hope the other two of you understand how important it is to put the children first—no more protecting those who don't protect them. Do we understand each other? Any questions?" She paused for the briefest of moments before saying, "Good."

She turned, picked up her cape, smiled disingenuously, and left the room, passing Christian in the hall without the slightest acknowledgment. The teachers listened as her footsteps grew quiet, not speaking until they heard the door at the school entry shut.

Ms. Woolhauser spoke first. "Oh my," she said once all was quiet and she knew she wouldn't be overheard. "Wasn't that enlightening?"

Emily nodded. "I believe we understand her very well."

Ms. Woolhauser agreed. "It appears she's hired a proper protégé, someone to monitor us," she said. "We must walk softly with this Constance."

Up to this point, Annette had kept quiet, too embarrassed or ashamed for having been singled out. Now, in her usual, mousy voice, she asked, "The new teacher, what chance is there that she's even aware the old woman's a rattler? I don't mean to be disrespectful. Mrs. Owen is elderly, so I can call her an old woman if I want to."

"I wouldn't be worried referring to her as an old woman or a rattler if I were you," said Emily. "But say it quietly."

After a moment, Ms. Woolhauser, brows drawn, warned, "We cannot assume this Ms. Madison is anything like us. She may be a rattler herself. I wouldn't put it past Mrs. Owen to pick one of those."

The other two hadn't thought of that and, upon further reflection, agreed.

"We must watch ourselves," said Annette timidly.

I believe we're done here," announced Ms. Woolhauser more boldly. "We'll all be careful, won't we?"

They each nodded and stood to leave. Emily quickly hurried to Christian, who waited in the hallway. They hugged. Taking his hand, she urged him toward the door. "Let's go. I've had my fill today, and you are my remedy."

Chapter 34

After stopping by the Hampshires to ask for Uncle Alberts's consent for marriage and receive well wishes from Aunt Marjorie, Christian and Emily headed to the Salvatori home. The door stood wide open in anticipation of their arrival. The humid evening air flowed freely throughout the house and into the sitting room, where Tommaso and Marco sat patiently waiting. Tommaso had just noted that the candle on the parlor table needed changing when he heard the couple's footsteps on the front porch. He stood to greet them as they entered.

"Papa, Emmy and I have wonderful news." Christian turned and looked at Emily. "Would you like to tell them?"

Tommaso glanced at Emily, who answered. "No, they'd rather it come from you. You tell them."

"All right. Papa?"

Tommaso smiled while nodding.

"I'm certain you can guess," said Christian.

"Tell me you gonna marry. That's it?"

"Yes, Papa!" shouted Christian. Both he and Emily could barely contain their excitement. "We are, Papa! Are you happy for us?"

"Certainly am." Tommaso looked at Marco. "Your brother brings wonderful news."

Christian looked at Marco, waiting.

"Happy for you, brother," he said.

Tommaso turned his attention back to Christian. "*Mio ragazzo*, my boy, my boy." He moved closer and hugged them both.

Emily peered over Tommaso's shoulder at Marco, who sat quietly looking off into the distance until eventually meeting her gaze. Smiling shyly, he looked down.

Tommaso finally let go and stepped back. "I always say, Christian, 'When you gonna ask Emmy?' Hmm? Don't I say that? And now look at ya."

"He did," Christian agreed, nodding excitedly. "I mean, he does—asks all the time."

Marco stood and looked at his brother, seeing pure joy in his face. "Congratulations. You too, Emmy. Would you excuse me, please?" he said as he left them and headed to his room, the door closing softly.

Tommaso invited them to sit and visit for a while, but the hour was late, and Christian felt it proper to see her home safely. "We've time for that later, Papa. If that's all right?"

"Yes, all right. I'll wait up for you."

Emily and Christian turned to leave. "I'll be back soon," said Christian, "if you care to wait." They shared one last hug before Tommaso smiled and kissed each of them on their cheeks.

"You make me so happy," said Tommaso. "Now go. Get her home, son."

Once the excitement of the evening passed and Tommaso and Marco were alone in the house, Tommaso gently knocked on Marco's door. He cracked open the door to peek into the room. "Marco?"

"Just reading, Papa." He set his book on the bed beside him.

"May I?"

"Yes, of course. Come in."

Tommaso quietly entered and sat beside him, sensing that something troubled his son. He often handled such moments with stories from his youth in the old country. Tonight was no different.

"When I was a boy in Sardinia, I dreamed of a girl. Her name I'll never forget—Lucia. I watched her every day at the school. Her hair was long and dark like maple, and eyes, oh, her eyes—I can still see them now. And how her dress blew in the breeze. She was most beautiful. I could never, never be happy without her. I needed her. I did." Tommaso's eyes closed as if overtaken by the memory.

"One day, I sent her a letter. I wrote to her, 'I love you. Will you be mine?' Something like that, I wrote. The next day she gave me a note. So I read it, and she says to me, no. She says she like Leonardo or Lorenzo. I don't remember now. My heart, yes, my heart—oh, so broken." Tommaso pounded his chest, and his eyes dropped. "My life, it was over. But I loved her and wanted her to be happy. So I went to this boy, Leo or Lorenzo, after the school, you know. I says to him, 'I think Lucia, I think she likes you.' You know what he says to me?" Tommaso's eyebrows rose. He waited for Marco to answer, but Marco shrugged.

"He says . . . he says to me, 'So.' 'So?' I say. What is this, 'So?' You know. But he liked someone else. My Lucia meant nothing to him. Love—it makes no sense. Then I find my Caterina, your mama, and, oh, how she loved me back. So, it is good. I found someone who loved me back. Your mama, she's the love of my life. My only!"

"Yes, Papa. Emmy loves Christian back, so that's good."

Tommaso patted Marco's knee. "She does, and that's good."

"I know, Papa," said Marco. "I am happy for him. You know that."

"Yes, yes, I know."

Christian held a lantern as they walked hand in hand down the dark street. At that moment, all the fear smothering New Harmony was no concern of theirs. Instead, they found solace in each other, free from the worries that crept into every home.

As they stepped onto her porch, Emily hugged him and said, "I'm not afraid anymore. I will be your wife, and you will make me very happy." After they shared a passionate kiss, Emily slipped into her home, and the door closed behind her.

☾

When Christian returned home, the oil lamp in the kitchen glowed softly. Tommaso sat at the kitchen table, eating clumps of rye bread soaked in milk and honey. An envelope sat on the table. He handed it to Christian.

"For me, Papa?"

"For you."

Christian sat and opened it to discover a letter. "Your mama wanted you to have it. She say to me, 'Tommaso, you know when to give to him.' She wrote one for Marco, but . . . not yet. One day I give it to him. I will know."

Christian unfolded the letter. He recognized his mother's handwriting in the language of his childhood. The flow of her words brought the memory of her back to him.

My dear Christian,

My time grows short. It won't be much longer, but I'm not scared to die. My only pain is leaving you, your brother, and your papa. Very soon, I will be with the angels, my mama and papa, and my two sisters, Rosa and Maria Teresa. I will wait for you there. But while I am gone, I need you to be a good boy. Listen to your papa. He is a good man. One day, you'll be just like him, if you work hard and are honest.

As for love, there is so much to tell, and I've little time. The girl at school, the one you talk about, Emmy, she's a fine girl. So pretty. You must understand that love makes you vulnerable and can hurt deeply, but no matter. You'll be all right. And I promise it is worth risking love despite the uncertain future. Whatever life brings will be for the best. Accept what comes no matter what happens. Things are not always our choice no matter how hard we try.

Know, my son, that I am not choosing to leave. Every day you walk out the door for school, I miss you. If it were my choice, I would stay here with you, your brother, and your papa. But, alas, it is not to be. As I watch you leave each day, my heart groans, and soon you will have to say goodbye to me. It is as life intends. Sometimes the most difficult part of being human is letting go. But we all move on. You will move on, and that's all right.

Please don't take life for granted. You must live and love, and, yes, there will be days you cry. Even love, the most precious of all, will surely make you cry, as when we say goodbye. But it can also bring immense joy. I choose to be happy, my son, and know this: I will continue to love you, even when you cannot see me. I will always be your mother. And as my heart rejoices each time you return from school, one day, we will rejoice together, and there will be no more leaving each other, no more saying goodbye. Until that day, I love you always. Be a good boy.

There was silence for a time before Christian set the letter aside. "Papa?"

"Yes."

"Sometimes I feel her near."

"So do I."

"Papa?"

"Uh-huh?"

"It's one of those times, but I don't want to cry."

"It's all right, son," said Tommaso. "You can cry, and still you are a man." Tommaso hugged him, and together they shared their tears.

Chapter 35

Neither somber skies nor sodden earth could dim the beast's hope, nor could the scant prey he relied on to satisfy his cravings. Despite his curse or the voices that threatened to drag him to purgatory, he'd been granted a scrap of humanity, and that meant more than anything he could have imagined. He was more than a beast or monster. Inside the abomination that imprisoned him, he had a name.

I am Jonathan, and I am human.

The words replayed in his mind as he followed the game trails through the thicket of underbrush that led to the road. When the weather finally gave him respite from the downpour, Jonathan breathed in the scents of pine, sage, holly, and moss.

The forest felt deserted as he broke through the brush and passed between the white pines. Once again, he carefully avoided being seen, intent on staying alive. He slid down a ravine and followed a muddy wash that emptied into a small stream. The thunder showers had just resumed when he heard a troubling sound nearly hidden by the pitter-patter of rain. He stopped and took shelter in the bushes, his ears turned toward the sound, trying to guess how far off and from what direction it came. He heard it again, only louder. This time, Jonathan recognized it and crept closer.

He couldn't remember the last time he'd heard human voices, but that wasn't the cause of his disquietude. He heard something more than just words.

From the agitated tones that floated on the air, he knew something was wrong.

Crouching low, he crept ever closer, still hidden, the sound of his approach drowned by the rain.

He had to be careful not to make matters worse.

The closer he got, the more troubled the voices became.

Suddenly, a man shouted, "Now push!" It echoed through the ravine, causing a red-bellied woodpecker to take flight.

The voice of a boy cried, "I am, Papa. I am!"

Jonathan heard groans of defeat as he peered through the dampened hawthorns and honeysuckle to see a man and a boy desperate to free their cart from the mud-bogged road. They dug with their hands only to have the sludge fill back in around the wheels.

"Papa, it's no use—the mud!" the boy cried.

"We got no choice," said the man. "We need the meat. We got your sisters and mother are countin' on us. Just keep digging!"

In the wet and cold, the boy continued his futile efforts as the father pushed, both unaware that something watched them from the brush.

The beast caught the scent of the deer strapped to their cart, his saliva involuntarily pooling in his jowls and dripping from his tongue. He snorted and clenched his teeth. Hunger was his constant companion. But it was *Jonathan* who watched their plight unfolding. He stared at his paws and bulging muscles with all the strength his curse afforded yet felt powerless. He wanted nothing more than to help free their cart. But that was out of the question, and he knew it. All the while, his stomach growled.

The father stood over his son, watching him struggle to scoop the mud away from the wheel. As fast as his tiny hands worked, the muck rushed in to fill the void. The boy's hands shook as rain streaked his face.

"Take a rest, son. Over there, under the tree."

The boy got up and headed for shelter. His father leaned against the cart, clearly at a loss, the rain falling in sheets now. Finally, slinging the mud from his hands and shaking his head in defeat, he abandoned the cart to join his son. He sat next to the boy and put his arm around him.

Still peering through the thick vegetation, Jonathan watched the shivering child embrace his father, trying to stay warm.

"We must wait and pray the rain stops," he said.

Jonathan looked away. He couldn't resist staring at the deer, and as he did, he heard a voice, the same that delighted in his torment.

"You're hungry, aren't you, beast?"

Jonathan emitted a low growl. *Stop talking to me. I won't listen.*

"You can't deny what you are."

I know what I am, who I am. Your lies mean nothing now.

"Oh, beast, you are no longer Jonathan," said a smooth voice.

A dark voice whispered, "We know a secret about Jonathan, the Jonathan you once were."

How do I break the curse? That's all I want to know. Tell me that and nothing else.

"The innocent are not cursed. You know what that means, monster?"

"We cannot touch them, the innocent," they said in unison. "Yet you are in our grip!"

"What we can tell you," one said, "is that Jonathan, who you once were, was a monster—just—like—you!"

The sound of laughter filled his head. *I've heard this before. Now, go away. I'm not listening.*

He covered his ears but to no avail.

"Try to ignore us if you will," chanted the voices. "What you can't ignore is your hunger. Look, beast. See what we've provided?"

As Jonathan stared at the deer, his stomach growling. His eyes drifted to the man and boy crouched under the tree.

Suddenly, he felt something more powerful than hunger. He wanted to rebel against the curse and damnable voices and help the man and boy.

I am Jonathan. I am no monster.

At that pronouncement, there surfaced a feeling he'd nearly forgotten—empathy. He looked at the son and father, muddy and wet, and felt their frustration. He was stunned and confused, his primal instincts screaming for him to avoid all human contact.

Believing myself a human is bound to get me killed. But I am Jonathan, am I not?

His eyes focused on the man and boy even as the emptiness in his stomach screamed for his attention. "Hunger is hunger, and meat is meat. It's all the same."

He held up a furry arm and brutish paw.

If I were human, it would be different.

"Yes," came a raspy whisper. "Satisfy your hunger. Time for you to eat."

Jonathan let out a growl. *No.*

It pained him to deny his primal urges, but he was determined.

They will walk away. I will not—

His stomach ached at the thought.

I will not fill my belly with human meat.

No matter how the voices tried to sway Jonathan, they were no match for his sense of compassion. The man and boy would not forfeit the meat needed to feed their family, not if he could help it.

He moved impulsively, breaking free of the brush. Upon hearing the commotion, the man and boy looked up, startled, as Jonathan appeared in the mist and rain as if from a hellish nightmare.

"Papa, what is that?"

"Run! Don't look back!" the father screamed.

Abandoning their handcart and the food their family needed to survive, they fled as fast as their legs could carry them, splashing through puddles and slipping in the mud. They ran south toward the gorge and the town farther on.

Their flight triggered something primal within the beast, an overwhelming urge to give chase, to hunt them as prey.

What have I done? I don't deserve this.

He slowly moved in their direction.

I cannot allow them to escape, to leave the woods. They'll hunt me. If not them, then others.

The beast was upon them in moments. He broke wide and off the road, crashing through bushes and branches alongside his prey. It would be easy to snap their necks and live undiscovered.

It's only a matter of time before people in the town know of my existence, but it doesn't have to be today.

The fleeing humans heard the terrifying commotion. A predator stalked them. At any moment, they could be torn apart.

In exhaustion, the boy stumbled to the ground.

"Get up!" the father urged.

"I can't, Papa. I can't run anymore." The boy burst into tears.

His father stopped and staggered back to his side, placing himself between his son and the danger. Black eyes stared back at him through the foliage.

The man picked up a rock. "Leave us be!"

Mouth dripping with saliva, Jonathan stared, wondering what to do, when a voice said, "It's time, beast. Fill the emptiness. You must eat to survive."

The man gasped as Jonathan's massive frame emerged from the brush. Monstrous and powerful, he towered over him with wolfish teeth, savage and razor-sharp, and claws like a bear's.

The man fell to his knees. "Please! Don't hurt my son!"

The beast rose on its hind legs and howled, then came down on all four limbs, lowering his shoulders and positioning himself to lunge at the man.

Tears streamed down the man's face. "I beg you. Please don't hurt my son!"

The beast paused just long enough to hear the man's pleading. He saw they were cold, wet, and frightened, and he suddenly felt the self-loathing of the irredeemable. He staggered back into the brush, his sense of mercy trumping his hunger. Freezing rain poured down Jonathan's face, washing away any goodwill and leaving him feeling indignant.

I was only trying to help. I knew better. I may lose everything now.

He turned away, unwilling to watch as the man lifted his son to his feet and continued unharmed toward the gorge that led to town.

There was little reward for the mercy he had shown. But the deer, abandoned on the handcart, was his. This night, his hunger would be satisfied. With a heavy heart, he made his way back to the cart, tore the rope from the carcass, and dragged the deer back to his cave.

CHAPTER 36

Tommaso had just lit the whale-oil lamp when the door to the barbershop swung open.

Bronson Parrish slipped in and quickly shut the door. "Do you have a minute?"

"Ah, you see it's late, don't you?"

"Yes, please excuse the late hour," said Bronson. "Just that I rarely leave the house these days due to a particular conflict, you might say."

"Hmm, the town meeting. Yes, I remember. Happened to be there," said Tommaso.

"The very same. I've made some enemies, I'm afraid."

"Yeah, come in, come in, now. But best we lock up and close the curtains."

"Please do, Shears. I'd appreciate the privacy."

After closing the curtains and securing the lock, Tommaso nodded toward the chair. As Bronson sat, Tommaso fastened a cloth around him, wasting no time. With two fingers, the barber lifted hair and cut, lifted and cut. Suddenly, there came a tapping at the window.

"Come back in the mornin'. I'm closed!" hollered Tommaso.

Whoever it was didn't appear discouraged, and the tapping persisted until finally, Bronson sighed. "Aw, must be LeFev, my neighbor."

Tommaso peeked through the curtains, and, sure enough, LeFevre's head appeared in the window. A rugged older man, weather-worn and leathered, Lamont LeFevre entered with a broad grin that showed his missing front tooth.

"Forgive me, Shears. I tell him to stop worrying, but he insists on following me. I did my best to come alone, but he must have seen me leave the house, claims it's no longer safe for me until after the election."

Tommaso hesitated. "Should I . . ."

"Yeah, let him in," said Bronson. "He's harmless and a good man despite having insulted the entire town on more than one occasion."

Tommaso unlocked the door, and in slipped Lamont LeFevre, a man too old for social graces and too eager to speak his mind.

True to character, he hadn't even sat before he opened his mouth. "Shears, what do ya think you're doin'? If you're tryin' to make Bronson here any prettier, give it up, man! He's cute as a cottontail as is. When you're done with him, tie a ribbon in his hair—one of those big pink bows, the kind the ladies wear on Sundays." LeFevre snickered, knowing Tommaso was too kind to reply.

"Pay him no attention, Shears. He means well."

A sneer crossed LeFevre's gaunt, angular face. "Hey, Shears, while you're at it, tell Bronson how his little speech bumped a beehive. Likely to get stung by an Owen, no less." LeFevre removed his hat, placed it on his lap, and smoothed his unkempt dusty-gray hair. "I'm his guardian angel whether he wants my divine intervention or not. Always got my shooter at my side."

Bronson rolled his eyes. "I keep telling him, Shears. I could get every vote in town plus one, but it won't make a difference. The mayor will find a way to beat anyone who stands up to him."

"Like playing cards with a cheat who's got nothin' but aces up his sleeve," said LeFevre.

"That's right, LeFev. I'd have better luck pullin' knickers off the queen than draggin' the mayor out of town hall."

Tommaso waited patiently as the two men exchanged lighthearted banter. "Can't do more, Mr. Parrish, not till you hold still."

"Forgive me, Shears," said Bronson, who then warned LeFevre not to say another word, and they remained quiet while Tommaso worked.

A bowl of warm water and a towel flung over Tommaso's shoulder kept the straight razor clean. The barber scraped upward, the snowy, white cream piling up on the silvery blade.

Outside, a commotion caught their attention. LeFevre stood and peered through the curtain. "Hey, Shears, is it always this busy after dark?"

"No."

LeFevre scratched his head and sat back down.

"Almost finished," said Tommaso after a few more swipes of the razor. "Finished."

Just then, there came a rattling and a pounding at the door. "Papa, are you in there?"

Bronson and LeFevre looked inquisitively at Tommaso. "It's Marco, my son."

Marco's voice sounded urgent. "Papa, open up if you're in there."

Tommaso quickly took the key from his apron pocket. As soon as he unlocked the door, Marco rushed in. Upon seeing Bronson and LeFevre, he nodded a greeting, then turned to his father. "Papa, something terrible has happened. People want to hear what the mayor has to say. Come with me."

Tommaso appeared confused. "We didn't hear the bell."

Marco grew impatient. "No one heard it. There was no bell, only word of mouth."

"Well, what's the problem? What are they saying?" asked Bronson.

"Just that there's been an attack. Here, look!" Marco pulled the curtain back to reveal a large crowd walking and holding lanterns, some running, all headed toward the town hall.

Tommaso untied his apron and hung it on a peg near the door.

An anxious Marco motioned to his father to close the shop. "Just hurry, Papa."

Bronson wiped his face with the damp towel, unfastened the cloth, and threw it onto the chair. The streets bustled with activity, rare for this time of night. The town was already on edge since the eclipse. And now, an attack would likely drive them close to hysterics.

Chapter 37

Lightning bugs kept a vigil, their tiny lights twinkling in the bushes and gardens beyond the picket fences as people hurried down the street, carrying lanterns. Marco, Tommaso, Bronson, and LeFevre stepped out into the night, mingling with the crowd streaming toward the town center. When they arrived, Main Street bustled with townspeople wrapped in thick coats and blankets, the tension in the air palpable. Even without the bell ringing, enough people had packed in that latecomers had to stand in the park opposite the town hall.

Bronson peered over the heads in the crowd to see the mayor exit the building, the sheriff in tow. Both stopped at the top of the steps and glared down at those gathered. Although close enough to notice the fatigue on the mayor's face, Bronson tried to stay hidden in the shadows and swarm of people surrounding him. Despite the cold weather, he could see the gleam of sweat on the mayor's forehead as the crowd grew more restless.

Vernon Davis, a farmer from north of town, hollered, "What's going on?"

The crowd around him became agitated, also wanting answers.

No doubt the first to arrive, Abigail Williams shouted, "Mayor? Any truth to the rumors?"

Another woman farther back in the crowd cried out, "Are we safe?"

That question caused an uproar, and in mob fashion, a handful of people climbed several steps closer to where the mayor stood, the sheriff rushing forward to cut them off.

"Move!" he hollered. "I won't ask twice. Now, back!" Then, using his long rifle like a battering ram, he pushed the frightened crowd back down the steps.

To further quell the disturbance, the mayor shouted, "Patience, everyone!"

"Quiet! Our mayor is trying to speak!" Abigail added.

The mayor glanced at Abigail, who gave him a wide grin.

The crowd quieted as the mayor whispered something to the sheriff. The sheriff disappeared into the building, only to return with a muddied and tattered Phillip Wallace and his son, Lewis. They stood at the mayor's side. Upon seeing their condition, the crowd went completely silent.

Seeing the crowd settled, the mayor called out, "Listen here! Not one of us is in danger! Do you hear me? What reason have we to fear? For now, there has only been an alleged attack far north of here, beyond the gorge, and we're investigating. I repeat—we are investigating."

Old Man Taylor hollered, "Perhaps no harm will come to any of you here in town, but what about those of us on the outskirts? Can't say we are not in any danger."

"That's right, Mayor," said Vernon. "We're not leaving here until we know what's out there in the dark."

Again, the mayor urged calm. "We are all exhausted, and at this late hour, patience is advisable. Stay where you are. I'll return and make a statement shortly. Until then, I urge calm, everyone."

The mayor turned and ushered Phillip and his son into the building. The sheriff stayed outside, preventing the crowd from climbing the steps.

While the people stood outside, waiting, the tale of a beast stalking New Harmony circulated like weevils in cotton sacks of wheat. With each retelling, the story grew more terrifying. Bronson listened to the parts and pieces, all propagated by Wallace's encounter with a supposed monster.

Turning to Marco, Bronson asked, "Make sense of this for me, would you? What did you hear? I trust your version to be more reliable."

Those within earshot listened as Marco related the account as he'd heard it, careful not to embellish. "Mrs. Folsom claims Mrs. Williams told her a monstrous beast of some kind attacked Mr. Wallace and his boy, nothing more."

Those listening to Marco hung on the word *beast,* most claiming Marco omitted the worst parts, by which they meant to say the best parts. A few disagreed, arguing that the entire encounter was greatly exaggerated.

Vernon interrupted. "Listen. I heard the same thing. Phillip and his boy was north of the gorge when they say they was attacked. When they got back, they went straight to the sheriff's office. That's all!"

In a daze, Tommaso turned to Bronson. "What do ya figure? Bears?"

Bronson nodded. "What else is there? The woods are full of bears, especially up north, and occasional attacks aren't unheard of."

Among the eavesdroppers, Boyd Kensington leaned in. "Aint no bear! I give you my witness. I seen 'em. Phillip and his boy came stumblin' into town screaming, 'Monster!' They said it pinned 'em down, whatever it was. Attacked the boy first while his pa tried to shoot, but his powder was wet from all this rain. Ball never left the barrel."

"Had to be a bear, then," Bronson concluded.

"I told ya," said Boyd, "ain't no bear! Not what Phillip said, and he ain't one to spin yarn. Says what is an' nothin' more."

LeFevre shrugged. "I don't know 'bout that. We were drinkin' once, and he tells me he stomped a badger till dead. Mean little creatures, so I doubt that."

Boyd's eyes bore down on LeFevre. "Don't care what any of you say. He wasn't drinkin' when I saw him with his boy, and he didn't say nothin' 'bout no bear."

"Ain't ya an educated doctor now?" LeFevre asked Marco.

"I suppose you can say that," Marco answered.

"Well then?"

Marco looked into the faces of those gathered. "Hmm," he said. "I'm guessing here, of course. Perhaps a general psychosis. That's the most probable thing, brought on by stress, I imagine."

"What does that mean?" asked Boyd.

"Huh. Not certain," said Marco. "Just that monsters live in our imagination. I believe he saw something. I just can't be certain as to what he saw."

"It's settled, then—a bear," declared Bronson.

LeFevre, however, wasn't so sure. "Spent my life trappin', and I can tell ya, I've heard things out there in the dark, in the woods. And I know the difference between a bear and, uh, and whatever. No tellin' what's out there."

"No," said Bronson adamantly. "The kind of monster people are talkin' 'bout is beyond reason, and I'm not saying Phillip isn't a good man, but—a monster? You believe that, LeFev?"

LeFevre shrugged. "Why not?"

Boyd shook his head, taking it all too personally. "LeFevre ain't the only one who spent time in the woods. I believe 'im. I sit by the Wallaces in church, and he ain't no liar."

At twenty minutes to midnight, Phillip Wallace and his boy exited the building, followed by the mayor. The Wallaces stood quietly off to one side in the darkness just outside the lantern's reach. The sheriff began yelling orders as he climbed the steps and came to stand shoulder to shoulder with the mayor.

Sensing the growing unrest, the mayor called out. "Listen to me, everyone! At present, we know little to nothing. However, Phillip Wallace's report is credible enough to raise concern. The responsible thing now is to wait while we investigate."

With overalls frayed at the seams, Boyd Kennington pushed through the crowd and began climbing the steps uninvited. The sheriff intercepted him, seizing his arm to escort him back into the crowd.

"I will say my piece!" yelled the bedraggled farmer, resisting the sheriff and refusing to budge.

The mayor raised a calming hand to the sheriff. "Let him speak," he ordered, fearing a heavy hand could turn those gathered into a mob.

Boyd stood defiantly before the crowd and shouted, "We are under siege, I tell you! A curse! There *is* a beast! The Wallace monster is real, and we are in danger!" He whipped the crowd into an instant frenzy, those who believed and those who thought the report outrageous yelling and arguing.

Suddenly, a screeching, high-pitched voice pierced the night. Abigail Williams stood at the top of the steps. "Evil has befallen us. The voices—you all hear them and must give heed. They are our only hope."

"Yes, them voices!" Boyd shouted over her, his weathered face filled with fear. "The eclipse, the darkening—that's when it all started! And that damn wind, whether retribution from God or the devil himself, it nearly brought my house down. Blew my cornstalks to pieces! I'll be in arrears for sure this season. And the sun gone dark? Like blowin' out a candle and leaving us in hell. And the unceasing rain? I've lost too much already, and now a monster that could tear us apart roams the woods?"

The mayor had heard enough and nodded to the sheriff, who, in turn, held up his long gun, aimed it at the sky, and pulled the trigger. The crowd silenced, and the attention shifted back to the mayor.

"I need you all to listen to me. No one mentioned a monster. We have ourselves a bear, one resembling a beast and nothing more! We've dealt with bears before, so enough of this nonsense!"

"No!" shouted Phillip Wallace, stepping into the light.

Every person in the crowd listened eagerly, wanting to hear from the victim himself, which meant the mayor had little choice but to allow him to speak.

"Wasn't no bear. It was . . ." Phillip hesitated as he searched for the words. People held their breath until he finally said, "No bear. It was twice as large as any I've seen. And no wolf, either, nor anything of this world. Fangs, claws, and eyes black as the pit of hell, it could tear you to pieces!"

Boyd pointed at Phillip and shouted, "Ya hear what he said? Who here hasn't heard the story of Cain, who murdered his brother, cursed to roam the earth forever? And now, Cain himself has come to New Harmony to do the devil's biddin', and this evil is upon us. It's a curse. Mayor, I beg you to listen. Since the eclipse, we are all cursed!"

With a hoarse voice and solemn face, the mayor said, "We all heard Mr. Kensington. No more for tonight. Go on home, everyone!"

The mayor nodded to the sheriff, who pulled Boyd from the steps and pushed him back into the crowd. All the while, Boyd hollered, "Ya gotta do somethin', Mayor! Aside from the monster, we watch our crops drownin', and I've five mouths to feed! We can't just up and leave. This month of Sundays must end!"

"I've young'uns myself!" shouted Mrs. Folsom. "When winter arrives, will there be enough? Should I be worried?"

Before the mayor could answer, Abigail screamed, "Course you should be worried! You should all be worried!" The sheriff climbed the steps and took her by the arm to escort her away, but she jerked free.

"Let her speak," ordered the mayor.

Abigail, still halfway up the steps, faced her friends and neighbors. "You hear the voices! My witness is they are not demons, as some suppose. They speak to me concerning your welfare and, as such, chose me to warn you." Many in the crowd gasped, while others dismissed her as a prevaricator, a known gossiper. She continued. "I knew of the monster, but dare I admit to having foreknowledge?" She glared at the startled faces in the crowd before continuing. "Would you have burned me at the stake? And who among you would have even believed me? But here we are—a monster in our midst."

She looked over her shoulder at the mayor and winked, which did little to assuage his growing discomfort. Abigail's attempt to appease the mob was not what he'd bargained for in allowing her to speak. Before he could dismiss her, she turned back to the crowd. "We must give ear to the voices. They are guardian spirits, not evil demons. We must do as we are told, heed their warnings. Therein lies our salvation. If still you seek a sign of their benevolence, I offer you this. Hear me now. I'll tell you what the guardian voices whisper to me: 'The seventh day draws nigh, and the mayor's words will come to pass.' So, you see, when the sun next rises, it will dispel your unbelief."

As the last words left her mouth, she smiled and peered at the mayor.

Bronson watched intently before eventually turning away and whispering to LeFevre, "I've heard enough."

They weaved their way through the crowd. Tommaso and Marco followed, leaving the bedlam behind.

The mayor's eyebrows narrowed, and a corner of his mouth twitched. He grabbed the sheriff's arm, drew him close, and whispered, "The bear attack was the perfect distraction from my promise of sunshine, but now, with Abigail reminding everyone . . . If the morning disappoints, I'll look a fool. So stay alert."

The mayor stepped forward to dismiss the crowd, but many refused to leave. "Nothing can be resolved tonight. If, as Phillip insists, there is a monster, we'll know it soon enough. Until then, hurry home—for your safety. Now go!"

The mayor and sheriff stood watching the glimmer of lanterns disappearing into the night. Once they were alone, it was the sheriff who spoke. "What do ya think, sir? You believe this nonsense? Wallace's story?" The sheriff looked intently at the mayor, unsure whether he, too, should be worried.

The mayor gave him a tormented, sideways glance. "You weren't in the room when I questioned Phillip and the boy. There are things, Weasley, things I'm just becoming acquainted with, things not of this world. I'm afraid I do believe." He turned and looked at Mount Erebus. "Go home," he said. "I'll let you know when I need you."

The mayor watched as the sheriff hurried down the steps. After watching him lock his office door and extinguish the streetlight in front of the building, the mayor listened to the sound of the sheriff's boots on the hard clay street fading as he went. Once everything was silent, a familiar sound reached the mayor's ears—the eerie cawing of a blackbird. A moment later, the bird landed on the steps next to him. The mayor froze, fearful of making any movement. It hopped close enough to peck at his shoe and stared off into the distance. Then it cocked its head, and one black eye fixed on at the mayor.

Time was running out. Tomorrow was day seven, and his thoughts had become desperate. He stared down at the bird. "I know who you are," he whispered, "and I've been waiting. Is it for your comfort that my back is against the wall? If the morning brings no sun, I will look a fool. Is that what you've intended all along? Is this for your amusement?"

Within his worried mind, he heard a song, its lyrics embedding themselves in his memory.

> *Absent an alliance, your affluence fades.*
> *With the withering fields, your world decays.*
>
> *The floodwater's coming. Act now or drown.*
> *Choose blight and doom or a jeweled crown.*
>
> *But choose you must before the last granule falls.*
> *The hourglass empties when the blackbird calls.*
>
> *Impatient are we, so don't make us wait.*
> *On your own accord, enter Erebus gate.*

The bird's inhuman black eye stared up at the mayor, then blinked not once but twice, after which the creature squabbled and cawed. It then hopped away before taking flight, circling not once but twice before disappearing in the dark, the screeching of other blackbirds sounding as it flew toward Erebus.

"Weasley!" yelled the mayor as he briskly descended the steps and chased after the sheriff, who heard him and stopped, a lantern in hand. The mayor panted as he turned the corner. A dozen yards ahead, the sheriff turned and looked back at him. The mayor hollered, "Check on me at the ranch in the morning like before. If I'm not there, head up the same trail where you last found me, like before."

"Like before," the sheriff called back.

"Yes, like before," shouted the mayor, who turned and walked to where his horse waited behind the town hall. As he turned the corner, he thought, *I mustn't forget my coat. It's going to be a cold night.*

Chapter 38

The lyrics ricocheted inside the mayor's skull. As unsettling as being summoned by strange creatures was, he knew he had little choice. It was the alliance or ruin. It had been a long, restless day, and although his back hurt and his brain was tired, he mounted Buck and headed north. Like before, Buck ascended the mountain, illuminated by the moonlight. Ahead, a pinpoint of light appeared. The mayor stared curiously as he approached. Lying in the dirt alongside the road was the lantern he'd abandoned on his first trip. And although days had passed, a flame still flickered from within as if whale oil burned forever—a demonstration of the dark powers. *I must remember to retrieve it upon my return*, he thought.

Growing more fatigued, he slumped in the saddle, the steady clomp, clomp of Buck's hooves threatening to lull him to sleep. He held the reins tight but felt his grip slacken with his consciousness. He nearly slipped off his horse and tumbled down the mountain before jolting awake and grabbing the saddle horn.

The moonlight gave the clouds a silky glow and softly illuminated the trees around him. Unfortunately, the same silvery light revealed how badly the trail had fallen into disrepair. Erosion and rockslides made parts of it nearly impassable. Up ahead, debris blocked his way, but Buck continued unabated, weaving around and over all obstacles, never looking up.

Suddenly, a wave of nausea washed over the mayor and he felt a painful thump to the chest, followed by a deafening crack. Dazed, he covered his ears and squeezed his eyes against the onslaught. He felt as if he'd been torn apart and put back together again, the pain gone as suddenly as it came. He opened his eyes to complete darkness. His heart stopped beating as time passed for what could have been an instant or eternity. He couldn't tell. Slowly, his vision and heartbeat returned. In front of him he saw a well-maintained trail, the way it was before erosion had taken its toll from years of neglect. The mayor pulled on the reins, and Buck came to a stop. The mayor waited a moment while catching his breath.

He had to tread lightly. These sisters, whatever they were, wielded the power to twist and bend time.

When Buck turned at the last switchback before the ridge, the mayor expected to see the wall of oozing, bubbling smoke; it was how he imagined the gates of hell, where unrepentant souls were cast into the underworld. But there was no such apparition, and for that he was grateful.

The old guard post was dark and full of shadows when he arrived. Crumbling under the weight of vines and beyond repair, it was just as he remembered from his youth. He peered into the rubble but saw no movement. Instead, he felt someone or something watching him. He looked up, at first seeing nothing but the dark of night, but then, out of the shadowy canopy, came the blackbirds.

They dived down and flew into what was left of one of the guard post's windows, disappearing into the void. A moment later, a flash of light shot out from the toppled ruins, leaving what appeared to be a flickering flame in the fireplace. The stones and decayed wood lying about began to shake, then came together, right in front of his eyes. A door materialized, and panes of glass suddenly filled the window frames. Stones jumped off the ground, piling on top of each other. A chimney rose high into the sky, just in time for smoke to begin bellowing from the top. Only seconds before, the door, no more than decaying pulp, had hung from broken hinges.

Next to the mayor, an old stump sprouted branches and leaves like yellow-and-green butterflies just opening their wings. He tied Buck's reins to the same low branch as before and stared at the old fort. *So this is how it must feel to meet the devil. I'll never get used to it.* His blood curdled as he slowly made his way to the door. And though it wasn't his first time here, it didn't make it any easier. He'd just stepped into the black hollow when the door slammed behind him.

Chapter 39

"Beast!" A voice inside Jonathan's head stirred him awake. "Wake now!"

His eyes flew open, and his claws shot out, poised to kill. His breath was hot and labored as he peered into the darkness of his cave. His keen eyesight scanned the void that bedeviled him. Above his head, a spider hurried up a silky thread and hid in a small crack in the rock ceiling.

He spoke to what woke him. *I know you're here, and I don't care what debt you hold over me. I only wish to see how we might settle this situation of ours.*

He could sense the wickedness in the air. It brought with it a hatred for everything, including him, and flooded him with thoughts of paranoia. He scrambled to the entrance of his cave and peered out into the night. A brilliant luminescence bathed the meadow, the dew-sprinkled holly berries and sage grass glistening under the moonlight. Hunched on all fours, he sprinted through the field and south to the gorge, pausing when the gorge opened before him, his lungs laboring with the effort. The heat pulsating from his fur hung about him in a blue mist. Hot, mucousy vapor rose from his flared nostrils. His salivary glands frothed, foam dripping from his mouth. He was angry, and he was hungry. He felt the hatred, the mindless inclination toward violence rising within him. He tried to resist, but found it difficult, so overwhelming was his fury.

The corruption of the beast grows.

He ran farther south, through the gorge and into the valley on the other side of the mountain. The faint glimmer of lights from the town appeared in the distance. He caught a scent, and his stomach growled. He weaved through poplar trees, scanning his surroundings like a predator. The lights from town grew brighter as he rounded an embankment buttressing a road that ran alongside a stream. On the other side lay a pasture, and beyond that, a house. The windows were dark, and he could make a kill undetected. He smelled the wind, inched closer, and peered over the embankment to see several cattle grazing in the moonlight. Suddenly, they sensed his presence and stared back at him. They began moving nervously, then broke into a stampede, triggering something inside him.

He sprung over the embankment and broke through the wooden fence that skirted the pasture. A heifer had abandoned her calf, an insufficient offering for his appetite. His eyes focused on the largest animal in the pasture, a bullock. The bull turned and kicked at the air, its horns thrashing about, but it was useless. The beast lunged, digging its claws into the animal's hide and sinking its teeth into its neck. The bull bucked and spun about, doing all it could to rid itself of the creature. Within minutes, however, the beast had crushed the bull's windpipe and the animal collapsed lifelessly onto the sopping-wet field. The cattle stopped fleeing and watched, sensing that the predator, now gratified, no longer posed a threat.

The beast had filled its belly, its killing instinct satiated. Jonathan looked at the lights in the town. He now felt hunger of a different kind—a hunger for human companionship. Leaving the pasture, he inched his way through the sleepy town, maneuvering through the streets and creeping in between houses, always keeping to the shadows.

From the darkness, an imposing black dog leaped at him, teeth bared. His reaction sudden and instinctual, the beast grabbed it and held it by the neck. The dog barked only once.

"Beast," came a gnarly voice. Jonathan let out a low growl, then quickly quieted. "Dog meat? That's what you care for even now that you've tasted cow?"

Jonathan pretended not to hear.

But the voices hounded him. "We say kill, and you kill not. We leave you to your devices, and look at you." The voices mocked. "Once you have human meat, nothing else will satisfy."

The taste of the bull's blood was still bitter in Jonathan's mouth. *I'm a killer, but I'm no cannibal.*

"Not a cannibal?" hissed the voices.

"You're already that. Are you not a beast? Look at yourself," said the high-pitched, sickly-sweet voice.

"And what did you just eat? A beast, no less!" said the more ancient voice.

"A cannibal eats its kind. If you fancy yourself something other than a cannibal, you must try human meat. Nothing satisfies more. Once tried, you'll never crave wild meat again."

Jonathan's anger turned to himself. *They're right. I am a beast. I kill. I want to kill.* The mere thought pressed down on him, and he released a blood-curdling roar that cracked the stillness. He tossed the carcass of what had been somebody's pet into a nearby hedge.

The beastly howl rendered in the dark of night, in the heart of the witching hour, was heard in every house in New Harmony, rousing people from their sleep. Children cried, their mothers trying to comfort them. Light from oil lanterns and candles appeared in windows, and the curious peeked from behind closed curtains.

But there was nothing to see beyond the dreary gloom that persisted even into the night hours. The beast was gone.

Almost as if on cue, the music that typically lulled the people of New Harmony to sleep each night took a dark turn. From hauntingly beautiful melodies came something altogether different, something altogether frightening. The music was more ominous and mysterious tonight, and the words in their heads brought dread.

> *Bar your doors. Open your eyes.*
> *Something's in the mist.*
> *Listen close, we warn you now,*
> *Or bones be chewed to bits.*

All your needs we provide,
No time for hesitation.
Our warning is but a courtesy.
Your fear is your salvation.

Pay attention. Let us in.
Allow yourself to fear.
Purgatory gathers strength.
Your demise draws ever near.

All your needs we provide,
No time for hesitation.
Our warning is but a courtesy,
Your fear is your salvation.

Those not woken by the howling were stirred awake by the incantation. Riveted to the voices, they longed for days filled with sunshine and the promise of a plentiful harvest. But now, their fear of a monster grew, and some prayed to the voices for deliverance.

Chapter 40

Inside the dark old fort, the mayor rubbed at the goose bumps on his arms and buttoned his coat against the bitter cold. He looked with disgust at the meager flame in the firepit. The quivering light seemed to fear the otherworldly presence as much as he did. Ghostly figures shifted in the inky blackness, just as before. And just as before, time flickered, contorting reality.

The mayor leaned against the inner wall and waited for the effect to clear. *Careful,* he thought. *No telling what harm they can inflict.*

Where only a moment before birds had flown, now, shapes in black, tattered fabric, faded and tarnished as if dug up from the earth at an ancient site, swirled about. A funnel of air stirred the scent of trash and decay. He buried his nose in his sleeve and shivered, realizing then that the chill he felt came more from conjurers of the unnatural forces than from the open windows or stone walls.

"You kept us waiting," a scratchy voice complained. "What took so long? You always keep us waiting."

"You sent for me, and I came straightaway," said the mayor curtly, knowing his voice sounded more tired and irritable than intended.

"Careful, you," warned a voice from somewhere over his left shoulder.

The mayor stumbled for a moment, and his vision blurred. "I, um, I haven't slept. Please forgive me."

Within the murky shadows of a black hood, one of the aged crones turned her head to the side. A black eye peered at him and winked, not once but twice. "Much better. So, tell us, what brings you? Figured it out, have you?"

"Your message . . . what you sent me . . . what you said you would grant me. I'm left wondering what it means."

Behind him, a voice like sandpaper scratched at his eardrums. "What would you have us grant you?"

"We must first hear it from you," said another.

Though the limp flame in the fireplace offered no warmth, sweat trickled down the mayor's forehead. "You know what I want, so why do you ask? Why must I—"

"Quiet!" snapped the more ancient of the voices. "Dare you keep us waiting again?"

"Tell us!" demanded the harsh voices. "We must hear it from you."

Struggling to regain his composure, the mayor hastily replied, "Not certain I dare ask."

He heard a whisper in his right ear and froze. "We know everything, so say it."

"All right." The mayor turned and looked at each of them as well as he could. "I'm here because our crops are failing due to lack of sun and the overabundance of rain. And now there is a report of a bear or large beast causing unrest, which could potentially cost me the election. The timing couldn't be worse. If this continues, I am sure to lose. Things have gone from manageable to impossible since that damnable eclipse and cursed wind. Perhaps a coincidence, but I must ask. Since both occurred upon your arrival, what, if anything, have you to do with all my troubles?"

To be so direct with such vile creatures bordered insanity, and he immediately regretted it. He felt a rush of icy air as a pair of obsidian-black eyes stared at him from above a crooked nose.

"Such impertinence!" the creature shrieked.

"Know you not with whom you speak? You fail to recognize opportunity, stupid human."

Having roused their anger, he felt the oppressive weight of all three sisters bear down on him, threatening to rob him of his breath. He collapsed to the ground, nearly suffocating, while their voices pounded in his ears. "Time is up. What is it you seek? Say it now!"

The room began to shift, the ground beneath him wobbling. He struggled to fill his lungs while stabilizing himself on his hands and knees.

"I, uh, I want to . . ." The mayor felt like he'd almost lost his grip on reality. Finally, the spinning in his head slowed enough for him to gather his thoughts. He yelled as loudly as his constricted lungs allowed. "I want to win the election and eradicate my enemies—anyone who would take it from me!"

Eerie voices hissed from above him. "Power is what you want, so say it."

Stripped of his inhibition, the mayor blurted, "Yes, power. That is what I came for."

As the words left his mouth, all went silent, like the world and every living thing on it had suddenly passed from existence. There was only the sound of his breathing and a feeling of relief at still being alive.

Minutes passed, and the mayor's vision began to clear. As his eyes fixed on the swirling shapes hovering above him, the withered sisters started to reveal themselves, coming into full view as he picked himself up off the ground.

"Was that so difficult? Why keep such worthy desires to yourself?"

"Worthy is right," said the mayor, brushing the dust off his pants. "I want what's rightfully mine. I've earned it. I deserve it." He felt a surge of self-satisfaction. He'd said what they wanted to hear, he meant it, and they knew it.

"And in return? What will you give us if we grant power the likes of which you desire?"

"Whatever! I'll give you whatever I can grant as mayor. So again, it is an equitable proposition. What can I do for you?"

A hiss emanated from the figures. "S-s-sustenance. We desire s-s-sustenance—an equal portion of the bounty."

"So let it be," said the mayor without hesitation. "We have an alliance."

"Not quite. There's one small detail, a contingency." The dark entities circled closer.

Sensing the deal was near completion, the mayor became more emboldened. "Tell me now. You'll find me eager to comply. Anything."

"The monster," chanted the voices. "Yes, our monster."

"The bear?" he asked, thoroughly confused. "What about it?"

"Sisters," said the more ancient figure. "He thinks it's a bear. Much like he thinks us witches."

Eerie laughter filled the space, followed by a flash of light that blinded the mayor, and a blast of heat, like a hot brand, that seared the side of his face.

And just as quickly, all returned to normal. The air chilled, the mayor's sight returned, the faint flame continued to burn in the fireplace, and the side of his face no longer burned.

"Robert. Dear, dear, Robert," they all chanted so perfectly in unison the mayor wondered if they shared the same mind.

"A bear? Oh no. No! It's no such thing," they mocked. "Not a bear but a hideous monster—our monster. The beast is in our debt and serves us, as we may soon serve you, so leave it be. If the beast dies, our alliance ends and a transfer of penitence applies. Whatever debt remains, the balance becomes yours. Understood?"

The terms of the supposed deal were turning dark, even threatening, and the mayor questioned the wisdom of doing business with the sisters.

But then he heard a soft, sensual voice behind him. He turned around to see the more ancient one assume the visage of the enticingly beautiful Aphrodite.

"Don't be troubled," she assured. "You see, we are not witches. We are whatever we desire to be, whatever we need to be, whether beautiful or terrifying. What's more? We are here to serve you."

The mayor watched in astonishment as all three took on the form of feminine beauty. Their graceful curves moved alluringly beneath white silken fabric that only moments before consisted of tired rags. He knew he had fallen under a spell, but he didn't have the strength to care. He listened gladly as the more ancient one assured him that the terms of the arrangement were to his liking.

"And as for the monster," she explained, "he is useful. You will see. The monster will serve you as he serves us. And thus he will be your monster and your responsibility. So you must make certain nothing harms him, or the consequences will be dire, for a debt will be unpaid. But never fear or worry yourself over assuming what another owes, for you shall not fail us, and, as a reward, great power is forever yours."

The voice was so soothing it slowed his anxious heart. The words *great power* echoed in his head.

"I won't. I won't fail you," he said.

Suddenly, he felt a sharp pain in his right index finger, and a drop of warm blood appeared at the tip. The mayor stared at it. His brow furrowed as his gaze moved to an apparition of ethereal beauty floating above him in the air.

"Look here," said the angelic being. A young, delicate finger reached out, pointing to a piece of parchment with ancient writing also floating in the air. "Touch the paper. Do it now."

As soon as the mayor pressed his finger to the parchment, the door swung open and a swift wind blew in. The meeting was over. He slowly made his way to the door.

"Robert," said a voice from inside. "You'll know what to do. Now, enjoy the sunshine, but never lose the darkness."

As he stepped outside, he heard the three devilish creatures giggling. It still unnerved him to know they knew his name. Their voices entered his mind as the door slammed behind him, followed by a loud crash. "Enjoy the sunshine, dear Robert. With enemies underfoot and a harvest to your credit—the future is bright."

Just before the tree withered to a stump, he hurriedly untied Buck's reins. Mounting his horse, he stared at the old post, now in ruin. Since Buck knew the way home, the mayor simply sat, rocking back and forth, contemplating what had just happened and what it could mean.

Chapter 41

Light seeped through the open shutters as the fragrant smell of morning filled the air. A warm breeze moved the white cotton curtains. Sparrows reveling in the sunshine chirped at one another from the garden beyond the yard. Martha stared at the bed to her left, the blanket neatly tucked and undisturbed.

Why hadn't Robert come to bed?

Alone in their bedroom, she slipped into her robe and walked barefoot through the house until she stopped in the hallway leading to the kitchen. Staring at the light beaming in from the window, she called, "Robert, look! You did it. The sun—it's shining!"

To her surprise, there came no answer. She went first to the dining room, but her husband wasn't there. She peered into the den, but he wasn't there either. Before looking elsewhere, she glanced out the back window above the leather couch. Robert sat on the porch swing, slowly rocking back and forth. She called more loudly. "Robert!"

He continued rocking as if he heard nothing.

Martha went out the side door and walked around to the back porch, stopping only feet away, but he appeared not to notice her.

"Robert, you're not answering me." Even with her proximity, he failed to respond. She yelled, "Robert!"

Only then did he look up at her, but even still, he said nothing.

"Are you awake? Because your eyes, they're open, so I'm assuming."

"Barely," he finally answered, "but yes."

She sat on the porch swing next to him. "Darling, the sun, look! You did it. I've been trying to tell you."

"Yes," he said. "I'd forgotten how warm it could be."

"It's wonderfully warm, and *you* did this." As she rocked back and forth, she gazed at their vast holdings bathed in sunshine. Golden fields of grain waved in the breeze. Rich green pastures stretched for miles. A freshly painted barn blazed in spectacular red and white. The white stable was so bright it hurt her eyes. It had been so long since the sun had shone she had nearly forgotten the vibrancy of their ranch. They sat in silence for almost an hour, admiring the grandeur.

Martha hesitated before breaking the silence of such sublime surroundings. "Robert? You did this. You said it would happen, and look."

She stared at him in awe, wondering how he could have known that this would happen in precisely seven days or whether he'd made the sun shine by willing it. Then she noticed his red, puffy cheeks and tired expression. His eyes were half closed, his chin nearly on his chest.

"Robert, my dear. Are you ill, and why did you not come to bed? Have you been awake all night?"

Robert swung back and forth a few more times before giving in to the conversation. "Martha?"

"Yes, darling."

"I do what I have to do, what I must do. You understand that, don't you?"

Martha stopped the swing and stared at him, confused. "Of course. I most certainly do, but why ask?"

Robert looked down at his feet, now resting flat on the freshly painted wood slats of the porch. "I do what I must," he repeated.

"What are you saying? But of course you do. You are a great man. Look at all this." She waved her hands, drawing his gaze to their spacious property. "Is this the estate of a beggar?"

"No, Martha."

"That's right. All this, everything we have acquired, is because you do the difficult things lesser men, poorer men, can't or are unwilling to do. No one handed us a damn thing. We took it. It's ours. All of it! And we've done for others as well. We've kept this filth of a town thriving, you and me."

She stopped talking and waited for a response. She didn't have to wait long.

"Martha?"

"Yes, dear."

"Remember when we first moved into the ranch house?"

"Of course I remember. We lived in the room above the stable before that. What about it?"

"Just that after father died, we moved into the house to see to Grandfather's care."

Martha nodded. "He was always bathed and fed. We saw to it."

"Yes, we did."

"What is this about, Robert?"

"You might recall the evening Grandfather asked to speak formally with me after dinner. He told me to keep our conversation to ourselves. Then, that very evening, he signed everything over. All of this. He did so but not without securing a promise."

"I assumed I'd heard all your stories, Robert. But I don't believe I've heard this one. What promise was that?"

"I promised we'd never sell. All you see out there must stay in the family, as grandfather put it—the land, the water, the cattle, all of it—our life, our blood. It must all be passed down. Without it, the Owen family is nothing, like everyone else."

"Just like everyone else in this godforsaken town," Martha agreed. At that, she took his hand in hers and squeezed it reassuringly. "We'll keep that promise."

"I'm not so certain anymore. Our son—so spiteful! After all we've done for him. Look at all this. One day this will all be his, yet he considers his birthright of no value. And he hates me, his own father. And to be honest, I'm not sure I've any love left for him. I'd sell my soul to keep Grandfather's promise, and I'm afraid I've done that. And for what?"

Martha turned to him, lifting his chin so their eyes met. "Think of Eugene no more, my love. He may come around eventually, but it doesn't matter."

"But he's our son, darling."

"I know that, Robert. But don't forget. We also have a grandson."

Chapter 42

To the east, beyond the fields of golden grain and distant rolling hills, the morning sun streamed into the valley below. The blanket of clouds that once obstructed the sun's life-giving energy dissipated and with it, the heavy gloom that hung over New Harmony. The continual downpour ended, and living things drank in the sun's rays. Even the puddles that drowned crops and made life seem unbearable began evaporating, and not a day too soon.

Amelia Taylor stood on the back porch of her home on the outskirts north of town. She stared into the pasture, a hand shading her eyes from the sun. Her bright-yellow summer dress moved in the gentle breeze on what should have been a carefree day, but it wasn't to be. To the south, someone approached on horseback, someone she expected.

Vernon Davis rode straight to the house and greeted her warmly. "Good morning."

"Certainly should have been," said Amelia, fidgeting nervously as he dismounted and wrapped the reins around the fence post. "We appreciate your coming."

"My pleasure, ma'am."

"Mr. Davis, pardon my asking, but did your wife sleep well last night?"

"I'm afraid not. We got little more than a wink between us."

"So you heard it, did you?"

"We did."

"Well, perhaps you still fared better," Amelia said. "My husband is in the north pasture. I see you arrived alone."

"Mr. LeFevre will be along shortly."

She turned and looked over her shoulder, out into the open field. Pointing, she said, "Henry's out there."

"I see 'im," said Vernon. He tucked his pant legs into his boots. "Try not to worry, Mrs. Taylor. Whatever tomorrow brings, we can't help that, but today? It's bright and sunny."

She brushed back her hair and nodded. "It's been some time since we've seen the sun. After such a terror last night, it's a welcome relief."

"Yes, ma'am. Always somethin' to be grateful for. Now, would you excuse me? Don't want to keep Henry waiting."

"No. Please don't. Henry's anxious as it is."

Just then, Old Man Taylor spotted Vernon and waved for him to come and see. The ground was still soggy, and Vernon's boots sank to his ankles as he walked through the pasture to where Henry Taylor stood, hands on his hips, puzzling over the carcass of his prized bull.

"I did as you requested. LeFevre will be here shortly," said Vernon. He looked down at the bloody mess. "You weren't exaggerating, were you?" He squatted for a closer look. The throat was missing, and entrails spilled from the abdominal cavity onto the ground. Large chunks of meat were also missing, as were the ribs. The rest of what was once Henry's prized bull remained untouched except for the buzzing flies. Cows watched without eating, bunched against the fence as if fearing another attack.

"Look here," said Henry. He leaned down and pointed to the lacerations above the rib cage. Four bloodred slashes cut deep into the black, hairy hide, each evenly spaced and running parallel.

"Claw marks? That what that is?"

Henry nodded. "That's my guess." He placed a hand over the wound, spreading his fingers as wide as possible, trying to put one finger over each slash, but his hand was far too small to reach. "What sort of predator can do this?"

"None I'm familiar with," said Vernon.

Henry scratched his head and looked away when he noticed Amelia standing near the back of their house with someone beside her. "Appears LeFevre's arrived."

Vernon recognized LeFevre in his wrinkled, baggy, gray wool pants and plain cotton shirt. "Why LeFevre and not the sheriff? I would have fetched either."

"Mr. LeFevre's the best hunter in town," said Henry. He whistled and shouted, "Over here!"

The Frenchman waved back. A moment later, he headed their way, walking through the muddy field, not bothering to roll up his pant legs. To their surprise, he didn't take a direct route. Instead, he crisscrossed the field and circled the kill sight, stopping once to pick up a gnawed rib bone. He turned it in his fingers, carefully studying it before tossing it aside and heading toward them. As he approached, he looked them up and down as if they were part of the puzzle, then turned his attention to the heap of bloody guts at their feet.

"Thank you for comin'," said Henry.

LeFevre nodded and looked north, over the horizon. "Noticed ya got bags under your eyes, both of ya. Why?"

Henry slipped his hands into his pockets and tilted his head toward his wife, still standing on the back porch, staring at them. "Wife kept me up all night sayin' she heard howling. My hearin' is not so good, but I heard those damnable voices in my head tellin' me to bar my doors. I heard 'em, all right. Then this mornin', I find this."

They each listened to the buzz of flies as they stared at the slaughtered animal until LeFevre nudged Vernon. "What about you? What's your excuse?"

"No different. Wife heard the same, but it didn't matter. The damnable voices wouldn't let me sleep for nothin'."

LeFevre grinned. "I slept like a baby." Then, turning back to the kill, he said, "Now, what have we got here?"

"Predator," said Henry, wiping the sweat from his forehead with his sleeve. "I forgot how hot the sun can be."

Vernon groaned. "I'm sweating like a pig."

"Pigs don't sweat," said LeFevre as he examined the length of the lacerations, then ran his finger along the inside of the cuts, measuring the depth. "Hmm. Quite the predator."

"Henry and I figure it wasn't no bear," said Vernon. "Pack of wolves maybe?"

LeFevre shook his head. "No."

He took hold of a hind leg and said, "Let's turn 'im over."

Henry and Vernon took hold of another leg and rolled the animal onto its left side.

LeFevre examined the animal. "There," he said, pointing to the jugular. "Never mind the claw marks. Look at the wound at the throat. That's the death blow."

"I see," said Vernon. "But why not wolves, the more likely of predators?"

LeFevre didn't bother looking up when he answered. "The kill ain't picked clean."

"Sounds reasonable. But if not wolves, then—"

"It doesn't matter," said Henry quickly. "Any wild animal and my losses are no different."

"No," said LeFevre.

"No, what, Mr. LeFevre?"

"Your losses are the same, we agree. But it was no wild animal."

"What? Tell me you don't suspect someone from town of doing this?"

"No, Henry."

"Then who, or what?"

Before Henry could question him further and satisfy his curiosity, LeFevre asked, "Ya gonna report this, tell the sheriff?"

Henry shuddered at the thought. "I'd rather not."

"Why?" asked Vernon.

"I've said enough and dare not say more."

A wry smile crossed LeFevre's face. "I suppose I ain't alone in my disdain for the man."

"I also have my distrust," admitted Vernon, "but I'm curious. Do you consider him dangerous? Do I hear fear in your voice?"

"Perhaps," Henry nervously admitted. Then, looking to either side and assuring himself they were alone, he whispered, "Wife and I were friends of the Stewarts. Theo and I shared harvesting chores."

Vernon interrupted. "Henry, you're whisperin', and I can't hear. We're in the middle of a pasture. There's no one to hear you other than Mr. LeFevre and me, and, certainly, you can trust us not to say a word."

Henry nodded. "What I was saying is that Theo Stewart and I were friends. Before they left town in such a hurry, that is. But you must swear never to speak further of this next part."

"We already promised," said Vernon.

"Well then," he continued, his voice still just above a whisper. "Before the Stewarts went missin', Theo tells me he knows things . . . about the mayor, and not just speculation. I believe he saw something he wasn't supposed to."

"What?" asked LeFevre.

Henry brushed his hand through the air to chase off a fly, then shrugged. "Wouldn't say, only that it was for my own good that I didn't know. He always complained the sheriff never let up, always pokin' at him, tryin' to see what he knew. Said he pretended, played *ignorant*, but when his boy got in a scuffle with the mayor's grandson, Theo feared for his life and that of his wife and boy."

"Explains why they skipped town," said Vernon. "Who can blame 'em?"

"Ain't nobody skippin' town," said LeFevre. "They've gone missing. What? Ya didn't know that?"

"Stands to reason," said Henry. "I never heard from Theo after they were gone, no correspondence. Nothing! But there isn't a thing nobody can do about it. Mayor's got half the town in his pocket and the other half afraid to open their mouths."

"Can't go to the town council either," said Vernon. "You'd have to deal with Mrs. Owen. The entire council has nose rings by which she pulls 'em along. They aren't gonna do nothin', not without her sayin' so."

"There's one unafraid, though, one willin' to do something about it. Don't forget him," said LeFevre.

"Your neighbor, Mr. Parrish, the teacher?" asked Henry.

Vernon said, "Of course. Who else? The town hall meeting—never seen anything like it."

LeFevre said, "We gotta vote for 'im is what we gotta do."

"I intend to," said Vernon. "But my wife may insist I vote otherwise."

LeFevre became thoroughly annoyed. "Why? Can you do no more than complain?"

Vernon looked up at the azure sky, not a cloud in sight. "Wife woke this morning, damn voices all night givin' her the shakes, and she sees the sun shining, just like the mayor promised. She insists we do as the mayor says, or else."

Henry quickly agreed. "First thing Amelia says this mornin'—'Look, the mayor made the sun shine.'"

LeFevre was incensed. "May I remind you, gentlemen, the mayor is nothin' more than a man and crooked as a goat's horn. Now, we've got ourselves a chance at a real election."

"No need remindin' me, Mr. LeFevre," said Henry. "I pay 'im a lease for my land. Mayor pats my back and tells me how grateful I should be. He could charge me more, he says, like I'm stealin' from him, more like he's doin' me a favor."

Vernon nodded at every word. "My situation is no different," he said. "If he suspected I support your neighbor, the mayor could pull my land out from under me."

"I wish it weren't so," said Henry, "but nobody's beating the mayor and gettin' away with it. Not the Stewarts, not even the teacher. Nobody."

"Now, you listen here," said LeFevre. "Are you both familiar with the guillotine?" Henry and Vernon both nodded. "Well then, women ain't the only ones to wet themselves when escorted to the device. Men suffer the same public embarrassment. Nobody chooses to face danger. Now, Mr. Parrish is willin' to lay his neck out, so what are ya willing to sacrifice to end this tyranny?"

"I suppose you're right," said Henry Taylor. "I'll vote for your neighbor, but I ain't tellin' nobody, not even my wife."

"I intend on doin' the same," said Vernon.

LeFevre grinned. "I suspect ya ain't alone, gentlemen. Mr. Parrish will win, you'll see. The mayor only wins if he intimidates us, and we can't allow that."

"No," they agreed.

With nothing further to be said, LeFevre prepared to leave. "Nothing more to do here."

"Wait, Mr. LeFevre," said Henry. "I sense there's something you're not telling us."

LeFevre shrugged. "Well, perhaps. Suppose we just gotta wait and see."

There was silence as they stared at the carcass. Then, as they turned to leave, Henry asked LeFevre one last question. "You said it wasn't a wild animal. What makes you say that?"

"Animals scatter bones, leaving nothing," he said. He peered around the kill site. Whatever did this, it took its meal over there." He pointed at an indentation in the grass. "It sat there and ate, left a large pile of rib bones, a femur, vertebrae, and whatever else *stacked neatly.*"

Shocked, the other two men stared in disbelief. "If not an animal, then what?" asked Vernon.

"Exactly," said LeFevre.

"Could it be the Wallace monster?"

"Don't know, Vern. S'pose that's why we'll have to wait and see."

Chapter 43

Christian felt the warmth as the early morning chill surrendered to the radiant beams of sunlight shooting over the eastern horizon. The streets were mostly empty except for the occasional person hurrying along. Before entering the post office, he peered through the window to see if Walter was in. All was clear. He fumbled in his pocket for the large brass key that fit the front door. If he hurried, he could have the ballots sorted before Walter arrived. Once inside, he set to work, hoping Warren would bring packages for him to deliver that afternoon. After all, Emily's aunt Marjorie had invited his family for supper this evening. She insisted on them dining together while discussing preparations for the wedding celebration. The sunlight beaming through the window brightened Christian's mood.

After placing a ballot in each post box, he recalled the growing pile of unclaimed letters addressed to the Stewarts in the drawer, not sure what to do with them. Finally, he opened the drawer and added a ballot to the pile.

If you're back in time, here's one for you.

Walter intended to forward their mail once notified of a forwarding address, but no such address arrived.

Only minutes before opening time, through the window, Christian saw Walter crossing the street. He quickly unlocked the door and let him in with a cheerful greeting. "Good morning, sir, a wonderful sunny morning. There won't be tracks of mud to sweep all day. That's a good thing, right?"

Walter lumbered in, dragging his feet. In the middle of a yawn, he asked, "How long have you been here?"

"Early, sir. I promised to make up time. And anyway, the mayor entrusted me with the ballots for the election. He wanted them ready this morning. I have them sorted. They're all done, though I only just started on Warren's delivery from yesterday. But it won't take long."

Walter's voice was hoarse. "That's good," he said. "Please see to it." He lifted the hinged section of the counter and walked through. "I'll be in my office."

"Sir, are you feeling well?"

"As much as anyone," he mumbled.

"Huh?"

Walter turned to face him. "I take it you didn't hear it last night."

"Hear what?"

"Dear boy. All Harmony is talking about it. You're certain you heard nothing?"

"What was I supposed to hear?"

"The howl, or roar, or whatever it was."

"I might have," Christian answered thinly.

"Huh. You might have? What about the voices, the singing of doom and despair? You hear that?"

"Yeah? I suppose," answered Christian. "May I ask, sir, what this is about?"

Walter let out a deep sigh. "Last night," he said, "there was a howl, but it wasn't a coyote, wolf, or anything else around here. It was loud—loud enough everyone heard it. Everyone! Terrifying!" Walter's voice sounded anxious as well as weak and tired. He pressed the palms of his hands to his forehead.

Christian stared nervously at his employer. "What do you suppose it was?"

"I've no way of knowing. What's worse—the voices, they warned of a monster." Walter suddenly leaned against the wall. "I'm dizzy. I need to sit." Without another word, he retreated to his office.

In the silence, Christian peered through the front window at those passing by. He expected them to be happy with the sun shining so brightly. Instead, he saw fear and worry in their faces. He called back to Mr. Buchanan. "Sir, I hate to bother you, but may I ask something?"

From his office, Walter answered, "What is it?"

"Could it be that Mr. Wallace told the truth? Is there really a monster?"

"I don't know, son. But whatever you do, don't be out past dark or alone, at least not now, not for any reason."

Chapter 44

Someone knocked at the front door. "I'm coming!" Bronson called as he dried his hands and left the kitchen. Coot rushed past him, barking as he went. Bronson cracked open the door to see LeFevre standing on his porch, his shoes caked with mud. Bronson squinted as the sunlight streamed in. "I keep telling you, just come in so I don't think it's the sheriff come to arrest me."

LeFevre grinned. "Yeah, you mentioned it. Why else do ya think I bang on your door?"

"Figures," said Bronson. "You're a genuine reprobate, LeFev. Don't just stand there. Come in!"

"I'm all muddy. I oughta stay out here."

"Lose your shoes and come inside or just leave them on. I don't care. I own a broom."

Leaving his shoes on, LeFevre clomped into the house, following Bronson into the parlor, clumps of mud trailing behind him. "Good thing ya own a broom," he said.

Coot curled up on a Hudson Bay blanket with red, indigo, green, and yellow stripes. It was thrown over the plush couch with the high-arched back. The blanket was a gift from LeFevre, a remnant of his previous life hunting and trapping. Bronson pushed his dog off the couch and onto the floor, allowing them to sit.

Preferring other seating arrangements, LeFevre dragged a chair in from the kitchen. Once settled, the two men stared at each other, LeFevre still grinning.

"What's with the mud, LeFev? Been in a fight? Looks like you lost."

LeFevre stood and walked to the window. "Never lost a fight. Lost a tooth. Never a fight." He pulled back the curtains, and the colors in the parlor turned vibrant. "Too dark in here. Why ya keepin' the sun out? Have ya noticed the sun's finally doin' what it was meant to do?"

"Yep, mayor's orders, huh?" said Bronson. "Seven days. How the hell did he know?"

"In league with the devil, but it don't mean ya can't beat him. People out there are gonna vote for ya. You'll see."

Bronson rolled his eyes and shook his head. "The man tells the sun what to do and when. We can't all win our fights, LeFev. This fight I'm certain to lose."

"That's your tired brain talkin'. Up all night, weren't ya?"

Bronson nodded. "What about it?"

"So ya heard. Not the voices but that other thing?"

"Yeah, I heard. Phillip Wallace's story seems more likely now."

"Perhaps," said LeFevre. "It's what I come to tell ya."

"And that is?"

After a brief lull in the conversation, LeFevre said, "I stopped by Old Man Taylor's. It appears Wallace's monster killed his breeder, assuming that's what did it. Unlike any kill I ever seen."

"You certain?" asked Bronson.

"Saw it myself."

"His bull?"

"Yeah, his breeder."

Still lost in disbelief, Bronson heard tapping on the wood floor as Coot strolled into the parlor and jumped back onto the couch. He snuggled up to Bronson, tail wagging and ears flopped down. "Whatever is responsible, so long as it attacks only cattle, no one gets hurt."

LeFevre's eyes narrowed. "And what about Phillip and the boy? They was attacked. People say they're lucky to be alive. But you watch. The mayor's gonna use this to his advantage. That's what I come to tell ya."

"Use what, the monster? I could argue for it being a disadvantage."

"Either way, he'll use it. Every cheater I ever knew used everythin' to their advantage. You ever play poker?"

Bronson shrugged. "I can't help but agree. The mayor is certainly that—a cheat. What if it was a mistake, my running for mayor?"

That only irritated LeFevre. "Too late now, but ya haven't lost yet."

"Yet!" agreed Bronson. Coot yawned as Bronson scratched him behind the ears. "And after he defeats me, he won't just stop there, not until he destroys me. Perhaps I was a bit impulsive thinking I could change things."

"Why ya sayin' all this? Givin' up without so much as a fight? Don't tell me you're not the man I thought you were."

"LeFev," Bronson pointed at the window, "you see that? The light beaming in? The mayor told everyone the sun would shine. He believes himself a god, and now, how many others believe him? Besides, the sun shining may save the town from hunger. So admit it. There will likely be a Mayor Owen in this town henceforth and forever."

"What?" LeFevre protested. "He's not so powerful as that. And if he is, more likely he dimmed the sun in the first place. Besides, there are things worth fightin' for. And I swear to you right here, right now, the mayor and the sheriff must go. It's a matter of how we make it happen."

Bronson stopped petting Coot and looked hard at LeFevre. "Now I'm worried. What exactly are you suggesting?"

"He's the devil, and you know it," LeFevre said unflinchingly. "And he's smart as the devil. That's how he got his fingers in everyone's pockets and droppin' coins in the right hands. He knows what he's doin'. He won't face justice unless . . ."

"Unless what?"

"Unless we do somethin'."

Bronson shook his head and looked down at Coot, now asleep beside him. "I've done all I can, and it may cost me my life. Even so, people don't bother changing things they can ignore. Can't fight human nature."

"Ya don't know that," said LeFevre. "The Good Book says it: Knowin' the truth will set ya free."

Bronson frowned. "And there lies the problem. They'll never recognize the truth, not if they've been fed on lies."

Chapter 45

With the mail sorted and the floor swept, Christian sat at the counter, peering out the front window. Outside, he saw the sheriff heading his way on his black horse. His hat cast a hard shadow across his angular face, leaving only his thin lips bathed in the warm sunlight. His horse slowed as he pulled back on the reins. With his other hand, he held the reins of another horse, a painted horse that trotted behind him. "Mr. Buchanan, sheriff's coming!"

Walter approached the counter and made himself look busy as he watched the gaunt figure loop his horse's reins around the hitching post. It was always a bit discomforting to see the sheriff. "Get on back," he told Christian quietly, so quietly Christian didn't hear.

"What, sir?"

Before Walter could tell him again, the door opened, tapping the bell that hung above it. "Morning, Sheriff." The sheriff only stared. Walter promptly turned to Christian. "Go see if the sheriff's got any mail." Christian quickly slid off his stool and headed to the back.

Fond of making others nervous, the sheriff watched as the two scrambled. "Didn't come for my mail."

Christian glanced at the sheriff after noting that the box was empty. It was a rarity that a letter ever arrived for the man.

Walter immediately stopped what he was doing. "Then what can I do for you?"

"Not you, him." The sheriff pointed at Christian.

Walter's brows rose. "Christian?"

"You have another employee here?" The sheriff looked about, seeing only Christian.

"No," said Walter. "What I mean to say is, is there any trouble, Sheriff? Why do you need Christian?"

That only seemed to irritate the sheriff. "What ya askin' for? If I say I need him, then I need him."

"Well, I don't know. Isn't there anyone else you could ask?"

The sheriff stepped within a foot of Walter. "You gotta problem, Postman?"

Walter took a step back. "I don't see how it's unreasonable for me to ask."

"Unreasonable or not, what does it matter to you?" The sheriff's beady eyes bore down on the postmaster.

Walter stuttered. "W-well, it would be helpful to know how long you'll keep him."

The sheriff shrugged. "Rest of the day?"

"And you need Christian, only him?"

The sheriff nodded. "Yeah. Him."

Nobody moved until, finally, the sheriff stepped back. "I don't have to tell you nothin', but I'll tell you anyway. The mayor left town this morning to ask the governor for help, and he asked me to investigate Wallace's story. Told me to take Shear's boy to keep me company." The sheriff leaned over and looked in the back at Christian. "You're comin' with me," he said, leaving no question to his authority.

"Me?"

"You're Shear's boy, ain't ya?"

"My pa, ya."

"Well then, yeah."

Walter shrugged and looked back at Christian. "Perhaps you made an impression on the mayor the other day."

The sheriff nodded. "He did. Mayor said to mention something about working at the bank."

"He said that?" asked Christian.

"In so many words."

"What bank?" asked Walter.

The sheriff sighed. "I ain't got all day." The tension in the air was palpable. "Get your things."

Christian slung his sweater over his shoulder and tucked an apple from his lunch in his pocket while Walter mustered his courage and asked, "Can you assure me he won't be in any danger? The woods have become dangerous as of late."

"He's a grown man, Mr. Postman, if ya hadn't noticed, and all your talk is scarin' 'im."

"I'm not scared, sir. I just need to know if I'll be late for supper. I'm recently engaged, and our families will share a meal tonight, and I promised I wouldn't be late."

"The longer we stand here fussin', the longer it's gonna take," said the sheriff.

"Mr. Buchanan, would you please let my family and the Hampshires know I might be delayed? And please, no mention of a monster."

"Of course, I'll let them know, son." With eyes downcast, Walter put his hand on Christian's shoulder as he walked past.

Christian looked back with a half grin as he followed the sheriff out the door. The bell rang as the door shut, and Walter found himself alone in the quiet of the post office.

The sheriff pointed at the spare horse tied to the hitch. "Let's get a move on. I don't intend on bein' out past dark."

They headed north, down Main Street, folks turning to stare as they passed. A woman called for her young children and hurried them into the house. At the edge of town, the sheriff stopped and waited for Christian to catch up. The horse he rode moved about nervously. It kept trying to turn around and head back to town.

"You're makin' her nervous," said the sheriff, pointing his chin at Christian's horse. "You calm down, and so will she."

Christian steadied the horse, patting her on the neck. "Easy, girl. Easy, girl."

They rode past pastures and fields of corn, barley, and wheat until the road climbed through the cedar trees just before the gorge. The sheriff stopped and waited for Christian to ride up alongside him. "We're not goin' so far as where the Wallaces got attacked, but keep your eyes open."

Christian nodded.

The sheriff pulled the reins to one side and turned his horse. "Follow me."

Christian tugged at the reins and clucked his tongue, his horse following the sheriff's as they approached the gorge. A cold breeze blew as they drew closer. He saw the shadow of Mount Erebus up ahead. It would be a welcome relief as the hot sun descended into the western sky. Christian threaded his arms through his sweater and pulled it tight around him. In front of him, the sheriff rocked back and forth with the rhythm of his horse, his head never turning, whereas Christian kept a close eye on the trees and bushes along the road, looking for movement and listening for anything out of place. Though he heard and saw nothing, the farther they traveled, the more worry built in the pit of his stomach. There was a monster, of that he felt sure. Worse, he was headed straight for it, unarmed and unprepared.

Chapter 46

Monday morning saw Constance Madison sitting on the steps of the New Harmony School, wondering why she had taken a teaching position so far from home. Young and with an insatiable urge to see more than her hometown, it was no wonder Mrs. Owen so quickly convinced her to accept the position. Although she had high expectations for her new life, nearly the moment she arrived, she began doubting her decision to leave her home in Bloomington.

Her long, dusty-blonde hair reached the swell of her back when let down, but she elected to keep it pinned up or tucked tight in her bonnet. Her figure was that of a schoolgirl with a modest waist. She wore a pale, rouge-colored dress over white cotton pantaloons trimmed with a subtle strand of thin lace below the knees. Having arrived only days earlier, Mrs. Owen had already given her the assignment to ring the morning bell, one ring and no more, saying that doing so reinforced the need for punctuality. But the teachers soon learned it was her way of reinforcing her role as boss.

As Constance sat clicking the heels of her boots, she wondered, *What was I thinking? Was it a longing for something new that brought me here, or leaving the past behind? And now I fear I may have lost my mind. It's never good to hear voices that are not your own. Why am I here?*

She needn't have wondered for long. She knew very well the answer. Now, it was only a matter of resolve. She'd chosen to come to this place where everything—like the gray stone church across from the school and the businesses along the Main Street void of any fancy lettering in the windows—appeared strange to her now. But the thing

Constance found most unnerving was the unfamiliar faces and curious looks she got. Indeed, whatever charm there was in New Harmony escaped her but for the lavish Owen ranch. Mrs. Owen presently afforded her lodging in a room above the stable, an arrangement the woman stressed would be temporary. Constance would need to find an accommodation in town as quickly as possible. Though the ranch was extravagant by her standards, there was little kindness. Even the help seemed cold and unfriendly.

To make matters worse, Constance sensed she had either lost her mental faculties or the town was cursed. Her first night, she'd been awakened by voices, not in her room or beyond the walls but in her head, warning of impending danger—of a monster, no less. Her heart had raced as she soaked her pillow with tears, drowning in a toxic mixture of fear and remorse. It was all she could do to keep her wits about her.

Constance looked down, still clicking her heels, a nervous twitch made worse by her strange surroundings. Forcing herself to still her feet, she took a deep breath and held it until her heartbeat slowed and her mind calmed. Then came the children's voices in the distance, and her nervousness returned. She stood and straightened her bodice as several students arrived. They didn't approach her. Instead, they stood about the schoolyard, staring at her while whispering into each other's ears.

Just before the appointed hour for classes to begin, women, whom she assumed were teachers, started walking past her. The first, an older woman, matter-of-factly said, "Good morning, Ms. Madison," and nothing more. At least she knew her name.

A younger woman, also someone she assumed to be a teacher, moved past with only a curt "Morning."

Yet another young woman, obviously a teacher more Constance's age, smiled and said, "Lovely morning, isn't it?" She also quickly disappeared into the school, but at least she'd smiled.

Unprepared for the indifference, tears burned in her eyes. For a moment, she felt homesick, a feeling that came as a complete surprise. Constance had a good reason for leaving home. But now she wondered if finding a new life away from Bloomington was realistic. When the clock marked the hour, she grabbed the rope and pulled, maybe too hard, as the bell rang twice. For a moment, she feared Mrs. Owen had heard her break the first rule—ring the bell only once!

As soon as the bell sounded, children poured into the schoolyard from all directions. As they walked past, the few who risked looking at her did so out of the corner of their eyes, their faces drawn and serious. Even the mothers bringing their children seemed worried, if not scared. Gathering her things, she followed them through the front door.

Once inside, the older woman who had walked past her minutes earlier introduced herself.

"Ms. Madison, I'm Ms. Woolhauser. Would you allow me to show you to your classroom?"

"I would very much appreciate it, Ms. Woolhauser."

"Think nothing of it. And please excuse my frankness. Times are dire, and people are frightened. Now, allow me . . ."

Ms. Woolhauser started to walk away when Constance stopped her. "Ms. Woolhauser?"

Ms. Woolhauser paused and looked over her shoulder. "Yes?"

"What is everyone so afraid of?"

"In truth, several things."

"Is a monster one of them?"

Ms. Woolhauser lowered her gaze and nodded. "Yes. Now, if you'll follow me."

There was little time for conversation as they arrived at her assigned room, the one vacated by the latest headmaster.

"You'll do fine," Ms. Woolhauser assured her, promptly excusing herself and leaving Constance alone at the door. Peeking inside the classroom, she saw the tired faces of children all staring at her.

"Good morning. My name is Ms. Madison," she said as she entered. "That's what you may call me, Ms. Madison. Any questions?"

No one raised their hand as they stared, seeming confused and disoriented.

Well, she thought, *this is going to be interesting.*

And then it suddenly occurred to her. *Perhaps I'm not alone in hearing voices and losing my mind. This place is cursed. That's what it is—cursed. I shouldn't be here!*

☾

The Friday-afternoon sun beamed into the main hall through the transom windows above the classroom doors. Emily waited for Christian to come and walk her home as usual, but he never arrived, and now the hallway stood empty. All was silent, and she assumed she was alone in the building. She was picking up several papers from the scuffed wooden floor when she heard a noise and stopped. Now keenly aware that she wasn't alone, she waited until she heard it again. Careful not to make a noise, she moved down the hallway and hesitated near what had once been Bronson's room. The classroom now belonged to the new teacher. Her door was shut but for the transom window, which was tilted open. From it, Emily heard the sound again. This time, it was unmistakable—whimpering.

I haven't time for this, thought Emily. *I promised Auntie I'd come right after school and help prepare the meal for Christian's family. I've waited far too long as it is.*

Emily turned, intending to walk away, but guilt arrested her steps. She stopped midstride, closed her eyes, and turned around.

I'm better than this.

She heard sobbing and felt the weight of responsibility. Returning to the closed door, she reached for the doorknob, paused, and then tapped on the door.

In a little more than a whisper, she called, "Ms. Madison, are you in there?"

Among the sniffles, she heard a meek voice answer, "I'm fine," and then nothing more.

"It's Ms. Hampshire. I assumed the school was empty and was about to lock the door. Are you all right?"

When Emily didn't hear a response, she persisted. "May I please come in?" Emily slowly turned the knob and peeked into the room. Sitting hunched over at her desk, Constance quickly looked away to hide her swollen eyes.

"Ms. Madison?" Emily stepped into the classroom, closing the door behind her and waiting until Constance looked up. Emily's heart ached as she watched Constance try to compose herself.

At that moment, it didn't matter to Emily if Mrs. Owen already recruited her to keep an eye on them.

Mrs. Owen recruited all of us, including me, she realized. *But, of course, none of this is the new teacher's fault. All we've done is confirm we are as rotten as Mrs. Owen told her we'd be.* Perhaps that was Mrs. Owen's intention, dividing them and thus gaining an ally in Ms. Madison.

Emily gently touched Constance's shoulder. "Please forgive my ill manners. I sincerely apologize. I've meant to extend my friendship," she said, her tone soft and conciliatory. "We need to talk, you and I. You see, there are things you couldn't possibly understand. I certainly wouldn't expect you to. But they are not your fault. None of this is your fault. But I believe everything will become clear over time. More importantly, you'll be embraced once everyone understands each other. You'll see. In the meantime, please be patient with us."

As she spoke, Emily noticed the late-afternoon sun casting the shadows of the desks and chairs on the far wall. "It's getting late. I'd make time now, but I truly can't. You see, I'm expected at home. I've recently become engaged, and his family dines with us this evening.

Again, my apologies. I do ask your forgiveness. You and I are going to be close friends, I'm sure of it."

Constance nodded. "All right," she said meekly. Emily leaned over and hugged her. Then, for the first time, they saw each other through watery eyes. "I desperately need a friend," said Constance. She withdrew a handkerchief from her vest pocket and wiped her eyes. Emily took her hands in hers, and they shared a quiet moment. "I won't keep you any further," said Constance. "Moreover, I congratulate you on your engagement."

"Oh, thank you, Ms. Madison. May I call you Constance?"

"Yes, please. Ms. Madison is far too formal."

"All right, then, and you can call me Emily, or Emmy, as do my friends. I do look forward to our talk later. Now, may I ask a favor?"

"Anything," said Constance.

"Would you see to securing the building? I'm running late and expected at the house any minute."

Chapter 17

Though the hour was late and dusk fast approached, it remained bright outside, even hot. Emily tipped her bonnet back, shading her eyes as sweat dampened her underclothes. As she turned the corner, she noticed smoke coming from the chimney, which could mean only one thing: Marjorie had started preparations without her. On the porch, an empty bucket waited to be filled, a cotton towel neatly folded inside the bucket. Emily pumped the water, filled the pail, and hefted it into the house.

Upon entering, she heard Marjorie bustling about the kitchen, unaware it was Emily who came in. "Albert? Bring in the water? I left you a towel."

"Auntie, I've got it right here." Emily set it on the kitchen floor.

"Oh, Emmy, thank goodness you're home. Be a dear and peel the potatoes."

Just then, with the assistance of Cormac Folsom, Barbara's nephew, Albert came in through the back door with an extra dining table in preparation for their dinner guests. There was a pleasant odor of Irish stew, lamb boiling in a cast-iron oven, and Aunt Marjorie chopping onions and cabbage.

Emily saw the onions, carrots, and parsley chopped and ready to go into the pot of boiling water. She threw on an apron, filled the washbowl with water, and rinsed her hands.

"The paring knife is in the top drawer," said Marjorie, pointing to a bucket half full of russet potatoes by the back door. "No time for bein' dreamy. Get buzzin'."

"What can I do?" asked Albert.

"In our room, dear—the bottom shelf. Get the extra tablecloth."

"Thank you, Cormac," said Albert as Cormac excused himself. Albert disappeared into the bedroom.

Emily could tell her aunt felt giddy, but not as much as Emily. Tonight, the topic would be the wedding, and plans would be made for the beginnings of her life with Christian. It was to be a magnificent evening, and Emily stared at the clock, willing it to move faster.

Chapter 18

The sheriff and Christian continued north, following the road along the stream that snaked toward the gorge. The sheriff rode stiffly in front of him, rarely looking back. Christian stared at the sheriff's blue-striped cotton shirt as it waved in the warm breeze. The rounded shadow of his wide-brimmed hat lay heavy on his back. The effect hypnotized Christian until they entered the gorge and the shadow disappeared.

No sooner had the canyon closed in around them when the sheriff's horse stopped, Christian's horse following suit.

Without turning around, the sheriff called back, "Come alongside here, boy."

Christian quickly rode up next to the sheriff, waiting for the lawman to speak. The spotted horse on which Christian sat brayed and swung its head side to side before relaxing, leaving only the sound of buzzing insects and the bubbling stream.

Finally, the sheriff asked, "Do ya believe in monsters? Do ya, boy?"

"If I saw one, sir, I would. But I'd rather not see one."

"No one wants to see no monster, boy, but it's what we come for—to see one. That happens, we may be hightailin' pretty quick."

"Fine with me," said Christian.

"All right. Stay close. Stay alert. Holler if you see anything."

Christian nodded, and they continued making their way through the gorge.

A chill radiated from the rock on either side of them, a welcome relief from the valley's heat. Lush green vegetation followed the stream to their right. To their left, on the other side of the road, rock walls towered above them. The gorge twisted and turned, carved over eons by the gentle stream, the melody of the water rushing over river rocks bringing up happy memories for Christian. Here, he and Marco passed the time fishing after church.

So familiar was the gorge that Christian knew every bend in the road, every boulder large enough to sit on as one waited for a fish to swallow the bait. It had been a place of refuge, of safety, but not now. Even the evening light that filtered into the canyon felt unsafe. His eyes darted about, focusing on the shapes and shadows in the bushes. The farther they traveled into the mountain, the more nervous he became. With each mile, he became more concerned with the time.

If we go any farther, I'm certain to be late for supper, and for what, to see a monster? This makes no sense! How much farther did the sheriff intend to go? Even if they turned around now, they'd be lucky to arrive home before nightfall. And if there was a monster, he'd rather not encounter it in the dark.

Besides, he had family waiting. He couldn't be late!

As he contemplated how to express his need to return home without upsetting the sheriff, Christian saw something unexpected. Ahead, Mayor Owen sat atop a small boulder near the river's edge, his arms resting on his ample belly. Even more bizarre was that he seemed unsurprised to see them. Why would the sheriff tell Mr. Buchanan the mayor went to the capital if he knew they would meet here?

Buck, the mayor's horse, pulled up tufts of grass alongside the water. The mayor stood as they approached. There were no greetings, only hard stares.

"Got him," said the sheriff as he stopped and dismounted. Christian stayed on his horse, hoping that at least now they would turn around and head back.

"Yes, I see," said the mayor.

"Been waitin' long?"

"Long enough to want this over."

Christian looked at both men suspiciously. What was this? He felt an urge to ride away, back to town.

When the mayor noticed, he waved Christian off his horse. "No reason to be scared. Please, come on over here."

"Ya heard him, boy," said the sheriff. "Get over here!"

"Now, Sheriff. No cause to make this young man more nervous than he is."

Christian stared when the two continued talking as if he didn't exist. Slowly, he dismounted and led his horse to where they waited for him.

They stopped talking and stared back at Christian. "Give her to me," said the sheriff, taking Christian's reins and leading the spotted horse to where the other horses grazed by the stream.

"Mayor, sir. Pardon me, but I need to return home immediately. You see, I can't be late for—"

"Please stop talking," said the mayor.

Christian immediately hushed. Then he noticed how tired the mayor appeared. "Something's wrong, sir. Are you well?"

The mayor shut his eyes and massaged his temples. "No, I'm not. It's Christian, right?"

"Yes, sir. Do you recall me coming to your house?"

"Of course." The mayor opened his eyes and looked at the young man standing before him. "How could I forget? You asked a lot of questions, curious boy. That I remember." The mayor took a deep breath and looked to where the sheriff waited. "Christian?"

"Yes, sir?"

"I'm sorry you had to see the extra ballots."

"Why, sir?"

"Then I'm sorry Theodore Stewart entrusted you with that letter."

"The letter, sir?"

"Yes, the letter. Just know that I'm sorry."

Confused, Christian looked at the mayor, who nodded to the sheriff behind him. Without hesitation, the sheriff stepped forward, and before Christian could turn around, he felt a blow to the back of his head. He went down, face-first, into the dirt. The sheriff and the mayor stood over him, staring, as his body went still.

"Out cold," said the sheriff, who knelt at Christian's side and placed his right hand over his mouth and nose. Christian's body kicked and squirmed, but the sheriff applied steady pressure, and the struggle ended with a quick twist of the neck.

The mayor looked away, preferring to order execution from a distance rather than witness it up close. He walked to his horse, pulled a rope from his saddlebag, and tossed it to the sheriff. "Here, you'll need this."

"You want me to put him with the others?"

"Of course not." The mayor leaned down, picked up a jagged rock, and tossed it to the sheriff. "Make sure to scratch him up good. Make it look like a monster savaged him, then take him to his pa. Meanwhile, I need to leave. We can't be seen together."

Without a second look, the mayor pulled himself into his saddle and headed toward town. It took only a moment before he was gone.

Meanwhile, the sheriff thrashed Christian's face, chest, arms, and hands with the rock. He looked down at the lifeless boy, his stomach convulsing at his handiwork. It took several attempts to heave the body over the horse. With each failed attempt, the body slumped off the horse and slammed to the ground, adding to the gore. Finally, he positioned the dead weight over the horse and tied it down.

He looked at his hands and shirt, now splattered with blood. He hung his wide-brimmed hat on a branch, walked over to the creek, and knelt to wash away the grime.

A flutter of leaves sounded in the still air. He looked up as the horses began backing away, snorting and kicking. Then, suddenly, there came the realization that he was not alone.

"The monster," he whispered.

The sheriff's blood ran cold, and he shook with fear. He stood alert, listening, hand on his pistol. The sound bounced off the rock walls, making it impossible to determine where it came from. Finally, in his peripheral vision, he saw movement and turned to his left, struggling to find the source of the sound in the dim twilight. Something moved through the underbrush near him, coming directly at him. He pulled his pistol from his black leather holster and pointed it toward the sound. It was enormous, whatever it was, snapping large branches and disturbing leaves like a boulder crashing down a mountainside. Then came the splashing of water. The pistol in his hand shook.

He staggered to his horse and flung himself into his saddle, then reached for the reins of the spotted horse weighed down with Christian's body. He peered back over his shoulder only to see a dark shadow in the vegetation.

"Yaaah!" He kicked his horse's hind quarters, and both horses took off at a gallop. He couldn't go too fast or the body might slide off. If it did, he wouldn't be able to stop. So he rode as fast as he dared, wanting nothing to do with whatever he'd encountered near the river. As he raced away, he suddenly realized that next to the pool of blood and hanging on a branch was something he had left behind.

Chapter 49

The wind kicked up as Jonathan moved to the middle of the dusty road, seething with anger as he watched the man ride away with the body. He looked down at the pool of blood, his stomach growling as he dropped to all fours. Sniffing the blood, the beast felt a shift of emotions.

"No harm in tasting," said a trio of sultry voices. "Wet your tongue. Quench your thirst. Calm your aching stomach."

Jonathan forced himself away from the murdered boy's blood and peered into the twilight. There was no need for him to wonder who spoke. In response, he violently shook his head.

The taunting continued. "Why not taste it? You did nothing. Is it a sin merely to dip your tongue?"

With that, Jonathan raised himself like a man. *Is this why you woke me, what you wanted me to see? The boy was unaware. Why must I witness a murder?*

The reply was quick and laced with feigned concern, several unembodied voices taking turns.

"Yes, indeed, it was we who woke you. We knew of these murderous intentions and wanted you to witness them."

"You heard them, didn't you? The killers, they cast aspersions on you!"

"Did you hear them scheming?"

"Their guilt they force upon you. They blame you for the evil they have committed."

"The sin is theirs, but who will pay the price?"

Though he heard every word and his claws flexed as saliva dripped from his jaw, Jonathan pretended not to listen.

"They'll blame you, and now men will come."

"Yes, they will come."

"For you!"

"Be careful, beast, until your penance is paid and you are free."

Jonathan's brows drew down in a scowl. He closed his eyes, drew a breath, and held it. He tasted the air, searching. He had the image of the men responsible for their treachery in his mind and willed himself not to forget it. He scanned the area, looking for anything left behind, anything that held their scent.

I will hunt these men, and I will be the last thing they ever see.

"Their sin, not yours," said the trio of voices.

Jonathan lowered himself to all four limbs. *Their sin,* he agreed, *not mine.*

Chapter 50

Christian's chair sat empty, his bowls, plates, and utensils untouched, the candles in the middle of the table half spent. Everyone sat waiting, except for Emily, who paced from the kitchen to the parlor and back, staring out the window into the moonlit street.

Tommaso took hold of Marco's arm and whispered in his ear. "Say again. What did Mr. Buchanan say to you?"

"Only for us not to worry, Papa. Christian said he may be late."

"Nothin' more?" asked Marjorie.

They both looked surprised that she had overheard. "No, ma'am."

"You're certain that's all he said?" asked Albert. Their conversation now belonged to everyone.

"Yes, sir, but for one thing I hoped not to mention—not that it is all too important."

"What's that, son?" asked Tommaso. They all stared at Marco, curious.

"Only that Mr. Buchanan said the sheriff came and got him."

"What for?" Tommaso, like the others, became instantly alarmed.

"I don't know, but he left the post office with the sheriff."

"Is your brother in trouble?"

Marco shrugged. "It's what I'm telling you, Papa. I don't know. Before coming here, I went to the sheriff's office, but no one was there and the door was locked. I even peeked in the window, but it was dark."

No longer able to contain her growing anxiety, Emily shouted, "Something's wrong! I can feel it. What do we do?" She looked at each as they sat around the table and stared back blankly.

"We're gonna remain calm, is what," said Marjorie. "No trouble in us waitin'. I'll keep the meal on the coals." She stood and hefted a cast-iron oven back to the hearth. Then, with a poker, she scooped hot coals from the firebox and set them on the oven. "On second thought," she said, "Frettin' won't help. Christian said he'd be late and not to worry. Mr. Salvatori, your son will join us when he's able. Let's begin. Besides, eatin' while we're waitin' will put our minds at ease."

Albert smiled reassuringly and said, "Yes, dear. Let's."

Marjorie quickly began portioning out the stew.

Emily sat, too nervous to think of anything to say, her arms stiff as boards at her side. Marjorie handed her a bowl of stew, but Emily merely stared at it, watching the steam rise into the air. "It's not like him, Auntie," she finally said. "Nothing could keep him. He'd never—"

Marjorie interrupted. "I know. I know, dear, but he said we should not worry. So let's not."

Marjorie smiled and placed a bowl of steaming stew in front of Marco, who pretended not to be overly concerned, hoping his brother would be along shortly. "Christian tells me you're a fine cook, Mrs. Hampshire. He goes on and on about it."

"So long as you think so after dinner." Marjorie watched as he leaned over, inhaling the aroma.

"It's certain I will, ma'am. Smells wonderful."

"You remind me of your brother. You're so much alike."

Once everyone was seated, the bowls were filled, the bread and butter set on the table, and, hands joined, Albert said a well-rehearsed grace. "Bless this food that Thou impartest. Let it be for our good. Bless those without and always watch over us, friends, family, and . . . Christian. Amen."

Whispers of "Amen" followed.

Suddenly, they heard a loud knocking at the door. Emily sprang from the table, her chair falling to the floor, the others following her. She opened the door to see Walter Buchanan on the front porch, bent over catching his breath.

"Come quick! There's been an accident!" He looked up to see Tommaso and Marco among those staring at him. "Shears, so grateful you're here. You'd better come quick. They're taking your boy to your home."

Emily's world tilted, and time slowed. "What happened?" she shouted. "What did the sheriff do to him? Is he all right?"

Marjorie went quickly to Emily's side, holding her tightly. "It's gonna be all right, dear. We'll stay here. Marco's a doctor. He'll see to his care."

"No," cried Emily. "I must see him. What if he's seriously hurt?" Her voice cracked, but her determined eyes held Marjorie's gaze. "You can stay here if you like, but I'm going!"

"All right, dear." Aunt Marjorie hurriedly gathered her shawl, and they headed down the street toward the Salvatori home.

As they turned the corner, they saw in the flickering lantern light a crowd of curious neighbors gathered in the Salvatori's front yard. Terrifying recollections of the last day she saw her father flooded Emily. She could still hear the pounding on the door as the sheriff stood on their porch. She could still see the panic on her mother's face. Her life changed forever that day. And now she sensed that her hopes and dreams were about to be torn away again and that nothing would ever be the same.

Chapter 51

Mrs. Harper, the neighbor from across the street, shouted, "Here they come!"

The crowd's attention shifted to them as they arrived. Without further commotion, people parted, allowing Emily to pass through the gate first, followed by the others.

The sheriff stood in the middle of the yard, smeared with dirt and blood, shouting orders. "Move, everyone!" He pushed the crowd back as neighbors craned their necks, trying to get a peek at the young man lying motionless on the front porch. A dimly lit lantern illuminated his body.

As the families approached, the sheriff stepped aside, allowing only the Salvatoris and Hampshires to pass. Upon seeing the lifeless body, Emily released a torrent of pain. "Christian! No!"

Marco held his father, who shook violently, overcome with horror and disbelief. Marjorie quickly took hold of Emily, trying to turn her away from the gruesome sight. At the same time, Albert surrounded them with his arms, doing all he could to suppress his rising emotions.

Sobbing, Emily calmed herself just enough to whisper to Marjorie, "Please tell me this isn't happening."

Marjorie and Albert tightened their embrace until Emily pulled away, rushing to Christian's side and throwing herself over him, bathing him in tears. The crowd watched in shock as Tommaso knelt beside her and, while holding Christian's hand, joined her in weeping.

"You can't leave me, Christian! I won't allow for it! Please, don't you leave me." Emily softly placed her hand on his cold cheek.

Walter pushed through the growing crowd until he stood directly before the sheriff, staring into his eyes, not saying a word.

"What is it? What do ya want?" asked the sheriff.

"I want to know what happened."

"Ya want to know what happened?"

"Yeah. You came and got him. He was in your care, Sheriff. So what happened?"

"Step back, Mr. Buchanan."

Walter did as requested while the sheriff gazed at the anxious crowd, all watching and listening. "I've somethin' to say," he hollered as silence fell over the crowd. "The mayor sent me off to see about Phillip Wallace's story—whether there be a monster. Shear's boy volunteered to go with me. We were ambushed, not unlike what happened to Phillip and his boy. I escaped. Shear's boy didn't."

The sheriff looked over his shoulder to see Emily glaring at him. He met her unflinching gaze, then turned his head and again addressed the crowd. "What more can I say? It's sad." He pinched the bridge of his nose and closed his eyes as if overcome with grief. The crowd remained hushed. No one moved until, suddenly, the sheriff swatted at a mosquito on his neck and people jumped.

Emily sprang to her feet and rushed at the sheriff, slapping his face. Her aunt Marjorie followed after her, grabbed her by the arm, and pulled her back.

"Don't!" her aunt cried. "Leave it be, dear. Leave it be!"

Emily stared coldly at the sheriff as her aunt restrained her. His eyes narrowed and his teeth clenched, but he held his composure. She noted there were no tears. That was something the sheriff couldn't fake. She recalled the absence of tears the night her father went missing.

Albert quickly guided Emily and Marjorie back up the porch steps while looking at the sheriff. "We're grieving, is all. Our loss is more than we can bear right now. Please . . ."

More people gathered as news of the attack spread, forcing the sheriff to ignore the public display of disrespect. Reluctantly, he turned his attention to the increasingly unruly crowd.

Vernon shouted, "Where's the mayor? Why isn't he here?"

"Mayor's gone for help from the governor to deal with the monster. He'll handle this when he returns. Now get on home!" The sheriff held up his rifle, shooing them away.

Warily, people began to disperse, taking their lanterns and leaving the street in the dark. Albert, Tommaso, and Marco picked up Christian's body and carried it into the house. Emily and Marjorie followed close behind. Once inside, with the door shut, Marjorie hurried to the kitchen, retrieving a water basin and towels to wash Christian's body while Emily knelt and examined his wounds. She could feel the fracture in his skull and the dried blood and dirt in his matted hair. Emily began to tremble, and more hot tears streamed down her face.

Aunt Marjorie returned, set the basin and towels on the floor, and held her tight. "Cry if ya must, dear."

Tommaso knelt on the other side of Emily, tears streaming down his face, while Albert watched in stunned silence. Marco paced back and forth, repeating, "I should've been there. I should've been there. We watch out for each other, and now? Why wasn't I there? I should have been there!"

Tommaso stayed near, eyes closed, saying his goodbyes in silent prayer, and asked for Caterina to find their son and for God to guide him home. Then he steeled his nerves and dried his tears. "Marco?"

"Yes, Papa?"

"Stop what ya doin'. Your brother needs clean clothes."

Marco quickly left the room, Marjorie following. He returned with Christian's Sunday best—a white, round-collared shirt and gray wool trousers with black buttons.

Marjorie soon returned with a comb, washcloth, and more towels. Careful not to spill the water, she filled the basin and handed Emily a washcloth. Then she watched as Emily washed the blood and dirt from Christian's body. Marjorie noted the pain on Emily's face. She had seen it there before. It was a pain from a place so deep, a place where emotions went to die. She would have gladly taken it upon herself to spare Emily, but all she could do was watch.

Suddenly, they heard tapping at the front door. Albert left to answer it. Parson Burroughs and his wife, Hannah, stood on the front porch. Albert let out a sigh of relief. "Oh, thank goodness you've come. Please, please come in."

Albert moved aside, allowing Hannah to enter. Her attention went straight to Emily and Marjorie as they hovered over Christian. Parson Burroughs followed, nodding to Albert with a sympathetic smile.

"My dear," said Hannah, addressing Emily. "Won't you please allow your aunt and me to do this? We understand there are needful things. That's why you have us, why we have each other. Please."

Emily listened but didn't move. Instead, she kept stroking Christian's hair, combing it with her fingers as the others watched.

Marjorie turned to Albert. "Dear, did ya hear Mrs. Burroughs? Nothin' more for Emmy here. Best take her home."

"No, Auntie, please. I want to stay here, just for the night." Emily looked to Tommaso for permission.

Seeing the desperation in her face, he nodded. "Of course you may."

Marjorie agreed with the arrangement. "Now, all of you, head to the kitchen. Mrs. Burroughs and I will tell you when we're finished. Please, Emmy. You, as well."

At Marjorie's insistence, Emily waited in the kitchen with the others as the women finished cleaning and dressing the body. Hannah called on her husband three times to empty and fill a bucket from the well pump in the backyard. Nearly two hours later, they heard Marjorie call, "You can come in now."

Emily entered the front parlor first. Despite being scratched and bruised, Christian appeared at peace. Emily appreciated the care they'd given him. They'd even cleaned the wood floor where he lay. All stood around, quietly staring, until the parson finally broke the silence.

"Take your rest, whatever you can. Expect us in the morning. We'll bring the wagon, deliver Christian to the church, and make final preparations." He looked to Tommaso and waited for a response.

Tommaso nodded. "I'll expect you come mornin'."

"All right, then." As they left, they embraced, both giving and receiving until all that remained were Tommaso, Marco, Emily, and the calm after the storm.

"Wake us if you need anything," said Tommaso.

"I will, Mr. Salvatori," said Emily.

Marco entered the parlor with the blanket and pillow from Christian's bed, spreading them out on the parlor couch. "Anything else?"

Emily hugged him. "Not unless you can bring him back."

Marco attempted a smile his grief would not allow before he followed his father, leaving Emily alone, a candle burning on the small table in the far corner.

Emily removed the bedding from the couch and spread it over the floor next to Christian's body. After blowing out the candle, she lay beside him and wrapped her hands around his arm. Emily next tried sleeping, but sleep wouldn't come. Instead, she whispered in his ear in the late hours, wishing to hear his voice once more, but Christian was gone, and the silence was deafening. She touched his face, but he was cold, and she feared her heart would follow.

Chapter 52

News of the mutilation of Old Man Taylor's prize bull had rolled through New Harmony like an earthquake, and now the killing of Shear's boy whittled away at the hours people slept during nights that seemed to last forever. People worried for their safety. Fear of a monstrous and unholy beast stalking them from the northern woods kept everyone on edge as thoughts of slaughter and mayhem seized the town. Then came the beguiling voices that spoke more directly, especially now that evidence of real danger lay at their feet.

At three o'clock in the morning, as people tossed and turned in their beds, the voices sang the eerie warnings inside their heads.

The monster has killed,
And blood's been spilled.
Innocence torn asunder.

Save yourselves,
and bar your doors.
Wise to fear the monster.

Hearken to our warnings now.
No time for hesitation.
Our warning is but a courtesy.
Your fear is your salvation.

The rising sun saw the mayor standing outside the front door of the town hall, his fingers fumbling inside his vest pocket. He withdrew a key and was about to disengage the lock when he heard a voice behind him.

"Mayor?"

He sighed when he recognized the voice, then turned to see Abigail, Elizabeth, and Susannah charging up the stairs. The mayor yawned, "Ah, good morning, ladies. Have we an appointment?"

Abigail skirted the question and got right to the point. "Did you hear it last night, the message from the guardians?"

"What? Wait! The who?"

Abigail chose to ignore his apparent irritation. "The guardians!"

"Oh, them! Yes, I heard the, um, guardians." The mayor took a deep, calming breath. "Now, if you'll pardon me, ladies. I hardly slept last night."

"Neither did we," Susannah interjected.

"Not a wink for anyone, I'm afraid," said Abigail. "May we visit?"

"Yes, certainly. Come in." The tired mayor held the door as the three hurried inside. "In my office." He gestured toward his office door. "I'm short a chair. Just a moment."

Abigail interrupted. "I believe we prefer to stand."

Susannah and Elizabeth nodded.

The mayor sat behind his desk, hoping to hurry things along. "Go on. What can I do for you?"

"Well, Mayor, if you heard the message from last night, it's understandable that the town is in a panic."

"Yes, in a panic, sir," agreed Susannah, as did Elizabeth.

Abigail continued. "The streets are bare, with everyone in their homes, doors locked. We need you, our mayor, more than ever in such times of distress, but we have concerns." Susannah and Elizabeth smiled and nodded.

The mayor leaned over his desk. "And those concerns are?"

"Firstly, are you aware who told your wife of the headmaster's treachery—Mr. Parrish's role in the assault on your grandson?"

"Yes, Martha told me who, and I am grateful."

Abigail smiled. "It pleases me to hear you say that, and you are welcome."

"And now you need something in return, is that it?"

Abigail shook her head adamantly. "Oh no, Mayor, sir, not at all. The truth is, you need something from us."

"That's right, Mayor," Susannah agreed. The mayor looked at Elizabeth, who nodded excitedly.

"I see," he said. He opened his desk drawer and withdrew a Figurado cigar. "And what is that, may I ask?"

Before he could light it, Abigail answered. "Information, of course. Like before, about the schoolmaster."

"Mr. Parrish?" He calmly put the unlit cigar back in the drawer and shut it.

"Well, not directly—rather, things that have to do with him indirectly."

"What?" The mayor squinted and opened the drawer a second time. "You need to make things clearer." The irritation in his voice returned as he reached for his cigar.

"The election, sir."

The mayor paused, looked up, and shut the desk drawer again. "Go on."

"There are things assumed that bear no fruit, things unsaid that have consequences. We listen for these things."

The mayor drew a deep breath. "Now, what does that even mean?" He instantly regretted it and leaned back in his chair. "Pardon me. This conversation is making me weary." Then, while twirling his finger in the air, he said, "But please go on."

The mayor sensed the power shift, and now Abigail had his attention. He could see she relished the feeling.

"Mayor, there are difficult things for you to hear, but you must listen. There are rumors and horrible lies about you. They've circulated for as long as I can remember. Until now, I was uncertain of their source, but not since the town meeting, when it became clear."

The mayor's eyes narrowed. "What became clear?"

"Mr. Parrish. He is the source. He envies your power. His grandfather helped found New Harmony, just like yours, and he wishes to displace you. The guardians have confirmed it. You know, the voices we hear."

"Guardians, are they?"

"Yes, and they speak to me and have a message for you."

"And what is it they say?"

"Mayor, I can tell you verbatim. I am an excellent listener and remember every word. They said, '*On the other side of a razor's edge gather the mayor's foes. But no matter the means or method used, he must gain control. Harm may come and blood the cost; the devil's harvest is not lost. For all must know to bend the knee to him who saved New Harmony.*' That's you, Mayor, who saved us."

The mayor waited patiently, just to be sure she'd finished. Then, finally, he cleared his throat and spoke calmly. "You're not simply a good listener but good at repeating what you hear."

Abigail smiled. "I take that as a compliment."

"As intended, but what do you make of this message from the guardians?"

"Isn't it obvious? You must stop Mr. Parrish and put an end to his lying tongue. He envies you and curses you while coveting what's yours. You've great possessions, so why not him? Or so he supposes. Unfortunately, many believe his falsehoods in your regard."

The mayor leaned forward. Now she had his undivided attention. "Who believes? Can you provide me names?"

"No need. You already know who they are. They are the silent ones, those who keep their opinions to themselves. They're arrogant and presume to know everything. Unfortunately, they are many, and you will lose the election unless—"

"Unless what? Tell me and be clear about it!"

"Good Mayor, I will tell you, so hear me. Bide your time and listen to the guardians as I do. When the time is right, they will impart your instruction. Wait for the opportunity, Mayor. For the good of New Harmony, you must be patient and wait. Then, when the time is right, you must act."

Chapter 53

As in times past, Emily found herself walking down Parrish Lane. In front of her, a shiny black horse pulled an equally glossy funerary wagon painted black and trimmed with brass lamps, royal red curtains, and black silk tassels. She stared through the glass casement at the fine grain of the pinewood box.

Weston must have been up the last two nights making Christian's casket. She noticed the special care and delicate workmanship.

He once gave me flowers when we were children, and now this.

Emily wondered if he meant the extra care for Christian or her. Either way, she felt grateful, and his kindness did not go unnoticed. Sooner than she hoped, they arrived at the cemetery, where the procession turned and entered the gate.

To her left, Aunt Marjorie and Uncle Albert matched her stride. To her right, Marco and Tommaso walked beside her. Arm in arm, they made Christian's final journey together. She could hear Parson Burroughs and Hannah directly behind her. In his right hand, the parson gripped the Holy Bible. Behind the Burroughs, half the town made up the rest of the procession. All gave reverence as the long line of mourners passed. Off in the distance, Emily heard the ringing of the bell. It had always brought her comfort, but today, it rang with the agony of her heart. She might never be able to hear it again without it conjuring the pain she now felt.

The gate to the cemetery stood open when they arrived. The horse and wagon moved past wooden markers bearing the surnames of friends and neighbors until it stopped at a pile of dirt and an empty hole. An earthen grave waited, no less empty than Emily herself, the ground that swallowed the dead to dust about to receive everything Emily had lost. It wasn't fair.

The ringing of the bell stopped, replaced by the sound of the breeze as it passed through willow trees that wept and the leaves of the aged oak sentinels that guarded those who slept here. Parson Burroughs began speaking.

Just words, thought Emily as her eyes fixed on the dark hole in the ground. Next to her, Marco put his arm around her and drew her close. She hadn't the will to resist and melted into him.

Albert and Marjorie watched as four men eased the coffin into the earth with ropes. Marco hardly moved as it disappeared into the deep hole. Tommaso stepped forward and looked on in stoic silence as the coffin descended, coming to rest six feet deep.

The men pulled the ropes from the open pit, their task complete. Through sniffles and watery eyes, Emily stared at the open grave, a wound in the earth. When her knees went weak, Marjorie, Albert, Marco, and Tommaso kept her from crumbling to the ground.

Parson Burroughs stood with his hands clasped in reverent silence. He positioned himself beside the large, freshly shoveled pile of dirt waiting to blanket Christian's body in eternal slumber. From outside the gate, mourners still arrived. The parson quietly bowed his head and waited for them to join. Then all fell into hushed anticipation.

The long rays of afternoon sun bathed the proceedings with a golden glow. Like the tears on Emily's face, tiny yellow leaves trickled from the drooping branches of the cottonwoods that swayed gently to and fro in the breeze.

Behind Parson Burrough's back, the sun made his gray hair appear luminescent, and with each turn of his head, his long, gray beard captured a halo of warm sunlight.

Even in his advanced age, the parson's face appeared youthful. His was a gentle face with soft, symmetrical, handsome features. His blue eyes exuded warmth from behind the thin lenses of his tiny, round spectacles. When he spoke, it was in sincere tones.

Seeing everyone assembled, he began. "Christian Salvatori, cherished son, beloved brother, friend, and, recently, fiancé. Yes, a young man on the verge of marrying the precious woman he loved since childhood.

"Those who truly knew him will tell you that Christian embodied the best in all of us, if in no other quality than in his innocence. Besides that, he was honest, diligent, and faithful. So there is no doubt he leaves an emptiness in our hearts. Such are the memories of goodness and love he leaves behind that are equal to the sense of loss we all feel.

"More than merely observing this young man from afar, I had occasion to visit with Christian, who sought my counsel when his mother passed. Of course, much of what we discussed must stay between Christian, me, and the good Lord. But I can tell you that Christian wanted to know how he could be sure of seeing his mother again. The purity of his heart assures me he is with her now.

"God constantly reminds us that there is more than this place, more than this time, more than our earthly trials, sorrows, and worries. In our greatest despair, we must remember this simple truth: we are all in God's care. Have faith, and may we all look to Him and no other."

With words of comfort offered, the parson knelt and took a handful of earth from the large pile. "Christian Salvatori, we now commend your soul to God. Go forth from this world in the name of God the Almighty Father, who created you, in the name of Jesus Christ, Son of the living God, who suffered for you, in the name of the Holy Spirit that poured out upon you. Amen."

A solemn chorus of amens affirmed the parson's words. Then he sprinkled the dirt over the grave as the first shovelful of dirt echoed off the pinewood coffin.

Emily closed her eyes and silently whispered words only she could hear. As warm tears rolled down her face, she said, "Please, God. I'm confused and feel lost. This hurts so much. Please give me strength.

Guide me from this dark place, and I will follow. I'm listening. And please tell Christian I will always love him. Always!"

Then, for Emily, time stopped. Marco held her securely as she began to shake.

"Marco?" she whispered. He squeezed her arm to let her know he listened. "Promise me something."

"Anything."

"Promise me you'll kill the monster who did this."

Through her tears, she heard him quietly say, "I'll do it myself."

To the Reader

Did you enjoy this book? I'd love to hear what you thought about it. Please leave a review wherever you bought this book or wherever fine books are sold. It would mean so much to me as reviews are a book's lifeblood.

You can order As the Starlings Fly book 2, *Before the Coming Dawn,* on my website (see below).

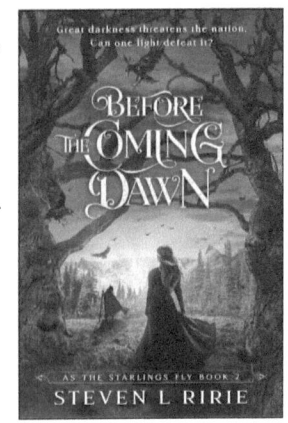

To contact me, learn more about me and Groundswell Books, or subscribe to my mailing list and be notified of future events and publications, please visit StevenLRirie.com.

A Sneak Peek at Book 2

Chapter 1

Perched on the ridge south of the gorge, the beast peered off into the distance at the valley below. His keen eyesight surveyed the town beyond the pastures and fields, the faint sound of a bell ringing and the procession of humans moving to the east end of town igniting his curiosity.

What is this?

Hungry to know, he sprang from the ridge, then followed the creek out of the gorge as it bent around fields and swung toward where the humans gathered. He moved swiftly through the vegetation, then crept slowly, crouching when exposed. The crowd entered what appeared to be a grove of trees on the outskirts. Here, the creek ran alongside the tree line, allowing him to approach undetected.

He'd intended only to keep an eye on the town, anticipating retaliation for something he had no part in doing. But the strange gathering of humans triggered a memory, something he recognized but lacked the words to explain. He hoped to reclaim a connection to his humanity by watching. He drew close enough to hear them breathing. Then, concealed by the brush that skirted the creek, he watched without fear of being seen while scanning the crowd.

Where were the humans who'd murdered the boy—those who would cause Jonathan harm with their deceit? He observed those who gathered, one by one, waiting for their heads to turn, looking for familiar faces.

Too many, too closely gathered.

Jonathan sniffed the open air. A good breeze found him downwind. He drew in another breath and held it, searching for a scent. *Yes,* he thought. *They're here.*

As he followed the scent, he noticed a young woman, her expression of grief unmistakable.

She sorrows.

Then he saw the pinewood box and looked once more at the woman's anguished expression.

He finally knew what this was—a burial. The young woman must belong to the murdered boy. This was his funeral.

Jonathan felt empathy. He looked hard at the grief-stricken woman and the young man comforting her. Nearby, others mourned the dead and newly departed. Jonathan's eyes drifted through the crowd until he saw them. Behind the grieving woman stood two men, their expressions blank.

There you are. Liars. Murderers.

He tasted the breeze again.

Yes, now I see you.

He'd found what he'd come for, which was enough for now. He would return later, preferring to hunt in the dark. A gentle breeze stirred the leaves, allowing him to retreat undetected, and he was gone.

About the Author

Steven L Ririe is the founder and chairman of the Silent Heroes of the Cold War National Memorial Committee. In 1998, he uncovered the details of a top-secret plane crash near the peak of Mount Charleston, Nevada. USAF 9068 was en route to Area 51 when it crashed into the mountain on November 17, 1955. Due to the classified nature of the mission, the families of the fourteen men who perished were kept in the dark as to the fate of their loved ones. Thanks to Steve's efforts, these families were notified, their loved ones recognized, and a memorial built in their honor.

The fate of Flight 9068 and Steve's quest to bring closure to the victims' families was featured on the Travel Channel's *Mysteries at the Museum,* in the Russian edition of *Newsweek,* and in the *Smithsonian Air and Space Magazine.*

Steve has been a Las Vegas, Nevada, resident since 1961 and is a member of the Association of Former Intelligence Officers. In June

2002, Steve testified before Congress on preserving Cold War historical sights and artifacts while recognizing the Silent Heroes of the Cold War National Memorial with a Congressional designation. Both memorials were dedicated in May 2015.

In addition, for nearly two decades, Steve has volunteered in a ministry at the Southern Desert Correctional Center, overseeing the spiritual needs of the inmates there. He lives with his wife, Marianna, has four adult daughters, and is a proud grandfather. Learn more about the 1955 top-secret plane crash on the Facebook page *Silent Heroes of the Cold War.*

To learn more about Steve and his books, check out StevenLRirie.com.

About the Series
As the Starlings Fly

The setting is the mid-1800s, just before the American Civil War, a period that closely mirrors our world today. Today, citizens of the United States are divided, just as in the mid-1800s. This was when Robert Owen founded a utopian socialist experiment in New Harmony, Indiana. To Steve's knowledge, Owen pioneered socialism. Steve believes that while Owen's intentions were noble, he created the poison apple that is communism, granting far too much power to the government at the expense of the people.

Now, some may read the series only for the story. Others will come away with an understanding of the spiritual implications and hidden meanings found in the intricate workings of humanity that either bring freedom and prosperity or authoritarianism and poverty. Steve hopes his series finds its way into the hands of a new generation that is unaware of the nuclear threat they face at every moment, day and night. He hopes his words will help them know they can be the light that outshines those who would plant fear and rob them of freedom and the pursuit of happiness.

www.ingramcontent.com/pod-product-compliance
Lightning Source LLC
LaVergne TN
LVHW091533070526
838199LV00001B/34